ANOTHER WEEPING WOMAN

ANOTHER WEEPING WOMAN

Donald Zochert

HOLT, RINEHART and WINSTON
New York

Printed in the United States of America

For Corey, John, and Mike

But puppets themselves have passions. They will bring a new plot into what they are presenting, and twist the ordered issue of vicissitude to suit some whim or appetite.

OSCAR WILDE

1

The thing I'll remember most is the car horn. The sound of that car horn just after dawn—filling the little valley with its wounded cry, echoing off those cliffs and rising up the cirque in that cold September air to the face of the Grasshopper itself.

It was a cry for help. A very mechanical cry for help.

Pug Collins heard it first.

He was only two hundred yards away from it, minding his own business, and it scared the hell out of him.

You don't expect to hear a car horn out in the middle of nowhere. Not in the sad September of the mountains, when the tourists and the dopers have all gone home. Not at sunrise in a silent place, when the aspen leaves are drifting upward in the copper light.

You especially don't expect to hear a car horn that doesn't stop, that just goes on and on and on, as though someone had fallen dead against it.

Pug Collins was alone in the ranger's cabin at the entrance to Grasshopper Campground when he heard the sound of the horn. It brought him to the door. What he saw was the mist and the tents and the blue car, and beyond the car, up past the head of the little valley, the distant face of the Grasshopper—cold and glassy in the high light. It was the color of roses, as in goodbye forever.

Pug ran for the car.

He ran directly between the two tents, and he did not notice that one of the tents was down.

2

Two girls were in the car. Their faces were ghostly white. They looked like they were drowning. The one behind the wheel was mousy and had straight brown hair and a very large mouth when it was open. It was open now. Pug could see the word she was screaming over and over, even though he could not hear it over the curdle of the horn.

The word was: *bear!*

He turned and glanced back at the tents. One was slashed to shreds. The tooled aluminum alloy poles stuck through the fabric like fresh bones. Inside the cocoon of ripstop nylon and the tangle of guy ropes he could see the dark taffeta of a sleeping bag.

It was alive. It beat like a human heart. Larger, smaller, larger, smaller. For a moment, he was afraid.

Pug turned again, toward the car, and saw the bear. It was up at the head of the valley. The mist was heavy. The bear was only a bad shape. It had its muzzle down in something.

Right there he should have gone back to the ranger's cabin and rung for help. That would have been prudent. You don't go after a grizzly bear by yourself. I asked him about that later. He didn't have an answer either.

When he got up to the head of the valley the bear was gone.

The girl wasn't.

She lay where the bear had dragged her. She had on pale blue bikini panties but no bra. The bear had taken out one breast, the left one, and part of the abdomen. One leg was in ribbons, white and red. The bear had gone into her skull like it was a beehive. A honey pot. She may have been a pretty girl. Pug wasn't sure.

That's the way you start a story, isn't it? Once upon a time.

She died about the age of nineteen.

Pug came back down toward the car. The Mouse was still grinding her palms into the hornbar. Her mouth was still flapping around that one word. And the sound of the horn—that high-pitched, wavering cry of terror—still begged for help.

Pug opened the car door and pried the Mouse out from behind the wheel and pushed her toward the little cabin across the campground. The other girl came scrambling after. She didn't need any encouragement. Then Pug went for the girl in the tent. She was still in the sleeping bag, all the way in and doubled over like a white slug touched by a needle, but the bag had stopped moving. He ripped it open. The lump came out head first, on all fours. A redhead. In Levi's.

He pushed her toward the cabin.

Pug finally used the phone. He rang up Headquarters and asked for help. Then he took the shotgun down from the pegs over the window and broke the gun open and closed it again.

He looked at the three girls. They were holding each other on the edge of the metal cot and rocking back and forth. They made little shuddering sounds.

Pug didn't say anything to them.

He left the cabin, closed the door behind him, and jogged up toward the head of the little valley in that lonely morning mist.

It was very quiet again.

She was still there at the edge of the yellow willows. One arm was thrown back over her head. The other arm lay at her side, broken backward at an awkward angle. It looked about as bad as her leg.

She was still dead.

I'd like to say what it was like, how it felt standing there in the plum mist on that deadly Sunday morning when it all began, not knowing who the girl was, or why, or what it would mean. I can't. All Pug remembers is the sunlight coming down the face of the Grasshopper and the willows starting to move in the wind.

And the white body in the dying grass.

It took forty minutes for help to arrive. There were fifteen of them, a couple of civilians, and all of them had guns. One of the rangers offered to stand guard where the girl lay dead in the grass, in case the bear decided to come back for more. The others broke up into twos and threes and headed into the willow.

They made a lot of noise. They were prudent.

It wasn't long before Pug heard one of them yelling. A high, excited voice.

Pug was deep in the brush when he heard it and he circled back into the meadow. The girl hadn't moved. But the guy who was guarding her was another story. He had moved very quickly up to the fourth branch of a big lodgepole pine.

The bear was on its hind legs beneath him—a grizzly, a big one, maybe eight feet from paw to paw. With a nice reach. The guy in the tree was standing on one foot. The other foot was waving in the air. The gun was on the ground.

Two of the regular rangers had come out of the willow brush before Pug. Three more heard the cry. They crashed out into the meadow, rifles high, arms protecting their eyes from the snapping willow.

They all opened up at the same time.

The bear came down heavily on all fours. And then all the way down—on its side. Its head twisted in the grass. Then it struggled to its feet. The rangers backed off. The bear stood a moment, shaking its head, and then ambled off into a dry wash as though nothing had happened.

By that time the other rangers had all come up.

They watched the willows. They watched the dry wash. Nothing moved. "Shit," someone suggested.

Then, as if to answer him, the bear lifted its head out of the bushes about fifty feet away and looked everyone carefully in the eye. They unloaded again, all at once. The bear went down with a crash.

The rangers waited some more. They were in no hurry.

Finally one of the hotshots from Headquarters moved toward the willow. Carefully.

He waved to the others.

One of the bears had fallen across the side of the other bear. Both of them were dead.

"Jesus," Pug said. "Two of them."

By then the mist was gone. The face of Grasshopper Glacier caught the full light of morning, three miles away. Everything was quiet.

And the girl was very dead.

It was just one of those things. Except for the bullet in her head.

2

Pug found me on the Little Spider a week later. It took some looking but he knew I'd be there. After all, it was September. And I was alone.

Almost alone.

On my first day in, Eddie Bauer was working a pool underneath some junipers about fifty yards upstream. At least I think it was Eddie Bauer. He was wearing an Eddie Bauer crusher hat and an Eddie Bauer chamois shirt and an Eddie Bauer vest, the one with 427 pockets, and Eddie Bauer twill trousers and Eddie Bauer waders. He was carrying a very expensive Eddie Bauer graphite rod. If he wasn't Eddie Bauer, he sure thought he was.

He didn't stay long.

As soon as he saw he had company he packed everything into an Eddie Bauer wicker basket and took off. I don't know where he went. Maybe page forty of the Eddie Bauer catalogue.

He didn't take any fish with him.

That left the Little Spider to me—the Little Spider and all its memories. It stayed that way until Pug Collins came thrashing through the underbrush up from the road.

"Put away the toys," he shouted when he reached the side of the stream. "Pack it in. Get out of the water. I've got something interesting for you."

His hands made a little megaphone around his mouth.

"Not interested."

He didn't go away. He never does.

Pug Collins always thinks he has something interesting for me. He sends me clippings from *The New York Times* all winter. Unsolved murders. Frauds. Truman Capote parties. All the evidences of civilization, down for the record. My wastebasket's full of them.

"The girl up at the Grasshopper," he shouted out again. "The one the bear got. You may not know about it—"

His voice barely carried over the sound of the water.

I knew about the girl up at the Grasshopper. Who didn't? I'd read about it two or three nights earlier, in the papers, when I was down in town. Coed mauled to death by grizzly. What else is new? Don't fool with Mother Nature.

"Wait a minute. Not interested."

I moved a few more steps out into the stream and dropped a stonefly into an easy pool on the other side, below a riffle. The fly drifted lazily over the water. Down where I was, there was no wind. Only memories. Up in the aspens the leaves were trembling. I heard Pug sputtering behind me, high on the bank. The sound of the water almost made me miss it.

"—a bullet in her brain—not the bear—found a goddamn bullet in her brain—"

I watched the water for a moment, fast and clear. Okay. Okay, I was interested.

An hour later we were down at Hungry Horse in the Golden Gate, which was nearly empty, watching the bartender wipe his hands on his red vest and put three more cold beers in front of us. One for Pug. One for me. And one for Pug's friend, a giant of a young man with a round face and features that were faintly Oriental, a plaid shirt that didn't want to stay tucked in, and two dull bronze eyes that didn't want to focus on anything too specific.

"I don't get it," Pug was saying. "Why would anyone want to put a bullet in the head of a dead girl? It doesn't make any sense. Or does it?"

He's funny. He wasn't fooling me and he knew it.

There are some things I like. Naps in the afternoon. Fishing. Driving at night. Soaring in the old Libelle out at Clearwater, riding the waves and thermals high enough to feel free of the earth. Good women. In about that order. All except the first and last are things you do alone. I've never had any trouble with alone. There are some things I don't like. Politics. Sociology for the millions. People who relate. People who are getting their acts together. I'm not crazy about Frank Gifford. The list is a lot longer than that. Don't get me started.

You can add Pug Collins to the list of things I like. He got out of a nasty business at a good time, at the same time I did. This report is not the place to discuss it, so you'll have to make up your own pedigree for him. As nasty as you can think of. Doctor. Senator. Salesman. Psychiatrist. Sociologist.

His face is full-moon, both chins are always clean-shaven, and his smile is goodtime-Charlie. Of course you've never seen him. But if you've got twenty-four bucks for one year, forty for two, you've heard of him. P. R. Collins, the celebrated writer. His stuff shows up in *The New Yorker* right along with that of Woody Allen and John McPhee, but not often enough to suit him. He lives in New York, of course. He has to. But he summers in the century before, in the mountains: Utah, Idaho, Montana. Mostly with the Forest Service, working lookouts. He's obviously got a split personality, but I'll leave that one for the psychiatrists. Pug writes about Mother Nature as though she were one of the family. His subject is solitude, and he doesn't know the first thing about it. He doesn't like being alone, and it's a handicap.

"Why would anyone put a bullet in the head of someone who's already been clawed beyond recognition by a grizzly bear?" he repeated.

"No. Not a bullet," his big friend whispered.

Pug ran his finger around the rim of his glass. I lifted my bottle.

"Give it to me again."

The dead girl was Margot Fraser. I'm sure you've figured it out. The bullet went into her pretty face before the bear did. She was twenty years old, not nineteen. She was in her last year at State, a very bright girl who had picked up credits by attending summer school. She'd already lined up two or three hard offers for graduate work. She could forget about them for the time being. Her major? Ethology, the study of animal behavior. It could have been worse. It could have been human behavior.

Margot Fraser and friends checked into the Grasshopper Glacier Campground shortly after noon on Saturday, the day before the bear came over the mountain. The friends were Emily Carpenter, Allison Carpenter, and Cynthia Farmer—Sin for short.

The first two were sisters, Carpenter and Carpenter, although from the way Pug described them you couldn't tell it by looking at them. Something about the gene pool. Emily was the mouse with the big trap. Allison was the redhead in the sleeping bag, and there was nothing mousy about her. Both were students. Emily was in Margot Fraser's class, a year older but just as bright, and with the same major—animal behavior. Allison was already in graduate school. Classics. That would mean Julius Caesar. I'm no dope. Cynthia Farmer was another story. She was blonde and good-looking. A dropout, naturally. She had to work for a living, which she did at a little data processing outfit called TechTronics, both *t*'s uppercase. She told the rangers she put the little holes in punch cards. Very demanding work, steady hand and so forth.

The girls arrived in Margot's blue Renault. It was packed full—the Renault, not the campground. Consider the season. They had the campground all to themselves, except for Pug Collins. And the bear.

The Grasshopper Campground is one of the smallest in the entire park, and one of the prettiest. I'm putting it in here for one reason. You might be a shut-in and never get to see it. Even if you're not, you might never see it.

The campground's out of the way, and they've never bothered to fix the road that winds up there through the mountains from Headquarters. That's on purpose. It discourages little old ladies. The camp's located near the border in a little valley that's cut back into the mountains, a nick in time. The flat of the valley is less than half a mile long. A stream with no name runs along the north side of it. The ranger's cabin is at the entrance, the east end, and a gravel road runs up the length of the valley with little turnouts at each campsite. The mountain comes down close to the road on the south, and it's covered with shrubs, moss, vines, and little trees that aren't going to get any bigger. The meadow itself rises gradually up to the willow and brush at the head of the valley. It ends in a stand of lodgepole pine. Beyond that you'll find rock. That's where you start the long climb up to the face of the Grasshopper, a very popular hike for the ambitious. The glacier itself spills down from an even higher valley, a gray slab of elephant skin that ends in a crumbling terminal face of ice about fifteen feet thick. It's nearly three miles up to the face of the Grasshopper and three miles down, with arguments the whole way as to which is tougher, up or down.

I vote for down.

Pug checked the girls into the campground that Saturday afternoon, as stated. They seemed to know what they were doing.

They pitched camp about halfway up the valley. When the two tents were up, they went for a hike. Pug watched them go. He didn't see them come back. But after dark he saw their lights in camp, a gas lantern and a couple of flashlights that bobbed around in the blackness like fireflies. They didn't make a fire. So much for the romance of the mountains. Once in a while Pug could hear their voices drifting down toward the little cabin at the entrance to the campground. He was playing Scrabble solitaire and thinking about New York. When he went to bed it was quiet. The next thing he heard from the girls was that car horn early on Sunday morning.

Pug Collins never did get a chance to talk with Margot Fraser's friends in the confusion of that Sunday morning. Headquarters handled it, the boys with clipboards and faint smiles that never left their faces. The two sisters weren't much help. The Mouse couldn't get her color back, if she had any to begin with, and Allison couldn't or wouldn't talk.

What they got, they got from Cynthia Farmer—who seemed very cool and efficient. A few details. The girls had hiked about a mile up the trail to Grasshopper Glacier. When it started to get dark, they turned back. They didn't cook because they'd brought cold chicken and cold beer with them. They hit the sack early. Fresh air. Margot Fraser and Allison Carpenter took one of the tents, which put Cynthia Farmer in the sack with Emily the Mouse. If you wanted to plot the relationship between the four girls, that's not quite the way it worked. Margot and the Mouse were fast friends—like a pair of high school sophomores, they were easy to tell apart but hard to keep apart. They were familiar with the Grasshopper Campground because they'd been there off and on all summer. Allison Carpenter had never been there—she wasn't the woodsy type, had nice nails and all that—but she must have heard Emily talk about it because she invited herself along on this particular trip. She also invited Cynthia Farmer along to make it an even foursome.

Between Allison Carpenter and Cynthia Farmer the line was pretty dim. They knew each other from somewhere. So do a lot of people. They were on a last-name basis, which is an improvement over most of mankind. Cynthia was the outsider. There was no line at all between her and the other two girls. She had never met Emily and wasn't impressed when she did. She didn't know Margot Fraser. She was along for the ride.

You have most of the rest of it. After the attack, Grasshopper Campground was closed down temporarily. The superintendent made the long trek up from Headquarters in his Buick to superintend. There was a call to the Interior Department in Washington. They talked about sending out a public relations man. Public relations men are always useful in an emergency. Some poor soul had to call Margot Fraser's mother and hand her some bad news. You don't get that in Wildflowers 101.

The two bears were loaded onto a flatbed and trucked down to the Fish and Wildlife Service lab at Bozeman. An ambulance eventually found its way up from Whitefish for what was left of Margot Fraser. They discussed the geographical niceties of the situation like cops in two different districts standing over a stiff on the dividing line and took the remains down to the coroner's funeral home at Paradise.

An official board of inquiry was convened at Headquarters the following day. The press was there. Those who knew bears, and who had looked over the campground, said the girls had followed all the rules in doubles. No perfumes. No food tossed around. No Natty Bumppo on the trails. Even on their little jaunt up toward the face of the Grasshopper, Margot had fitted herself out with bear-bells. She was no babe in the woods.

The board did what came naturally. It adjourned without reaching a finding. They needed an autopsy report on the two bears. They had their victim, poor thing. All they needed was the bear that did it. No one gave a thought to the autopsy on Margot Fraser.

As it turned out, both reports came in the next day within a few minutes of each other.

Bears first. Both bears had bloody muzzles. One had dried blood on the claws of its right front paw. It was human blood on the paw, same type as the blood Margot Fraser used to have. It was bear blood on both muzzles. That was unsettling. Stomach contents? Camas root, willow twigs, huckleberries. The usual. That was even more unsettling. There was nothing to indicate that either of the two bears shot by the rangers on that Sunday morning had done anything more than poke around in what was left of Margot Fraser.

Margot second. The coroner at Paradise had handled the autopsy himself, a sticky business at best. This is no place for details, you might be reading and eating at the same time. Except for one detail, which was not unsettling at all. The cause of death. The coroner said that Margot Fraser had died from shock and loss of blood. Sudden trauma, he called it. Just what you'd expect if you were eaten up by a bear.

The board of inquiry came to the only conclusion it could. Margot Fraser died from the results of an attack by a bear. The bear got away. End of inquiry.

I asked the only question I could.

"Where's the bullet?"

"Okay," Pug's friend said. He forced his mouth open a quarter of an inch. "Uncle Deadly lied."

"Uncle Deadly?"

"You tell it from here," Pug said.

The big guy had a lot of inertia going for him in the first place. Now that he'd put himself on the outside of four or five fast beers, he had a lot more. He weighed an easy two-seventy and it hadn't coagulated in any one spot. He looked like a lineman for the Washington Redskins. His curly, reddish beard made him look even bigger than he was, which was unnecessary, and his eyes still had that unfocused glaze that a bull has just before someone swings the sledgehammer.

Pug Collins adopts people—I told you he didn't like being alone—and he'd adopted Mononucleosis Oto when he walked out of the darkness one night up at Grasshopper Campground and slid a banged-up guitar off his sloping shoulder and started strumming away for all the wide-eyes who were gathered around Pug's ten o'clock campfire. Not quite John Denver, but be thankful for small favors. He was a free spirit of the sort that went out of fashion fifty years ago, before they invented IBM. He knew all the songs of Joe Hill, for instance, still a dangerous thing in some sections of Montana. The campground tourists had never heard of Joe Hill, of course, and the kid was a hit. He worked for the park, in maintenance, and he came back to Pug's campfire every night until the tourists went away, and then he came back some more because Pug was there and Pug likes dogs and orphans.

It's easy to see why Pug liked the guy. It's not every day you run into someone named Mononucleosis Oto. And he was an orphan. He was a Samoan. He'd wound up in San Francisco around the age of eleven and was passed around from one well-meaning family to another until he was formally adopted by a crazy couple who ran sheep in the Montana mountains. They were dead now, too. That made him an orphan twice over. This much I'd picked up from Pug down on the banks of the Little Spider while Mononucleosis Oto waited patiently in the Jeep. He preferred "Mono," and you can't blame him for that.

He looked at me and his dull bronze eyes tried to focus and I said, "Hi, Mono. Where's the bullet?"

"Let's be honest," he said. "I *knew* her. We went together. We broke up. But why would I kill her?"

"Wait a minute," I said.

"Margot Fraser."

"Who says you killed her?"

"His uncle," Pug said.

"I was drunk," the big guy continued. "What the hell. You would be, too. She broke up with me and I got drunk. I busted up a place, the Royal Flush. Did it real bad, I admit it. And I talked a little crazy, said I'd take care of her. I didn't mean it. Let's be honest."

His head was bobbing up and down, like he agreed with himself. His palm came down flat and hard on the bar.

"I didn't do it. My uncle bailed me out. He *thinks* I did it. What the hell."

"Your uncle," I said. I was trying to follow it. I didn't know Samoan.

"His uncle," Pug Collins said. "The coroner. Dud Dunlop. He's the one who—"

Mono turned back to me.

"Uncle Deadly," he said, and the way he said it was enough to let you know how he felt about it. "We don't get along. He's into death and politics. I'm not. But he's all the family I've got. I mean, he bailed me out and he said I was talking crazy, about killing Margot—"

"Listen," I said. "Let's be honest. The fish are biting and thanks for the beer. Have you ever heard of the police? This is somewhat out of my line. I lead a nice quiet life." I was talking to Pug.

All of a sudden Mononucleosis Oto looked a little ugly. Maybe because he'd finally focused his eyes. They were focused on me.

Pug said, "The kid's in trouble. His uncle called him down to Paradise yesterday, said he found a bullet in Margot Fraser's brain—"

"Not a bullet."

"A custom job," Pug said. He leaned across the big guy. "The point was filed down. He showed it to the kid, put two and two together. Mono knew her, they dated, they broke up. Life, right? His uncle thinks the kid did it, shot her with the damn thing—"

Mononucleosis Oto growled a little. He was crying.

"It's not in the autopsy report?" I asked.

"Hell, no," Pug said.

"What the hell," Mono sobbed. His eyes were closed as tight as fists.

"I don't get it," Pug said. "He didn't do it. Who did? Why would anyone want to put a slug in the brain of a dead girl?"

He looked into his glass of beer. It was empty.

"We also shot the wrong goddamn bears."

It was starting to get dark. My rented car was still parked up there on the road over the Little Spider. My tent was there, a half-mile in, and my waders, and all my gear. So were the fat browns, hanging over the gravel. If you work that pool just right, below the riffle, use a stonefly or a Matuka or a Goofus Bug, you stand a chance of getting something. Something very nice.

"Where the hell did that slug come from?" Pug was saying to no one in particular and me in general. "It doesn't make sense. Where did that goddamn bear go?"

I drew a deep breath myself.

"Three more over here," I said.

3

Everyone has his own little war. I didn't need this one. For one thing, I was a long way from home. For another, I was on a very strict schedule. Sleep and feed. For another, it had been two years since I'd taken on somebody else's troubles and I thought I was through with it, and Pug Collins knew it. No one involved in that little adventure had lived happily ever after.

I figured to bow out while I still could, grab my gear, and head on home. Home is on Delgany Street in Denver, northwest side, not much of a neighborhood but gray and empty enough to suit me. The house is a restored Victorian bordello with plenty of gingerbread and a lot of pleasant memories I didn't have the pleasure of having. Previous occupants: two kids out of college who fixed it up and then moved on. How I got the house is a long story but I can hold it down to one sentence. Mononucleosis Oto isn't the only one with an uncle. A rich uncle took a shine to me and remembered me in his will. He left me the house and the keys to five lock boxes, three in New York City, one in Berne, one in Milan. The lock boxes were worth about eight times as much as the house was worth, and the house was worth plenty. Make it four sentences.

The name on the little brass plate under the doorbell—if I had a little brass plate under the doorbell, which I don't—is Nick Caine. It's as good as any other name, and better than Mononucleosis Oto. I spent a lot of time on it. I considered others. Bodie Maginot. Zap Dancer. Sten Cody. Joe Barlow. Mickey Finn. Nick Caine comes close enough. Too close, maybe. I used to work for the government, sort of like a mailman. It's not necessary to say which government, or how much like a mailman.

Actually, there isn't even a doorbell.

The schedule is another story. It can be adjusted to fit circumstances. Under the circumstances, the circumstances weren't right. I tried to explain this to Pug out in the parking lot of the Golden Gate roadhouse, after we'd left Mononucleosis Oto blinking into his beer. Let's be honest, I kept saying. It didn't do any good. By the time we were halfway back up to the Little Spider, Pug was pulling the same old arguments out of the hat. Those rabbits didn't have any fur anymore. I'd heard them all before.

"I hate to see a grown Samoan cry," I said.

"He's a good kid. He's straight. He's—"

"He's not only dumb, he's stupid. Even if what he says is true, why did he even open his mouth? It's nothing but trouble. What are you? A priest? Let's be honest. You don't even know if what he says is true."

"I know one thing. You have no redeeming virtues. You shave twice a week. Probably less. Your boots are always scuffed. You dress like a bum. One tie, and it's red, white, and blue."

He made a sour face and continued:

"You watch too much television. Am I going too fast? Your brain is turning to mud. Television and the movies. You're a lump. Eisenstein, who is he? You hide out in that mansion of yours like a hermit. You're not on death row, Nick. Not anymore. For two years all you've done is fish. Let's analyze it. It's a great literary tradition. I'm a fan of Ernie Schwiebert, who is the best writer in the language, and I suppose he is a fisherman. But you always fish alone. Why? Because you're a recluse. That's an American word. It means, like, garbage. You go away for weeks at a time. No one can find you. You are the only man I've met who has no forwarding address. You have no redeeming virtues, except—"

"I heard this one."

"I was going to say, except—you can do things I've never seen anyone else do. That's a compliment. A professional compliment."

Pug was suddenly watching the road.

"I remember that woman who came to you from Argentina," he said. "How'd she find you? The countess, or whatever she called herself? I remember the Air Force colonel from Washington who found something interesting in his briefcase. I remember that dancer from the Bolshoi. There are probably more I don't know about. I'm sure there are. I'm not your keeper. Not anymore. All it takes is one thing, Nick. Get you interested."

"Nuts." I explained. "I'm a Trappist. I have my monastery and you're invited. I do my devotions. I stay as far away from trouble as I can."

"Yeah. I'm Porky Pig."

Silence.

"This kid's on the spot," Pug said after a minute or two. "Mononucleosis Oto. Forget about him. You can take him or leave him. Leave him. What I'm thinking about is the girl, Margot Fraser. I'm thinking about her up there in the mountains, in the darkness, dead. I'm wondering why somebody put a bullet in her brain. I'm trying to figure out why she was there in the first place, and what the redhead knows—she was in the same tent with her—and where the bear comes in. Why the bear? What is this? That girl was killed twice, Nick. Somebody wanted her dead so bad that once wasn't enough."

Silence.

The night swept around us. The dashlights glowed green on the underside of the windshield. The rented car was still where I had left it, just past the bridge over the Little Spider and nosed into the alders off the side of the road. The reflectors came up from out of nowhere. They gleamed at us, two fierce red eyes in the darkness. You forget how dark it gets.

By the time Pug got the Jeep stopped, I had a nice walk back along the shoulder. He turned the Jeep around and cruised behind me and then pulled off the road, waiting. The engine made a deep, throaty sound. Thumm-thumm-thumm-thumm. Oil and metal and camshafts, flesh and blood.

I put the key in the door of the Capri, turned it, opened the door, slid in, put the key in the ignition, closed my eyes, counted to three, and turned the key. In that order. Not a Trappist. A Penitente. Upstream on the Little Spider, my tent was empty under the September stars. A thin gauze of cloud was putting the stars out, two by two. It could stay that way. I had some things to think about, and they weren't the usual things I think about on the Little Spider. Or maybe they were. But that was no place to think about them. Not with the river whispering to itself in the darkness. Not with the silence crushing down. Not with bones pinned against the earth.

Not with the memories that kept coming back.

I pulled out of the alders, turned the Capri around, and followed Pug back down the access road. When we reached the turnoff, the Jeep kept going. I eased off the accelerator, tapped the horn, and turned to the left onto the asphalt, headed down toward Hungry Horse. I kept the window open all the way, because that's the way I like it, even when the rain started. The Golden Gate flashed by on my left, a blur of neon lights in the rain, and I wondered whether Mononucleosis Oto had figured it out yet, and if so, whether he'd switched to something stronger than beer.

After another forty-five minutes of blackness I picked up the gray smudge of lights from Kalispell.

You won't find the Hi-Vu listed in the motor club guides. Or written up in the Sunday supplements under gracious living. They wouldn't like the color of the big tile slabs it's built with (pink), or the neon (red and blue), or the mattresses (hard to very hard). The TVs are black-and-white, and the management's new every year. This year it's a couple of kids from Cleveland who got tired of watching the Cuyahoga catch fire and sold everything they had back East, including their future, so they could breathe fresh air and starve in the mountains. Maybe the same kids who fixed up the house on Delgany Street. Good luck. It's mostly locals who use the Hi-Vu, which means it's full on weekends and empty otherwise, except for the afternoon trade. Schoolteachers and salesmen and secretaries, hosiery clerks and tractor dealers and forty-year-old delivery boys. They're in and out in a jiff, which is fine. I only show up late at night, if and when the silence of the Little Spider gets to me.

The rain was steady—a gray, dismal, straight-down rain in the neon.

I parked the Capri in front of No. 7, unlocked the door, went in, closed the drapes the rest of the way, opened the bottle of Scotch (generic), capped it when I was done with it, and took a hot shower. A very hot shower.

Then I came out and sat on the edge of the bed. The television was next to the bureau. A chair was next to the television, and the newspapers were still piled very neatly on the chair. The *Kalispell Tribune* and the *Hungry Horse News.* They had a bad smell, wet and musty, like something a dog would leave under your shoe when you weren't looking.

The room was cold.

I looked at the face in the mirror over the bureau.

Why they call it dishwater blond I'll never know, but it fell down over his forehead. It covered the scar. The eyes were blue-gray, mostly gray. The skin was still tight over his cheekbones, although at the corners of the eyes you could see something that was no longer young and easy. The nose was not quite in plumb, but the teeth were still straight. The better to eat you, my dear. The chin was cleft just a touch by a dimple that had been deepened by too many feminine fingers saying nice things. Despite the other scar—the red, quarter-inch welt that came down at an odd angle from the lower lip. The man who put that there is dead.

It's funny about a man's face. Sometimes you can look at it and you can see the little boy it grew from—freckles and jam and all those little temporary abrasions that come from knocking into life and not giving a particular damn about it. Sometimes you can look at it and read it the other way, see all the sutures and sockets, the ligaments, the white bone, the valleys and channels it will eventually collapse into.

Not this one.

This one was just a point in time, without a past and without a future. It was hard to say where it could have come from or where it would go. It told you nothing, unless it happened to be your own face, and then it told you something you couldn't tell anybody.

The paper I wanted was the third one down. I shoved my elbow back into the pillow and lay back on the bed to look at it.

Her picture was on page one, a small picture, and under it were the words: "Margot Fraser." I wanted to say this is your war, kid. You lost. But she didn't have the look of a loser. Not by a long shot. She was squinting, probably looking into the sun over someone's shoulder. Dark hair, dark eyes. Her face had that expression runners have in the last few miles of the marathon. Pinched with an indefinable pain, hurting somewhere inside, but able to take it. When they're so young you think of them as vulnerable and easy. This one wasn't.

The story that went with the picture was eight inches of nothing new. A follow-up on the original story, the conclusions of the board of inquiry, the funeral arrangements. By now she was buried. I tossed the paper back on the chair and went to the door to check the rain. It hadn't changed to snow. Maybe it wouldn't.

I lit another cigarette and closed my eyes and drifted back two years to that last day on the Little Spider.

Two years is a long time. That day had started with a sliver of ice on every blade of yellow grass. By noon it had burned off, and the earth was soft and warm. September. It's not for the browns that I go back to the Spider in September.

We'd been there ten days, each of them different and better than the ones that had gone before, eight of them without seeing another soul. In the afternoons, eagles drifted out above the high bluffs next to the river, dark shapes pinned against a sky that was fading to amber. I'd put the problem in the back of my mind all that time, forced it down into the basement, slammed the door, threw the bolt. Pretended I was just like anyone else. I fished. She cooked. We did all the things the very young do, even though only one of us was very young. Her eyes laughed. Something very good was happening and she did not want to go.

In the blue shadow of the tent she cast her yarrow sticks and read to me from her book. Nine at the top means:

Perseverance brings the woman into danger.
The moon is nearly full.
If the superior man persists,
Misfortune comes.

Even then, they were already there. They were up in the hills—watching.

We broke camp at two o'clock in the afternoon, not knowing where we would go or what we would do. Knowing only that I did not want to stay, that I heard a sound, an ugly stirring, in that dark basement room.

I stowed the tent and lashed the pack. She lifted the two duffels and headed down along the bank toward the car. I was far behind her when she reached the road. She threw the bags in the back of the car, rolled down the window, and shouted something I didn't catch.

Then she turned the key in the ignition.

I saw it before I heard it, and I knew it was meant for me. The orange blossom of flame beneath the back seat—curling forward with its withering, black petals, filling the interior of the car. And then the spurts of flame reaching upward from under the hood. The sound finally came—it seemed like hours later—in two soft "carooomphs."

Instinct put me flat on the ground. I rolled over twice, came halfway up, and raced for the protection of the line of loblollies back from the Spider. I moved slowly through them, working my way down toward the road.

There was a soft hiss of rubber and plastic and flesh. Her arms floated on the flames. Her head was thrown straight back against the front seat. Her mouth was open. It was white.

It was then that I realized there was another sound. The sound of the car horn, which stuck when the explosives were detonated. A cry for help, where there was no help.

Three-thirty in the afternoon when I finally woke up. The heat had gone on in the motel room during the night. It had stayed on. The air was stale. Light seeped in between the window drapes.

I lit a cigarette, pulled on my pants, and opened the door to the room. Outside it was spring. A reprieve. The air was smooth and wet and glistening in the low afternoon sun. Winter would come. The cold would bite through the flesh to the bone. The snow would wrap itself around all the memories and smother them. But not today.

I found Pug Collins in the Chief Joseph Room of Bear Lodge, across from Park Headquarters. He was sitting at the long bar. He was alone.

He didn't even turn his head when I parked myself on the red stool next to him.

"I counted on it," he said to the mirror behind the bar. "Two years is too long."

4

Pug Collins said, "I'm relieved."

"I figured you would be."

"I don't mean that," he said. "I'm relieved from duty. For a week. They've closed Grasshopper Campground for a week and they've got two crews up there right now. Looking for the bear. I'm supposed to hang around Headquarters. My tour's up in two weeks anyway. When Good Housekeeping gets done I may go back up. But for now, I'm free. It's been a long time since—"

"One head is better than two," I said. "I work alone."

He took no for an answer.

But he'd already anticipated me. He'd gone ahead and done two things before I showed up that evening in the Chief Joseph Room of Bear Lodge. Neither was worth much, but they showed he was thinking. For one, he had cloned the official board of inquiry report on Margot Fraser's death and had a copy waiting for me on the bar. For another, he'd set up an audience with the park superintendent, an old coot from the Georgia pines who went by the name of Hoe Norse.

The board of inquiry report ran to thirty-six pages, single-spaced, and whoever wrote it has no future in government. It was in English. I read through it quickly. Pug had already covered most of the ground for me, so I found nothing there to knock me off the barstool. I wrote down a couple of addresses and noticed that Ms. Mouse—Emily Carpenter—Margot Fraser's close friend, had sent up a note from her doctor that excused her from testifying before the board.

Uncle Deadly's autopsy report was stapled to the back of the board of inquiry findings, half a page. Pug was right about that. Uncle Deadly forgot to mention anything about a bullet in Margot Fraser's brain.

Pug and I finished our beers and I straightened my tie, which is red, white, and blue, and went out the door and up the road.

Hoe Norse didn't have much of a future in government either.

He was a good old boy, pushing sixty further than it wanted to go. Somewhere along the line he'd pushed someone else the wrong way and they'd sent him up to the mountains to freeze. He didn't belong there. He belonged in a swamp. He was as slow and deliberate as an alligator, and his bite matched. It was long after hours when he saw me and he still had his dress uniform on, neatly pressed, which said something about the way he superintended.

We sat in wicker chairs in his rustic living room, up the road from Headquarters, and from the size of the fire you'd have to say he thought it was February. He sat very close to it.

"People die," he announced, his mouth barely moving.

"Most of the people who die in this park die from drowning. Fishermen. Sometimes we'll have a climber fall, or a hiker who doesn't know what the hell he's doing. Usually a kid. A hippie. You can't hold their hands. We have a lot of heart attacks. People aren't used to the altitude. We have people who walk in front of cars and get run down at fifteen miles an hour. We've had four people reported missing out in the back country who never turned up. Or if they did, they never bothered to tell us about it. Lot of lost kids. They get found. The last time this happened, someone put together records on it. I don't have any names. You don't want names. All I have are the numbers. You want numbers. Collins said you're—"

I was ready for it.

"Risk management," I said. "Tours. Little old ladies, schoolteachers. Something like this happens, the company gets nervous. Someone has to figure the odds, and figure a way to keep the odds down. You don't want some grandma from Oskaloosa coming through here on a bus and getting eaten up by a bear—"

"Okay."

It was enough for him. He waved my mouth shut.

"The last time this happened, I wasn't here," he said. "I was at

Ocala National Forest. Lake George. It's a damn sight warmer there. But when this Margot Fraser business came along, I dug out the records. This is Big Sky country, boy. There's no mystery to it. Lot of room for things to happen here, good things and bad."

I still don't think his mouth was moving. He didn't pause for a breath.

"Bears?" he continued. "These are bum bears up here. They're used to people and they're used to garbage. They're too goddamn civilized. We've got what we call a management policy. Manage the bears. But that's not the problem. The problem is, manage the people. Bears are bears. We're careful about the campgrounds, try to keep 'em clean. We're on most of the trails, not all of them, but most of them. That's a losing battle. You'd be surprised at the garbage we find in the back country. They go to the trouble of packing things in and they don't go to the trouble of packing them out. Human nature. The bears get it. The more people we have using the park, the more trouble we'll have with bears. We talk to the people. We're not bashful. But on the whole, we're lucky. The bears were here first—"

He sighed, but his face still didn't change its expression. Which meant his face still didn't have any expression.

"Margot Fraser?" he said through his teeth. "Previous to her, we've had three people killed by grizzlies in this park. More than sixty years. That's not a bad record, all things accounted for. These were girls, or women, or what-have-you. Two of them were attacked on the same night about ten years ago, in different parts of the park. One up by Saddleridge, the other at Moon Lake. The third girl caught it year before last, cooking wienies with her boyfriend. They had a cute little Skye terrier along with them on the trail, contrary to the posted regulations. At least the bear thought it was cute. The boyfriend went up a tree and waited for the cavalry. The girl wasn't so fortunate."

Maybe this is where Hoe Norse breathed in. I'm not sure.

"Risk?" he said. "You can't make odds on a bear. That's one risk you can't manage. We look into it, of course. What do we look for? Hell, I'm asking your questions for you. What we look for is, what provoked the bear? These babies are easy to provoke. They're not mean, just bad. They're bum bears. Too civilized."

He leaned back in his wicker chair, lifting the front legs off the floor, which I forgot to mention was linoleum.

"What did these girls do wrong up at Grasshopper?" I asked.

"That's a good question."

I waited for more, but there was no more. That was his answer.

"How did they provoke the bear? How come the bear picked on one girl and not the others? You shot two bears but they were the wrong bears. Where's the bear that—"

He came down with a thud, which surprised him, and his face showed it.

"Wouldn't we all like to know," he said.

The old dog smiled. His teeth were long and yellow, and it didn't take a genius to see where his allegiance was—with the bear. He rubbed his hands together.

"They been studying the grizzly for a long time now," he said, "these college boys, and Old Bear hasn't told them very much. No more than he wants to. He moves around, and there's no way on earth a two-legged man can keep up with him. Forty, sixty miles a night. Try it yourself. He's a mighty interesting creature, quite an animal, and he's—"

It was pretty clear where Hoe Norse was headed. A campfire chat. You don't need all of it. Let's just say he went on for about fifteen minutes, leaning forward with his elbows on his knees and shaking loose everything he knew about bears, which was plenty. I learned how to walk plantigrade and retrograde, and why the Indians worshipped the grizzly (they were afraid of him), and how there were six or eleven or thirty-seven different species of bears, depending on which college you attended. Finally he got so interested that he tipped back in his chair again, lifting the front legs off the floor.

I stood up quickly.

He came down with a thud again, and the same look of surprise turned his face on. What he needed was a rocking chair. What I needed I wasn't going to get from Hoe Norse. Did he know anything they didn't have room for in the official board of inquiry report on Margot Fraser? The answer was, plenty. But nothing about Margot Fraser. Somewhere out there in the dark mountains was a very smart bear. A bear you could trust.

The bullet in Margot Fraser's brain made it murder, and it was put there before the bear got to her. But the bear made it something more horrible. As in *Ursus horribilus.*

I checked in with Pug Collins, collected my gear—he'd gone up to the Little Spider to get it—and drove back down to the Hi-Vu. Before I left, he asked me how it had gone. I showed him how to walk retrograde.

The next morning I was headed back across the mountains. While I concentrated on the road, I gnawed on the bone of Uncle Deadly. Death and politics. I agreed with Mono. I didn't like the type. I'd rather walk away from it. But I couldn't. If there really was a bullet in Margot Fraser's brain and Uncle Deadly found it, then Uncle Deadly was in a hole. I wanted to keep him there.

"I'd like to walk away from it but I can't," I said when he finally came to the door. It was my turn not to take a breath. "Mononucleosis Oto. He's your nephew. I'm here to talk about it. There are two things I could do. I could try to softsoap you, give you a little song and dance, but the look on your face tells me you don't like singing and you're too tired to dance. Sit this one out. There's another thing I could do but we won't discuss it. You're probably not in the market. Withholding evidence of murder is a felony. Even in Paradise. Withholding evidence of murder on federal property is even more of a felony. I can't flash a badge at you because I'm not a cop. I can't put my hand out because I'm not in the market either. There wouldn't be enough money in Paradise to cover it. So it's your move. You're wrong about your nephew. He's a nice boy and he didn't do it. He's off the hook. You're not. You'll have to decide about that, but maybe you don't have much of a choice."

I smiled.

The idea is to talk fast. They don't expect somebody to come to their door and rattle the skeletons in their closet.

Uncle Deadly handled it pretty well. His yellow eyes didn't blink. His mouth flapped open and he tried to make a few words, but they didn't want to come out. His nose was so long and straight he could have used it for a gunsight. He did. He lifted it until he had me in the cross-hairs. He stepped back into the shadows of his funeral home and elbowed the door open the rest of the way.

He turned, and I followed him down a carpeted hallway with electric candles on the walls.

"Play *that* on your piano," he said to himself. His voice was dry.

We went through a doorway on the left and found ourselves in his office. Dearly bereaved. He took the desk, a big brown battle-scarred piece of furniture with nothing on it except a green blotter and the parched white skull of a steer. Remember, this is Montana.

Death and politics. He had a picture of the President on the wall behind him. Franklin D. Roosevelt. He was only seven or eight presidents behind the rest of us.

He reached into the bottom drawer of his desk and brought up a bottle.

"Rye whisky," he said. "I was out early. Three o'clock. Hunting rabbits."

He didn't make much of a ceremony about it. Up went the bottle and he drank from it. His eyes didn't leave my face.

Uncle Deadly was over the hill. White hair combed neatly off to one side, heavy white eyebrows, and a long, thin mug that had been scrubbed by more western winters than I'd ever live to see. Maybe seventy or seventy-one. I could see the gears working. He was wearing a pair of khaki drill pants, an old brown sweater with black patches at the elbows, a flowered Hawaiian shirt, and a smile. Only the smile didn't fit.

He took another drink, still not bothering with a glass, and when he brought the bottle down he pulled the smile down with it. The tic at the corner of his right eye was a little more active than it had been when he first opened the door.

"And you know Mono."

It wasn't a question, he was just telling it to himself. He could still look a man right in the eye, which he did. He paused a moment, considering it. Then he went on.

"You're right. Good boy, by and by. Make a hell of a football player and I keep telling him that and he don't listen. He's bullheaded. Samoan. Adopted, of course. Now he's on his own. Been on his own since his Ma drove on down Catamount Mountain on the wrong side of the road. We consider that an accident around here, but she was not a well woman. His Pa? He's dead. That's my baby brother. Henry Dunlop. Twenty-two years in the United States Navy before he come back home to run sheep. Leaves me as all the family that poor boy's got. Needs a lot of looking after. He's Samoan. Damned fool dropped out of school now, and he's just kinda floating around. Can't say I understand it, but I'm his family."

Uncle Deadly brought his hand up and rubbed his chin. He needed a shave.

"You want to sit down, son?"

Ten years ago he'd have put up a fight, and it would have been a good one. But he looked tired. He looked even more tired when he reached his hand down into the bottom drawer again and brought it up and let something small and shiny fall onto the green blotter pad.

It was a .22 caliber slug with the cap fluted and ground down to a point. He pushed it around in a small circle on the pad with his finger.

He talked to it.

"Most damn fool thing I ever done. Lots of times a man'll do a damn fool thing and regret it. Other times a man'll do a damn fool thing and he'll be the only damn fool who knows about it, and then it don't matter much whether he regrets it or not, except as it suits his mind to."

He looked up at me.

"I care for that boy," he said. "Don't regret it. I don't know what he told you, but I'd say you know a bit more than you ought to. I had good reason to—but that's neither here nor in the high country, is it? I'm an impulsive man. This's a mighty surprising business and if there's one thing you learn it's don't be impulsive. Keep your mouth shut. Stick to your side of the street and don't go looking for trouble. Those are rules to live by. Take care of your own. I generally can read a face. Can't read yours."

It didn't sound like a question, but it was. He was asking himself the question, wondering if he still could.

"You got me in a corner, son, and I'll tell you the truth. Don't know what to do about it. I been coroner in this county for forty-two years, seen a lot of things, never seen anything like this. This girl was shot in the head by a twenty-two caliber pistol. She was chewed on pretty good by a bear. Can't tell which of them things happened first. But both of them happened second."

The skin around his mouth tightened, and he looked straight at me.

"This girl was dead before the bear got her, and she was just as dead before the bullet was shot into her head. Now can't I convince you to have some rye whisky?"

5

Uncle Deadly wanted to make one thing perfectly clear. He was talking in hypotheticals. Assuming this, assuming that. So we did it his way; we played that little game of sand castles in the air. Both of us knew there was nothing hypothetical about it.

He hadn't had so much trouble with a corpse since seven illegals burned to death in a bunkhouse down at Two Sleep Canyon a couple of years before. They'd all crawled under the same bed and that's where they were found four days after the fire had burned itself out. He also hadn't handled the other girls who fell victim to grizzly bears in the park in years past. Those attacks occurred on the other side of the Divide, and the coroner at Kalispell did the honors.

Margot Fraser was another story. Her death was a mystery, a puzzle, and it contradicted everything Uncle Deadly had learned about human nature. What Uncle Deadly had learned about human nature was: make it simple.

There was nothing simple about a girl who had died three times.

Uncle Deadly admitted his mistakes. When he found the bullet in Margot Fraser's brain, the first thing he thought about was murder. The second thing he thought about was Mononucleosis Oto, his nephew. He put two and two together and got five. The slug would have made a nice message fired from a handgun with a silencer, nice and deadly and quiet. With some of the powder removed, you could fire it at close range—through a sleeping eye, for instance—and count on it coming to rest in the brain.

He didn't allow himself any reflection when it came to Mononucleosis Oto. He remembered that the kid knew Margot Fraser, he remembered Mono's drunken threats after the two had broken up, and he confronted the kid with what he had found. Mono denied it. But by then it was too late. Uncle Deadly had already decided to walk on the other side of the street and mind his own business. He had submitted his autopsy report according to his rule of human nature. He had made it very, very simple. For the kid's sake. Of course, we were talking in hypotheticals.

It was impossible to say where the bullet entered Margot Fraser's head. There wasn't enough face left to tell, and many of the bones had been crushed. A sleeping eye was as good a guess as any.

The most astounding thing Uncle Deadly found on the autopsy table was that the few centimeters of gray matter around the .22 caliber slug had not hemorrhaged. To him, that could only mean one thing. She was dead before the bullet hit her or the bear got her. Impossible to say how long she'd been dead. It could have been ten minutes. It could have been longer. Impossible to say what she died from. It could have been natural causes. It could have been fright. It could have been a million things. He wasn't there. He didn't know what happened up there at the Grasshopper in the Sunday morning darkness. The more he thought about it, the more he knew he didn't want to know.

As for which came first, the bullet or the bear, he leaned toward the bullet. Where was the opportunity after the bear got her? But if he had to get up in open court and swear on a Bible, something he very devoutly hoped he would not be obliged to do, he would be obliged to say he didn't know which came first. There was no sure way to tell.

And speaking of telling—he looked me hard in the eye.

"A damn fool is his own excuse," he said. "An impulsive old fool. But I haven't lived seventy-four years in this county without building up a sizeable collection of what you might call IOU's. From some pretty wild boys. Anxious to please. Handy with guns."

"We understand each other. I told you before, you're out of it. Mono's out of it."

"You realize I'm still talking in hypotheticals."

I began to like the old guy. He'd dug himself into a nice deep hole not because of death, not because of politics, but because of something to do with a brother who came home from the Navy and a woman who was not well and a big, bullheaded lug from Samoa who needed looking after.

When I reached out to pick up the .22 slug from the green blotter on his desk, he swallowed it up in his bony hand.

"I think not," he said slowly.

I walked myself to the door. Somebody had put glue on Uncle Deadly's seat. But after I got into the car and turned it down the driveway toward the highway, I saw that he had moved. He was standing at the door—inside, in the shadows, and the electric candles were flickering behind him. He wasn't waving goodbye.

By late that same afternoon I was down on the campus at Missoula trying to sort things out and not having much success because of the two blondes in tee shirts playing something called Crash Racer for two bits a turn in a joint that went by the name of L'Espresso. I was drinking something by the same name. Across the front of the tee shirts were the words "Afternoon Delight." They used a lot of body English. I know the language.

I wondered about myself. Why me? I got hooked on that car horn, that painful cry of things that can't be redeemed. It brought back memories, most of them bad. Maybe I was trying to pay back the past. If I read it right, that picture of Margot Fraser told me something, too. It told me she was like a girl I used to know. Self-sufficient. Self-contained. Tough and resilient. A woman in a world of girls.

Whatever happened up there on the meadow under Grasshopper Glacier was part of a world of danger and double-cross and darkness, of great power and small men. A world I thought I was forever done with. I could feel all the old instincts—the quickness, the alertness—moving into place within me, like pieces of a puzzle. It was a do-it-yourself job. I had a pocketful of questions and I needed answers. There was only one place to start looking for them—the three girls who shared that last, dark night with Margot Fraser.

One of them had an opportunity to kiss Margot Fraser goodbye forever. The one who shared her tent. The redhead.

Allison Carpenter.

I paid up and left 15 percent for the lady in white. Then I moved out into the afternoon. Down the block I cut across the street and took directions from a simp with red-tinted glasses and red suede shoes.

Two administrators with pimples sat behind the counter of the

Administration Building with nothing in particular to administrate. Maybe they were waiting for money from home. One was reading a comic book and didn't even look up. The other one was combing his hair.

I picked him.

I said, "I'm here to visit my kid sister; she's a student. I was just over to her place; she's not there. It's a surprise. Her birthday. I came all the way from Marengo. She sent me her schedule and I thought she had the afternoon free. Maybe yesterday and not today. I don't know. But now I can't find the damn schedule—"

I patted my pockets absently.

"Number?"

I looked down the counter. I didn't see any place to take a number.

"I'm the only one here," I said. "You're telling me I need a number?"

I knew colleges had rules. I just didn't know how strict.

"Her number."

"Her number. She's got a number? If I knew it I'd tell you."

The kid peered at me from behind his glasses. He still hadn't stood up.

"Her name."

"Allison Carpenter," I said. "We call her Snooks."

"Last name first."

"Oh. Carpenter. Allison."

I looked at him.

"Snooks," I added.

He was still sitting down, and it was starting to bother me. He was sitting down because he knew that sooner or later he'd have to sit down again, and why monkey with a good thing. He tucked his comb in his shirt pocket, swiveled around in his chair, and played the keys on an oversized keyboard. With one finger. The kid was a real ballerina.

He was done. His finger was poised over the keyboard. He waited a moment. Then a Teletype printer burst into noise across the room. That probably meant he'd have to get up.

He got up. Like it wasn't in the contract. The kid was probably pretty old for eighteen or nineteen, done a heap of living, and his bones hurt. He walked over to the printer, tore off a perforated sheet of paper, and brought it over to me. He took out his comb again.

"You, thank," I said.

"I think what?" he asked. He was spoiling for a fight. But I let it go. He had to be a business major. He wouldn't have understood.

I had her whole schedule in front of me.

It was a few minutes past four o'clock and Allison Carpenter was down for a two-hour seminar, English 421. Seventeenth-Century Wits. Unless she was home with the mumps there'd be no one there to entertain me, an idea I endorsed. I could get to know her real well, before I even met her. She lived in a rooming house on Woodbine Street, an address I had from the board of inquiry report, and it was only a ten-minute walk across the campus.

I walked it. Not too fast and not too slow, figuring I had plenty of time to find it and it would only take me fifteen minutes to make a clean job of her room, depending upon her upbringing. What I wanted to find was a gun. Allison Carpenter had a chance to use it. She also had a chance to ditch it, plenty of chances, but don't let that stop you.

I found the street easily enough and the number, 845. It was on a block off to the side of the campus. A pet hospital and a gas station were at one end of the block and something called the Engineering Club was at the other. Old houses, big mansions, once-upon-a-time lumber baron joints, were in between.

The other side of the block was all houses. You may wonder why I went all the way around the block. It's an old habit that I can't break, like many others.

From the looks of No. 845 you could rent out rooms to six or seven girls, more if they doubled up, fix the plumbing every so often, and still have plenty of time left over for television. It was an old gray stone house, two stories, with big bay windows on either side of the front door. The porch was wood and it needed paint. So did the eaves. That would still leave you plenty of time for TV.

The front door was cut glass set in a heavy frame, with gilt stripes and the address stenciled on it. The last one in or out hadn't shut it. It stood open about two inches. As in welcome stranger.

I checked the street both ways, it was empty, nudged the door with my foot, and stepped into a small entryway.

The door on my left was closed. Somebody's room. A three-by-five notecard was posted on it with a blue thumbtack: "Reggie—10 o'clock at Bombo's. I gave it a pass.

The stairs leading to the second floor were straight ahead, and on my right were a pair of large glass doors leading into what once had been the living room. The doors were closed but I could see through the glass into the darkened room. A mess—pillows all over the floor, a pizza somebody couldn't finish, a stuffed Superman doll laying on its back. There had been a party, but the party was over. The sound of a record player or radio came faintly from that direction.

"The things that I remember, the sorrows were so small," were the words. Sorry, I couldn't name it. I couldn't even tell you what it means.

Allison Carpenter gave her address as 845 Woodbine, 2A, and the 2A could only mean try the stairs. I did. They took me up to the long second-floor hall running the length of the house, doors on either side, all closed, and a small octagonal window at each end of the hallway to let in a little of the afternoon.

On the nearest door someone had written "2C."

I went on down the hall toward the back of the house and sure enough. Even her name was there, printed neatly with a steady hand on a small white card about a third as large as the one downstairs, and taped to the door just below a poster of something called a Frodo.

The door was locked. That took less than thirty seconds, proving there are some things you don't forget even if you want to.

I can't tell you what I expected to find inside Allison Carpenter's room. My mind was open on that point. But I can tell you what I didn't expect to find.

I didn't expect to find what I found.

6

Somebody had redecorated Allison Carpenter's room. Somebody with very bad taste.

I closed the door softly behind me and surveyed the ruins. The drapes were torn off the window rods. A reclining chair was reclining on its side. Books were scattered all over the floor, and that didn't leave very much room for the bookcase, mahogany, which was face-down on top of them. A floor lamp stuck its thin copper leg out from underneath the bookcase.

I took a couple of tentative steps into the room and clipped a fuzzy pink elephant with my elbow. The elephant was on a shelf full of knickknacks. It hit the floor with a crash. How a fuzzy pink elephant could crash, and why it was there at all, is explained by the fifth of whisky that fitted snugly inside it. Expensive, not generic. The Japs think of everything.

I was alone, that was obvious, but I didn't waste any time.

I did the desk first. Nothing to write home about. The chest was easy, just clothes and a couple of blankets. In the two bookcases that hadn't fallen over, the books were flush with the front edge of each shelf but I shoved them back into the case and satisfied myself there was nothing behind them. Except dust. Allison Carpenter didn't have a maid.

The bed hadn't been slept in, but by the time I was finished it looked like the seven dwarfs had played games in it. The closet took a little more time. It was an old walk-in, and it was full. She had nice taste in clothes and apparently she had plenty of money to spend on them. She had pitched her sleeping bag on the floor of the closet, down with the shoes and the slippers and the boots, like she was in a hurry. I pulled it out, turned it inside out, and pitched it back. Of course not. That would be too easy.

Then I checked the bathroom. A hair brush, a blow dryer, a box of tissues, and two cans of hair spray, both empty, were thrown in one corner of the floor. The blow dryer was broken. I would say they nabbed her in the bathroom—it was farthest from the door. Maybe she ran in there after they redid the rest of the place, or maybe they played catch the weasel on the way out.

I flipped open the cabinet over her vanity: razor, blades, powder, glazed copper lipstick, one nickel and two pennies, dental floss, eye shadow, aspirin, hairpins (rusted), petroleum jelly, Super-Lube, Neet. You get the idea. You've got one at home.

There was no gun, .22 caliber, with a silencer.

I told myself I hadn't really expected her to keep it as a souvenir. I was back at work on the desk, giving it another going over, when I heard her say hello.

The second thing I noticed about her was that she didn't need glasses, and if she did it wouldn't have made any difference.

The first thing I noticed was her eyes. Dark blue as the summer sky from ten thousand feet. She was wearing a trim beige suit flecked with black, in a style that was thirty years old but right up to date, with shoulder pads and a black patent leather belt that matched her hair.

"I know. Don't tell me," I said. "Audrey Hepburn."

She didn't even wrinkle her nose.

Her eyes took in the room and then they came to rest on me. I was still taking in her eyes. They made her face look white, like she was suddenly frightened.

"Where's Allison?"

She kept her voice to herself.

"I beg your pardon," I said. "A natural mistake. You only *look* like Audrey Hepburn. You live here, you're a regular, and you thought you'd come up to see whether anything was left in the pink elephant. If you're a regular, none of this would surprise you. Very much."

"Where is Allison?"

She made it a little stronger this time, but it was just as scared.

"How many guesses do I get?"

She looked at me for a long time, uncertain as to whether to take another step into the mess or turn tail and run. She stayed put, the easiest decision because it was no decision.

"My name is Lisa Mueller," she said finally. "Lisa with an *s*. I *do* live here. Right across the hall. Are you a friend of Allie's, or—"

She was having a little trouble with her lower lip.

"I'm her housekeeper."

She clamped her lips together. Then she relaxed them.

"I should have called the police."

"Go ahead. Where's the phone?"

"I should have called the police on Friday."

"Nick Caine," I said. I stood up. She didn't move. "I'm looking for Allison, too. She gave me her key." I shrugged.

Lisa with an *s* wasn't very sure about it, she was still biting her lip, but she took a couple of baby steps into the room. It was my turn not to move. She didn't shut the door. She took a cigarette out of her handbag, lit it, leaned against the wall, let her eyes wander around the room, and exhaled a cloud of blue smoke. That helped a little.

"I heard something."

"Just an elephant," I said. "Don't worry about it."

She glanced quickly at the floor.

"I heard something on Friday. Some noise. And I think—I think it was Allison crying. I should have called the police."

"Obviously she had company," I said. "Maybe she liked her men rough. Two of them, I would say. One couldn't do all this and take care of her at the same time. You would know, you're her friend, you live right across the hall—"

"Not that rough."

She swallowed.

"Not that much of a friend," she added.

She explained. This was graduate housing, and all the residents—eleven of them—were graduate students. Lisa was a graduate student. At three-thirty in the afternoon on the previous Friday she was taking a surprise quiz—between the bedsheets in her own room across the hall. Her adviser, a young anthropologist with a wife who didn't shave her legs, was there, too. He wanted to make sure she got the right answers. She was in the middle of the test when she heard the noise from Allison's room, and she couldn't very well drop everything to go investigate, not if she wanted a good grade. Grades were important to her. That much was obvious. She dressed too well for anything less.

Lisa Mueller didn't tell me all this, of course. Some of it I figured out for myself. When I add two and two, I usually get four, not five. I've been there myself. However, she did tell me the part about her boyfriend's wife not shaving her legs.

By the time the professor went home to see what was on for dinner, it was very quiet across the hall. Lisa tried Allison's door. It was locked. There was no answer to her knocks. She tried a couple more times during the weekend, but she knew there'd be no answer. Allison was never home on the weekend. Eventually Lisa put it out of her mind. Maybe she imagined the noise on Friday afternoon, and the sound of what she thought was a woman crying. The professor sort of wheezed while he breathed, something he picked up in Borneo, and his feet banged into the foot of the bed a couple of times.

"Got it," I said.

"Then a few minutes ago I heard the—"

"You heard the elephant."

"Yes. I thought Allie was back. Honest to God, I don't know her that well. I mean, we're all *strangers* here. A drink now and then. That's all."

Her eyes were calm. The blue was even deeper than before. There'd be nothing like them in Borneo, that's for sure. She looked over the debris of Allison Carpenter's room once again.

"Do you suppose—"

"She was mad as hell and wasn't going to take it anymore," I suggested. "She threw her fit and went away for a while."

"Do you really think so?"

"What I think doesn't matter. As for this mess—keep it under your hat. It's not a nice thing for a grown woman to do."

"Oh! I agree! We have a deal!"

She could add, too.

"Nick Caine?"

I heard her footsteps going on down the hall and then descending the stairs quickly. I checked the hall, closed the door softly behind me, and went down the stairs myself, two at a time.

As I was going out the front door, a girl with an armload of books was coming in. I raised my hand to where the brim of my hat would be if I wore a hat.

"Chow," I said.

"Really," she said, and brushed past me.

It was nearly dark. Thin streamers of cloud picked up the red of the dying sun like knife marks in the sky to the west. The air had suddenly turned cold.

I took a left at the corner and headed back the way I'd come, toward the business district and L'Espresso.

Some things are easy, some things are not. Allison Carpenter was not. She'd ditched the gun and left no traces, not even of herself. That wasn't easy. Her room told you a few things, but not much. She had a closet full of nice clothes, as stated, not only the blue fur jacket but also the Reggio satin and the Calvin Klein charmeuse silks, and she lived in an over-the-hill rooming house. A nice contrast. Either she spent all her money on clothes or somebody else spent a lot of money on clothes for her. Another thing: You couldn't buy clothes that slick off the rack in Missoula. Maybe Allison Carpenter spent her weekends in Paris.

Her desk told me not much. She was organized. All her paper clips were in a little green plastic frog that opened in the middle. She kept telephone numbers in her head or in her purse, and either one might have given me a lead on her but neither was available. Make do. When she doodled she wrote her own name over and over. In large bold letters. A psychologist might be able to make something out of that, besides a fat fee. Under the glass on her desk was a faded newspaper photograph of Jacqueline Bouvier Etcetera Etcetera, leaning over the railing of a yacht. That helped immensely. Maybe she wanted to be an editor.

The small business district was bathed in the pale, sickly glow of sodium vapor lights. What had been neat and clean by day looked like a bad movie by night.

I ducked into a corner drugstore, bought a pack of cigarettes, came back out, window-shopped down the street to a place called Alice's, saw a sign in the window advertising the world's best hot chili, and took them up on it. It wasn't. Next door was a joint called Butch Cassidy's, where you could get cold beer if you could stand the phony Old West atmosphere. I had a beer, one, but I couldn't stand the atmosphere.

Ten minutes later I was on the street again, looking up and down for the Royal Flush. It wasn't there. Mononucleosis Oto must have closed it down for good when he had his little tantrum.

I moved past an Army surplus store, glanced across the street, and stopped.

That's when I saw him.

Not Mononucleosis Oto. Monkey Man.

I moved, he moved. I stopped, he stopped. An amateur. I'd first picked him up out of the corner of my eye in the drugstore. His back was turned, but his head caught your attention.

Now I had a good look at him in the orange glow of the street lights.

I didn't like what I saw.

7

When he dies and the archaeologists get their hands on his skull, they won't be able to tell it from *Pithecanthropus erectus*. His brow hung down over his eyes in a thick, wide ridge of bone. His nose was only a hint. Give evolution a chance. In a couple of million years that nose might amount to something. His mouth was clamped shut and his jaw jutted out a good two inches before falling off into folds of fat and muscle. This gave his face a pitch backwards of about thirty degrees. It didn't help any that his ears were small and gristly, or that his gray hair was trimmed down to a quarter-inch stubble across the flat bones of his head. That he'd been stuffed into a business suit and let out of his cage was somebody's idea of a joke.

There was only one place he could have picked me up, and that was outside Allison Carpenter's rooming house. Here I was getting nowhere fast and somebody was taking a very active interest in my progress. Who? Not Monkey Man, that was obvious. He looked like he'd have trouble tying his shoelaces.

I glanced back across the street.

His shoelaces weren't tied.

The problem was, what to do with him. It would have been easy to let him catch up to me on a side street, where the lights weren't so bright, and scare something out of him. Such as why he had staked out a rooming house from which Allison Carpenter had been hauled kicking and squealing a few days earlier, and whether he was in the redecorating business, and where Allison was now. There were a lot of other questions. But he wasn't so bright either. And he didn't look like he scared easily. By the time I had him in the mood to talk, he wouldn't even be able to answer the easy ones. Such as what happened to your face.

I crossed it off. I needed some stretch time. I had a list in my pocket with three names and addresses on it, three survivors, and Allison Carpenter was only one.

Monkey Man managed to lose sight of me very easily. I don't know how he did it. Maybe he blinked.

If Margot Fraser and Emily Carpenter were thick as thieves, there was a reason for it. They lived together halfway across campus in a red brick residence hall, four stories high. The name was lettered in concrete over the big entranceway, Biehler Hall, and it wasn't until you got all the way up to the door that you could see what someone had added with a can of spray paint. "For Wayward Girls."

The doorman sat at a desk in the lighted lobby. She wore a pink sweater, a pony tail, and round brown specs, and her lips moved when she read. The book in front of her was *Love's Last Passion.* Something like that.

"Avon calling," I said. "I've got some things for Emily Carpenter. Lip brush, eyebrow pencil. Can you call her down?"

"Take the elevator. Third floor to your left. Three-ten."

It's called the old college spirit. She didn't even look up.

I walked on past her and through the empty lobby, spotted the elevator down a side hall, and took a ride. The number, 310, was the first one to the right when I stepped out at the third floor.

She opened the door all the way when I tapped on it, because she was liberated, and she looked me over with a frown.

The frown didn't do anything for her, but at the same time it didn't actually ruin it: red hair swept up on top of her head, blue-green eyes, a nice turned-up nose, a knockout figure, a green blouse with three top buttons she couldn't quite manage, and a white skirt.

I was impressed.

"You're Allison Carpenter," I said.

She laughed.

"You're not Allison Carpenter," I stated.

She laughed again. She had a nice laugh.

"You're Rhonda Fleming."

"Who?"

She turned around and said something into the room. "He wants your sister. Scream if he gets nasty." Then she squeezed past me and walked off down the hall. Loosely.

I peered into the room.

Only one light was on. I couldn't see it, but it cast enough of a glow to show me that the interior was very comfortable. So was the little bundle huddled under the afghan on the sofa across the room. Ms. Mouse.

"Emily Carpenter, I'll bet."

"Mmmmmmmnh."

I stepped past the bathroom and on into the room.

"You *are* Emily Carpenter?"

"Unnnngh."

"I'm looking for Allison."

"Mmmmmmmmnnugh."

"But that wasn't her?"

She pulled the thermometer from her mouth.

"Shit, no."

She did have a large mouth. I watched her while she squinted at the thermometer. Mouse just about covered the rest of it. The scraggly brown hair fell down to her shoulders, but no one could ever ask her to do a commercial. Her eyes were so puffy I couldn't tell their color. Maybe they had no color. Her skin was pale, going to gray. She looked like she could really use a lip brush. All over.

"Are you contagious?" I asked.

"Ninety-eight-point-six. Shit. That's normal. For most people, that's normal. For me, ninety-eight-point-four is normal. I'm running a slight fever."

She began to shake the thermometer, like she didn't believe it.

"You're a reporter," she declared.

"Pretty good. How can you tell?"

"Come in. Close the door. Don't worry, I can tell. I've seen enough reporters since this happened. Even *The New York Times*. Their woman in Denver. Did you see the piece in the *Bugle?* It was shit. You guys really have a racket. The hell with the facts, right? But don't let me stop you. I'm very cooperative. It's good therapy, right?"

She was still shaking the thermometer.

I was very understanding.

"I know you've gone over it a million times. But I thought if we got you and your sister together—"

She flashed me a sharp look. Despite the bad light I finally could see what color her eyes were. They were gray, too, just like the rest of her.

Ms. Mouse had gone over it a million times, but it wasn't enough. She wanted to talk. She *had* to talk. It was the biggest thing that had ever happened to her. For the first time in her life she was front stage center, Margot Fraser was dead and she was still alive, and she had to tell somebody about it. Anybody. It didn't matter whom.

I put myself in the chair across from her and nodded a lot, as if I'd never heard it before. She only interrupted herself once.

"Don't you take notes?"

I pointed to my forehead.

When she got to Margot Fraser's funeral down at Hellgate, back in the mountains, her gray eyes started to fill. She wasn't looking at me any longer. I could see it coming, and when she got to the little piece she recited at the cemetery, Margot's favorite poem, something by a Frenchman about how the destinies of men and animals are bound together, she suddenly stopped.

She threw back the blanket, swung her feet down to the floor, and let it come.

She was a jangle of elbows, bare knees locked together, head down, eyes twisted shut. I was surprised to hear such great sobs and wails and sharp rasping intakes of air come from such a tiny body. Her sister must have gotten all the good genes. This one was nothing but clacking bones and noise.

I half expected Rhonda Fleming to come rushing back into the room, but she didn't. Everyone must have known that Emily had a slight fever.

Ms. Mouse was a vulnerable kid. That was easy to see. Every time she closed her eyes she was back up near the Grasshopper, lying there in the predawn darkness, sensing the terror of sudden death all around her. She was a moth around the flame of her own private agonies.

I looked around for a pink elephant. She didn't have one. Brandy would have been good for her. It would have given her a different shade of gray.

I got up, went into the bathroom, soaked a washcloth in cold water, and brought it back to her.

"Thank you."

"That's okay."

"Thank you."

"It's all right."

"Thank you."

"Don't mention it."

She finally got it under control.

"Shit."

She dabbed at her eyes with the washcloth.

"You see what I mean? I'm sorry. It's therapy. My doctor says I need to talk it out. I have to deal with it. I'm sorry."

"Forget it."

Her face dried fast.

"Margot never did deal with it," she said.

She had my attention.

"She was obsessed with her father," Emily continued. "Classic case. I tried all summer to get her to see my doctor, but she wouldn't. She thought therapy was a crock. Sigmund Fraud, she called it. That's why we were there, you know. That's why she's dead."

Her lips had wrinkles. Emily had rearranged her face into a pout that contradicted the faint gloat in her voice.

"Why were you there?"

"Looking for her father. It's like waiting for Godot."

"Who's her father?"

"Her father's dead," Emily answered quickly. "That's the point. She couldn't deal with it. Margot grew up thinking her father was dead. I didn't know her then, but what difference does it make? It's a classic case. Obsession. She grew up thinking her father was dead, that he died when she was very young. Her mother lied to her, of course. Her mother's sick. The plain truth is that Margot's father left them. He abandoned them. He was weak, you see. It wasn't until last spring that her mother leveled with her, told her the truth about him, that he'd just run away. It was more than she could handle. Depression. Obsession. All the classic symptoms. Do you know Freud?"

"Wow," I said.

Emily leaned forward on the couch, like she was going to share a secret.

"We were looking for her father's bones," she whispered.

I nodded. "His bones."

"Yes," she said. Her eyes darted around the room. "The last thing

Margot's mother ever heard from Margot's father, fifteen years ago, twenty years ago, was a postcard. A picture postcard. And do you know what the picture was?"

"No."

"Right," Emily said. "Grasshopper Glacier."

She collapsed backward into the couch, shaking her head. There was a little flash in her eyes, a helpless assertion of superiority. Even smugness. The ones that live always feel it.

"Douglas Fraser was his name. That was the last anyone ever heard of him. Vanished," she said. She said it a little louder now, not caring whether any of the ghosts in the room heard it or not.

"My guess is he just dumped on them. Started a new life. He was *supposed* to be so brilliant. Margot thought otherwise. Not that he wasn't brilliant. She idolized him. Odysseus. The missing parent. But she thought he was dead, that something terrible had happened to him, he'd had an accident up there, fallen off a trail, something like that. You couldn't reason with her. He was *supposed* to be good in the mountains. But you couldn't reason with her. We went up there all summer, off and on all summer, covered that whole country—"

"Looking for a man who's been gone twenty years."

"Really. That's what I mean, an obsession. She put ads in a lot of papers. Chicago, New York, Hartford, L.A. She didn't really know whether he was dead or alive, not for sure—and that just took over her life. She couldn't deal with it. You have to act your rage, let it out. My doctor keeps telling me, act your rage. Margot kept it inside."

She agreed with herself.

"All four of you went up?" I asked.

"I was her friend. Her *best* friend."

"And Cynthia Farmer? Your sister Allison?"

She considered it.

"They don't know anything about it," she said finally. "It was just a day in the mountains for them. Even Margot and I hardly ever talked about it. Not openly. Listen. I don't think you should put this in the paper. Is that okay?"

She tried to smile at me. She was being confidential.

"They were just along for the ride," I said.

"They invited themselves. My sister invited herself. Shit. I don't even know Cynthia Farmer. Never met her before. She's an ice skater. Cermak's Ice Circus. I wasn't impressed."

"I thought she worked for some data processing outfit."

"Maybe she does. I don't know. But she skates for the Ice Circus. According to Allison."

"And your sister?"

"You'll have to ask Allison about Allison," Emily said sharply. If you could have seen her eyes, you'd know how she felt about it.

She gave me a minute to absorb it.

"People have been asking me about Allison all my life. Merit scholar, all that shit. She'll be happy enough to tell you herself. Don't ask me—"

"I tried to find her. Not home," I said.

Emily made a funny little noise, second cousin to a laugh.

"Shit," she said.

It was my exit line. We were back where we started.

"What newspaper are you with?"

"Thanks," I said.

This time I took the stairs down, not the elevator, and used a side door at the end of the hall just in case somebody was sitting on the front steps tying his shoes. It put me on a street with no lights. The stars were cold and icy blue between the branches overhead.

I got the message. It's always like that. Don't dig too deep. They were the best of friends. I wondered what it was really like between Margot Fraser and Emily Carpenter. Now that one was dead, the other was free. I suppose it could have been worse. They could have been sisters.

I left Ms. Mouse gnawing on her own heart.

The car was where I'd left it several hours earlier, down the street from L'Espresso. It was late, but there was one more name on my list. One more survivor.

I found the place on the north edge of town, rising out of the darkness off the interstate. Floodlights bathed the twin towers in a silvery light. The sign said Ginger Creek, luxury condominiums. But there was no need for it. The joint said money all by itself. It looked like someone was going to the moon. Two towers, each fifteen or sixteen stories high, with a green bubble growing from the ground between them. The green bubble was the pool.

I parked the car near the west tower and followed the curving footpath along the outside of the pool. Behind the steamy green glass the silhouettes of palm trees bent over the moving bodies below.

The lobby of the east tower said the same thing, even clearer. Money. Leather couches, gray statues, flowering plants in gold pots, a little pool with pennies in it.

The elevator was paneled with genuine walnut and it was very, very quiet. When the door slid open on the ninth floor, it didn't even whisper.

That's why I saw him.

He had his back to me. He was standing down at the other end of the hall, next to another bank of elevators, but you couldn't mistake those gristly little ears or that gray fuzz on top of what he called a head. When he finally heard me and turned sideways, his mistake, you couldn't miss that odd angle—thirty degrees back—of what he called a face.

He stepped into an elevator, which also made no sound, and vanished.

Suddenly I wasn't tired.

Her apartment was in the middle. I knocked, she answered.

I said, "Cynthia Farmer."

I was right. She didn't have her skates on, but who needed them? Everything that Ms. Mouse was, she wasn't. And vice versa.

She didn't want any.

"No. Go away. Out. Goodbye."

"Wait a minute, sister."

"No peddlers. I'll call the cops. Get out of here. Who are you? No reporters. Vamoose. I'll call security—"

She tried to slam the door shut, but it stopped about six inches from the catch, because of my foot.

Her smile was on the nervous side.

"Move your foot?"

I kept my foot where it was and moved the rest of me back a little.

"Okay, Goldilocks. Have it your way. I'm not selling anything and I'm not buying anything. Of course not. I'm the Boston Strangler. I never met a ballerina before, especially not one from Cermak's Ice Circus, and certainly not one who puts those little holes in punch cards. Very demanding work. My pleasure. Thanks. I was looking for your autograph, but what the hell. You're a picture and I'll remember you every time I close my eyes. While you're at it, give my regards to the plug ugly down the hall. The guy with the face that breaks mirrors. You know, the ape who took care of

Allison Carpenter and left her apartment for somebody else to clean up. Monkey Man."

I took a deep breath.

I pulled back my foot, spun around, and began to walk back down the hall. After five steps the door still hadn't slammed shut.

"To who?"

8

I corrected her.

"To *whom*. The guy who can't find his way back to the zoo. The goon who followed me. Beauty's only skin deep but ugly goes to the bone. This guy's all bone. And he knows what happened to Allison Carpenter. Monkey Man."

"Followed you? Here?"

I turned to face her.

"Not exactly," I stated. "He got here before I did. Maybe it was you he followed, not me."

The lights in the hall were very low—after all, it was a class joint—but she had her apartment lit up like it was the Fourth of July. It gave her hair an aureole of honey. Of course it may have been my imagination. She was blonde and she looked like gentlemen preferred her. Maybe she wasn't alone. She just stood there sizing me up, not saying anything, smiling the faint crooked smile, nervous, with the door to her apartment open six inches and the aureole of honey. So I figured it was still my move.

I glanced at the opening.

"I'll never make it," I said.

She opened it all the way.

She had recovered her composure, which consisted of gold-flecked eyes, a little turned-up nose just the right size, and a quilted crimson something that she had wrapped around her.

She was alone.

"I didn't interrupt something? A chess game? A crossword puzzle?"

"I was watching a movie. Paul Newman, *Never Give an Inch.* The *TV Guide* described it as frequently pretentious, and I wanted to see how frequently."

She was still sizing me up, even as she talked. She shut the door behind me, threw the bolt, fastened the latch, and turned the lock on the knob. I must have been the right size.

Every light in the place was on. She was afraid of the dark. I followed her down the hall and into the large living room, very modern. She directed me to something that looked comfortable, a long black sofa with white pillows, and I sank into it. It wasn't. It was too modern to be comfortable. Cynthia Farmer was modern, too. But she looked very comfortable.

She stood in the doorway to the living room, looking past me at the floor-to-ceiling windows that kept the darkness out.

"Sin for short," she said. She had taken the smile off her face and tucked it away somewhere inside her crimson robe. If she had instincts, she was trusting them. She looked like she had instincts. Good ones. I guessed she was twenty-three or twenty-four years old, and besides being twenty-three or twenty-four years old she was beautiful.

"Now, what's this about Allison Carpenter? Ever since this happened I've lived in a kind of—a kind of holy terror. I'm down to raw nerves."

She ran her tongue over her lips, they were dry, and walked briskly across the room to the little black bar in the corner, leaning over it to get at the refrigerator underneath. She had her back turned to me. She had a nice back. When she turned around, she had a beer in each hand.

She was about to say something, but I beat her to it.

"Allison Carpenter," I said. "I went to see her. She lives in a rooming house. She wasn't there. Somebody took her. I would say she didn't leave without an argument. The place is a mess. It wasn't as nice as this to begin with. Now it's a lot worse. And she's not there. When I left the rooming house, I picked up a little shadow. A real monkey. He was watching the place and he watched me leave and decided to follow me. How I got rid of him has nothing to do with it. He came here. He came here before I did. The only reason I can see that he came here is because you live here, because he figured I would come here, because you were one of four girls who went up to the mountains and one of three girls who came back down. I don't pretend to understand it."

She had the beers down on the table in front of me but she hadn't straightened up yet. She was paying very good attention.

"When I got here, he was standing down at the end of the hall. Out the door and to the right. Pretending to wait for an elevator. Let me describe him. He may be an old flame. Okay. Take one baby. Stand him on his head. Bring him down from the perpendicular just a little bit. Press hard, for four or five years. He looks like an ape and his face slants backwards and his hair is short and gray. His neck isn't worth mentioning because he doesn't have one. He was wearing a blue business suit. His mother didn't double-knot his shoes this morning. They keep coming untied. Do you know him? Have you ever seen him before?"

It wasn't that the color had gone from her pretty face. Nothing as dramatic as that. But there was a little battle around her eyes. She blinked a couple of times and straightened herself up. For a girl who was down to raw nerves, she was plenty cool.

I said, "There can't be too many like him around, unless they're in a museum somewhere. Stuffed. Maybe he lives here. If you use the pool, and you look like you might, you may have seen him hanging around. He'd go good in a palm tree. Ugly little ears, eyes like a potato's, very long arms—"

"No," she said softly. "I don't."

She backed up without moving.

"Margot Fraser was murdered."

This time she didn't even blink. She didn't show a thing. She hadn't shown much anyway, because she had something inside her that had broken and healed and made her stronger. It wasn't that she was older than the others, or that she'd lived more, although the first was true and I'd bet on the other. It was just that she could handle it. Whatever life served up, she'd take.

I gave it to her straight. She put herself in a chair across the room and she left the lights on, they kept away the dark, and she didn't let her eyes wander. We went back to the beginning.

Some of it I left out, of course, such as Uncle Deadly and Mononucleosis Oto and what had happened a long time ago on the Little Spider, the reason I was there, my own little broken ghost. The rest I included. A .22 caliber bullet and who could have fired it—Allison

Carpenter, although you couldn't prove it. A bear that was part of the act, trained and trusted and turned loose, and where did it come from and where did it go? Allison's room and what it told me, that someone was unhappy with her. Who? The man with the face of a monkey and the brain of a snail. Emily Carpenter, that butterfly hovering over the edge of nothing.

Cynthia Farmer took it all in silence. Only her eyes talked to me, and I couldn't tell what they were trying to say. They were the eyes of a woman who had been deep in more than one kind of darkness.

When it was her turn, the voice was under control—just like the rest of her. The face gave away nothing. Life happened to someone else.

She was twenty-three, not twenty-four. I'm always on the high side, sorry. She'd been born in Jersey City, and there was nothing she could do about it. Her father was the high school track coach there, doubling in golf. Glamour sports. Her mother stayed home and made apple pies. When she was six her family moved to Arkansas, living in a trailer. When she was eight, back to New Jersey. You don't need her life story. Her father went to work in a box factory. Cynthia took up ice skating.

She was a junior AAU finalist at the age of thirteen and she wound up on the front page of the hometown paper, with eleven other girls. Finalist, not champion. She was honest about that. Never a champion. Ice skating did something real for her. It gave her discipline, and it got the image of broken glass and weeds and factories out of her head.

When it came time for college she wound up in the mountains. She thought about Boulder but decided against it. Not enough money to cut it with that crowd. Her major was lit of the French variety but she never really got into it. She quit after three years to skate, this time with Cermak's Ice Circus, a road show that works the mountain states. The pay was good, not great, but that wasn't the reason. She thought she'd be a star.

Now she didn't know. Two years and lightning hadn't struck. Maybe she'd go back to school. She doubted it. Maybe she'd try for the Ice Follies. She doubted that, too. Suspended animation, she called it, the modern condition. She practiced four hours a day, sometimes five, very early in the morning. In the afternoons she worked at TechTronics. It paid the light bill. She had quite a light bill.

She went along with the other girls to Grasshopper Glacier because Allison Carpenter had asked her and what she usually said was yes. A small defect in her character. She wasn't the outdoors type, she'd never been there before, and she didn't want to go back. Who can blame her?

She'd never met Margot Fraser before. She'd never met Emily Carpenter before. Allison was an acquaintance. They were both regulars at a roadhouse called The Tarot, about fifteen miles south of town back in the foothills. Not really friends, but Allison was hard to miss. She was everybody's sweetheart, played the crowd, and never got serious about anyone. Or anything. Allison had shown up at The Tarot one evening with a real mink, blue, and that could only mean one thing. She had a man somewhere, a man with money. The way Allison dressed said her man was older than she was and didn't mind spending it. The way Allison was never around on weekends said her man was somewhere else.

These were Cynthia's observations, not mine, but I gave her good marks for observation. I gave her good marks for everything. But she had nothing to add on the events at Grasshopper Campground.

It was long past midnight when we finished asking and answering, and I suppose she had decided long before then. Maybe when she went to get more beer for the third time. Her robe had fallen open and what she had on under it was called see-through. I saw through it right away.

"Why did I do this, Nick?"

"Do what?"

"Let you in here."

She stood there and looked down at me. The half smile was back on her face.

"You're afraid of the dark."

"I'll get myself killed," she said.

She went around turning out lights.

I'd like to say I explored every curve and angle of her body, and that you could tell how good it had been for her because of the way she was breathing, but I'm old-fashioned and I only explored one angle and seven or eight curves. As for her breathing, she was. There was nothing suspended about her animation.

I hadn't planned on it, but what the hell. It's better than running a mile a day.

Whatever it was, she kept it to herself. She kept almost everything to herself, but not quite. I could only guess at it. Fear? A man who went away? A man who didn't run away? Maybe not. Maybe it was only desolation. Maybe it was only life. She got up three times and left the bedroom and came back, silent, to my side. Her hand searched for the covers.

I don't know about you, but I do my dreaming before I fall asleep. This time I wished I hadn't.

I was back on the Little Spider two Septembers ago, scrambling up the hill for a better look. The gun, a Margolin Special, had been wedged in the top of the tent bag and I had it out and in my hand. Black smoke curled below me, down the road. To the left, around the curve at the bottom of the hill, I saw them through the trees.

Two men, walking quickly along the shoulder of the road. Their car was off to the side, a quarter-mile away. I got there first. They never saw me. The first one never even heard me. When he stumbled and fell face-down on the gravel, the blood surrounding his head in helpless spurts, the other one looked up in my direction. His arms began to flop. His eyes went crazy. Then he fell backward on the empty road and was still. I took the big one first, dragging him back through the dust. The car was still burning. The windows were melted in. A dark shadow lay bent and brittle against the wheel. I hoisted him up to my shoulders and shoved. Then I went back for the other one. The bullet had caught him in the forehead, just above the right eye. There was no blood. I carried him back and got up close to the heat. He was already dead, but it didn't make any difference.

It was something to walk away from, and I did. By then the horn had stopped. There was no sound. Just the silence closing in through the steep and empty hills.

I woke up once during the night. She was weeping. I pulled her toward me. Her hair was soft and wet against my throat.

We all have something to dream about.

9

Burt Bacharach was right about a little loving in the morning. Her skin was like silk, only warmer. But it took three cups of coffee to get the rest of me awake.

I was on the fourth cup, the clock on the wall said ten minutes past ten, when she stopped being busy and sat down at the table in the little kitchen. The aureole of honey was gone, but she still looked good. Better, in fact.

"Dead wrong," she said finally. "A single woman is single. A married woman, a woman who's been married once, is unattached." She gave me Wednesday's smile, full of woe. "Nothing so popular as divorce. Just one of life's little tragedies."

She laughed softly. Reflex. But those gold-flecked eyes weren't having any part of it. The smile vanished, and she leaned toward me.

"I know who he is. The one you call Monkey Man."

That'll do it, too, just as well as coffee. I was awake, trying to read that earnest look in her eyes.

"I know I should have told you last night, but I couldn't. I hate to think about him. His name is Joseph P. Daddano and he owns The Tarot. It has to be him. Some people call him Big Daddy, because he likes that. I don't know anyone who calls him Monkey Man. Except you. But there couldn't be two people in the world like that, Nick. He looks like a—"

"Right. He looks like a guava that somebody chewed on for a

while and then spat out, because it tasted bad. What does he do at The Tarot?"

"He tends bar. Breaks up fights. Books the acts. Mostly he chases after girls."

Her eyes dropped toward her lap.

"The younger the better," she added. "He forgets to close his mouth. His tongue hangs out. He's a pig. You should see him when he smiles. He looks like a—"

"Right. He looks like something a moose would do after a big meal. Obviously he knows who you are, Cynthia. He wouldn't be here otherwise."

Her face was puzzled.

"I'm sure he knows who I am, but I've never seen him around here before. Never. Only at The Tarot. He once asked me for free tickets to the ice show. Thirty of them. He was very upset when I told him no."

I finished my coffee, checked the clock, and stood up.

"It's me he wants, not you. He's looking for a free something and it's not tickets. I had a shirt. Blue on blue."

She went to get it.

When she came back, she got very close to me.

I said, "Give me ten minutes to get the garbage out. Then come down. He won't bother you. He may not even be here. There's a motel down the road, a big green neon tree out front—"

"Callahan's," she said.

"I like the furnishings here better, and I haven't even been there. But let's leave you out of it. I'll check in at Callahan's. If you need me, call. Anything suspicious. They'll take messages. One other thing. The police. They can find Allison Carpenter a lot faster than I can, and I've got other things to do, and I'm going to let them have her. The police will come here. They might ask you about Margot Fraser. They might even ask you about me. I hope you've got a short memory."

Her eyes told me yes.

"All the things I told you last night about Margot? Forget it. That's the only way you can stay out of it. As for me—"

"I won't forget," she said.

I knew what she meant.

I cupped my hand under her chin and looked down at her.

"I never say goodbye, Nick."

I said it for her.

The hallway was empty in both directions, but that didn't mean anything. If Monkey Man and whoever worked his gears were really anxious to know what I was doing, and why, the Neanderthal would still be around. Somewhere. All I had to do was knock over one of those little trees in the lobby so he could find me.

When the elevator came to a stop and the doors slid open, I could see that the lobby was empty, too. Sunlight poured in through the high windows. It filtered through the leaves and plants and put patches of green shadow on the polished floor.

I took a sharp right from the elevator and crossed the lobby and was nearly at the glass doors when I realized where he would be. After all, he had the brain of an ape.

I doubled back past the elevators, hooked to the left down a short corridor, and pushed open the heavy door to the pool area. It was steamy. An old man sat in a white plastic chair at the far end, staring into the empty pool. Ponce de Leon, dreaming of Florida. He didn't even know I was there.

The door on the other side of the pool opened into another corridor. I took it. And then took half a left into the lobby of the west tower.

Except for him, it was empty.

He was standing at the entrance, making sure that my car in the parking lot didn't go away without him, and he was so wide he blocked the light. He made the mistake of starting to turn as I came up behind him, which put his face right in the way of my fist. That made his nose a little flatter, and it was just a suggestion to begin with.

He barked once, his head wobbled, and he started to bend.

My knee showed him why boys are different than girls. It straightened him up. He pushed off the glass door, bounced out to meet me, and said hello to my forearm. He still didn't have his hands up.

I grabbed one arm, his left, spun him around, and brought the wrist up hard behind him. When I let go the arm hung limply at his side. Not even the fingers moved.

He looked at me and coughed. The guy had no manners at all. He was trying to figure it out. He knew something was happening to him but he wasn't sure what.

I stepped into him with a left in the chest, just below the ribs, and caught his jaw on the way down, and he lay still. He spoiled the view. His foot kicked for a couple of seconds, but then even that stopped.

Cynthia was right. John P. Daddano's mouth was open. John P. Daddano's tongue was out. John P. Daddano was a human flytrap, and that's giving him the benefit of the doubt.

I didn't step on his face because I didn't want to confuse the archaeologists.

The air outside was bright and cold. I unlocked the car, got in, and began to do my count. Then I stopped. He may have been dumb, but he wasn't stupid. He wouldn't have wired the car and then parked himself behind a glass door to watch the fireworks.

Callahan's was less than a mile down the road. The land of the neon pine. I parked in the motel lot near the office, crossed over to the gas station next door, found the phone booth next to the apron, and filled it. The number I wanted was on the pay box.

When he answered, I said:

"There's a man on the floor of the lobby out at Ginger Creek. People have to walk around him because he's too ugly to look at. If he wakes up and his jaw still works, which it may not, ask him about the mess at eight forty-five Woodbine."

"Woodbine? Say again? Eight forty-five Woodbine?"

"Sure. Let me be kind enough to repeat it. There's a man in the lobby out at Ginger Creek. The west tower. He's polishing the floor and he's putting everything he's got into it. Whisper eight forty-five Woodbine in his ear and see whether his eyes open. His ears are those funny little things on the side of his head. You might miss them. Whatever you do, don't step on his face."

I heard the cop saying to someone else: "Woodbine."

I hung up.

There's no use pretending I liked having the cops in on it, but they weren't all the way in and I didn't think they would be. Once they opened the door to Allison Carpenter's apartment, they could do in a day what would take me a week to do. And I had other things to do.

I was counting on one thing. Monkey Man might open his eyes eventually, but once the cops started in on him his mouth would stay closed.

I stepped over the metal bumper, crossed the motel parking lot, and pushed open the door to the office. The desk clerk took my name and seventeen dollars and looked around to see whether I had any company. He was disappointed.

He slid the key over to me. I took it and headed for the room. At the corner of the lobby I passed a newspaper vending machine, green and white, gave it a glance, took a couple more steps, and turned around to look again.

I was wrong. Dead wrong, as the lady says.

No wonder the cop on the phone had a one-track mind. It wouldn't take the police to find Allison Carpenter after all.

Allison Carpenter had found herself.

10

I fed the machine its breakfast, a dime, took out a newspaper, and walked slowly down the hall to my room.

They found Allison Carpenter folded up in the front seat of her car shortly after midnight. She had been dead two or three days; it was hard to tell. The car, a gray Porsche 928, was parked on the street just around the corner from the rooming house at 845 Woodbine. I remembered it. The reason I remembered it is that the car had a tan dust cover tucked around it. The reason they didn't find Allison Carpenter sooner was the same.

A bored beat cop who had just come on duty lifted a corner of the cover, flashed his light inside, and felt faint.

They found the flexible hose when the crime lab boys arrived and lifted the rest of the cover. It was the kind of hose mechanics use when they're working on a car inside a service bay, and it was attached to the exhaust pipe. The free end went in through the window on the passenger side.

Suicide? Nobody was buying it. Who would gas themselves to death on a public street? There was no note. There were no obvious marks on the body. And Allison's apartment had been ransacked. None of the other girls in the rooming house had seen anything or heard anything. No one had seen Allison since the previous Friday. The circumstances were "mysterious." Autopsy scheduled. End of summary.

I chewed on it.

What did it mean? It meant that Allison Carpenter was there all along, all the time I was going through her apartment. It meant that Monkey Man must have been watching the car as well as the rooming house. It meant that the cops had been working on it for nearly twelve hours. Of course, it also meant that Allison Carpenter was dead. That's what it meant most of all.

I tossed the newspaper on the bed, didn't bother to read the comics, opened the door, and went down the hall to the lobby. The pay phone was in the corner. I dialed a number I'd learned that morning.

There was no answer.

She'd either gone to work or had company and couldn't get to the phone. I voted for the former. I considered putting a call through to TechTronics but gave it a pass. Cynthia would find out soon enough. Depending upon how strongly they doubted suicide, the boys in blue would be by to see her sooner or later.

I dug deep for another nickel. The operator upped the ante. This time I had an answer. A woman who had gone to school to learn how to talk through her nose. I told her who I wanted and she had to look it up. Finally he came on the line.

"Pug, Nick."

I told him where I was in case he needed some good company. I filled him in on the news about Allison. He didn't faint from surprise. It was his turn. He filled me in on the crews that had been out looking for the bear that mauled Margot Fraser for the fun of it. They had come back empty-handed, and what else did you expect? One thing. Back in the woods, a good distance from the campground, they had found an old chain secured to a tree.

"What kind of tree?"

"Didn't ask."

At the end of the chain there was plenty of nothing. That left us even. I thanked him and walked over to the desk clerk. He was standing in front of the motel switchboard.

"I'm expecting a message. Maybe more than one message. Save them for me."

I was thinking of Cynthia Farmer.

"Why don't you use the phone in your room?" he asked.

I looked at him.

Twenty minutes later I had worked my way free of the maze of noontime traffic and I was sailing south on the highway out of town, hoping I was still a step ahead of the cops. The needle on the speedometer pointed straight at sixty. There was little traffic.

Nevertheless, I almost missed it.

It flashed by on my left, a large compound of several white buildings set back from the road and surrounded by a high chain-link fence. By the time I saw it, it was too late to turn. I drove down another half-mile, turned the car around, and cruised back slowly, rolling an idea around in my head.

I parked inside the gate, next to the ark. The ark is what caught my eye. Thirty feet long and ready for the deluge, as in Noah. The wooden sign at its base, nearly hidden by the tall brown grass, said:

ANIMAL RESEARCH STATION
STATE UNIVERSITY

I went through the doorway into the darkness of the main building.

"You the boss?"

I knew she wasn't. Too young, for one thing. She had her hair drawn up in a bun, her nose was wrinkled with distaste, and the sleeves of her red chamois shirt were turned up above her elbows. She was standing underneath a bare light bulb that descended from the high ceiling, next to some packing crates that stood higher than her head, and she had her hands deep in a steel drum filled with something that didn't look good.

"There is only one boss and Professor Reimann is it," she said.

She didn't stop kneading whatever it was that didn't look good through her hands.

"Out back," she added.

The place was like a warehouse, front and back doors open, and it was cold inside. I went out the back door into the sunlight and saw him leaning against a split-rail fence in the distance.

His back was to me. He was talking to a long-legged crane on the other side of the fence, maybe about the weather, maybe about the egg market. He heard me coming across the gravel, turned his head, and went back to his conversation.

He straightened up when I got there and turned around. I expected a cold-eyed German, but he wasn't. He was young, he was thin, and his blue eyes were cheerful. They looked like they had secrets behind them. His hair was thinning, but even at his age that was professorial. He had a pipe stuck in the corner of his mouth and that was very professorial. The bowl of the pipe was bright orange; the stem was sky blue.

"Professor?"

"Yup," he said. He put out his hand. "They call me that. Otto Reimann."

You can add this: his voice was an octave too high. The doctor must have put two knots in his umbilical cord when he was born, instead of one.

I said, *"Times-Union."*

"Yup."

His head nodded in agreement. He'd heard of it. Most people do that. They don't like to talk to cops or strangers, but they'll talk to anyone who knows the name of a newspaper and who looks like he knows something he can't mention. It makes them feel real. They're honored. At last somebody's taking them seriously. I know the names of a lot of newspapers, including the *Rocket,* the *Item,* and the *Times,* and those I don't know I make up, including the *Rocket,* the *Item,* and the *Times.* It doesn't make any difference. They still talk.

He looked at me.

"You're the tail end of the parade," he said. "Yup. She was a bright girl, best we had. Her interest was grizzlies. You can make out of that whatever you want to, seeing as it was a grizzly that took her. Most of these kids ought to find jobs as vets or go work in a zoo. You know what I mean, nothing wrong with it. Margot Fraser was different. She was a damned sight different. She was serious about it. She put in her time, here and back in the chemistry lab on campus."

He tapped his pipe on the fence. The crane fluttered backward, stopped, and cocked its head.

"We do biology here," he continued, "animal behavior. Find out what makes these critters tick. It's called ethology, the study of—"

He wasn't looking at me anymore but he was still talking. It didn't take much to get him started. Like I said, professorial.

He decided to move away from the fence and scare up some coffee. I followed him, listening to his Margot Fraser routine. He had it down pat. After all, I was the tail end of the parade and he'd been over the same ground before.

Margot was working on something called sensory perception in grizzly bears. She was trying to find out what turns a grizzly bear on and what turns him off. It meant monkeying around with a lot of scents and odors—raw meat, perfume, human blood, sweat, essence of acorn. You get the idea. Add this, take away that, until you wind up with something that makes a bear want to shave and put on a necktie. He gets very excited. Or he gets sick to his stomach. Margot had three or four kids in the chemistry lab working on it for her, and she put in plenty of time there herself. Her goal was very practical. Come up with something that would make a grizzly go home to mother. Make the back-country trails safe for democracy.

Margot had already had one research paper accepted for publication by a fancy scientific journal. Accepted, not published. It would be published in about ten years. But it was still quite a mark for an undergraduate to hit, and the Professor was proud of her. He'd liked her. There was no doubt about that. He said he'd tried to talk her into going to Berkeley for the summer, even promised to pull some strings for a free ride, but she said no thanks. She wanted to hang around the biology station, work on her project, get up into the mountains.

"Yup," he said. "She was a damned sight different."

By the time he led me back to the main building and down an aisle between the packing crates and into the little cubbyhole he called an office, Reimann was talking about sticklefish. He had an eye on the main chance.

By the time he worked his way around behind his desk and wedged himself into a chair, he was talking about where the money was going to come from to keep the program going, and to keep turning out people like Margot Fraser, and wouldn't it be wonderful to have a story in the newspaper, and maybe some people would sit up and take notice of the great things State students were doing in the field of animal behavior.

"Ethology," he said. "E-t-h-o- . . ."

There was barely enough room for his big desk and a couple of stiff wooden chairs in what he called an office. The walls were covered with black-and-white photographs in black frames, most of them pictures of animals, but one wasn't and of course I spotted it right away.

Margot Fraser in a dress and a smile. She didn't look comfortable in either. She was facing three middle-aged men who didn't like photographers any more than she did, and their faces showed it.

The Professor was giving me a tour of the wall.

"That little bugger's an ocelot, smart but snappy. You've got to watch him. That bird up there is a saddleback bird, right there next to him. Took that photograph myself. There we've got a hawk, yup, and right adjacent to the same is—"

Finally he caught up with me.

"Yup, that's her," he agreed, pouring the coffee out of the glass pot, "and those three gentlemen with her, that's Rashad, Morgan, and Martin Augerman. Augerman runs Empire Industries. You may have heard of it. Corporation types. They give us a little money, thirty-five percent or so, and I wouldn't have that picture up there, tell you the truth, except for the fact that it's good business. You run an operation like this, you've got to keep one eye on the pot and the other on the kettle. Those gentlemen come back, they might like seeing that picture up there on the wall. Lets them know we appreciate all they do—to avoid taxes."

Reimann had a wry smile on his face, as though he was letting me in on a secret. He banged the bowl of his pipe on the top of the desk and added a few scraps of charred tobacco to his collection.

"Now that one next to Rashad is a timber wolf. We don't see him around much anymore—"

I interrupted.

"What was Margot Fraser doing in the picture?"

He sighed and lifted himself out of his chair. He pointed to something in Augerman's hand.

"You see that? Money. A certified check. They came up from Denver last winter and they wanted a ceremony—can't blame them—and we picked Fraser to take the money and run."

He chuckled to himself.

"Would you want to see Fraser's bear?"

"She had a bear?"

"A good old sow. Come along."

He squeezed out from behind the desk, stopping only to finish his coffee, and led me out into the cold sunlight again. He made sure I saw all the sights on the way—the fish tanks, the bird house, the reptiles. Any one would make a good picture for a newspaper story. You get the idea. I did, too. He led me around the corner of a building. We went past his friend the crane and finally stopped in front of a large pen, double-fenced.

There was a lean-to off in the back corner of the pen, and in the lean-to was a large pile of brownish-gray fur.

"Hey, Babe!" the Professor squeaked. "Sooey!"

He turned to me.

"Like calling a pig," he said.

The bear didn't move.

"She doesn't seem to be as smart as a pig," I said.

"Brainwise, about as much as the European brown. That's the one you see doing tricks in the circus. Babe's a grizzly. She's bigger, but she's smart enough. This old girl's hardly wild. A wild bear would be long gone by now. Yup. Babe does her share of tricks. Margot used to go right in there with her. I wouldn't advise it, but she—"

"What kind of tricks?"

He looked up at me, like he never thought I'd ask.

"You stay right here."

He walked over to a shed about forty feet away, did something to the lock, opened the door, and disappeared inside. When he came out he was carrying a stick in his hand, maybe twelve inches long.

I heard the bear coming behind me. She must have seen him.

"Hey, Babe!" he squeaked again.

He poked the stick through the fence at her, pulled it back, and then flipped it high in the air to the far side of the pen. The bear turned on a dime and loped after it, gracefully. She didn't bring it back. She chewed on it. I could hear it snapping between her teeth.

But the Professor was happy.

He squinted at me.

"Have to confess!" he laughed merrily. "There's a trick to everything."

He reached into his back pocket and pulled out an aerosol can. He held it up for me to see.

"Some of Margot's stuff," he beamed. "Looks like hair spray, doesn't it? But it's not. Thirty-five syllables just to get halfway through it. She cooked it up over at chemistry. A bust, not quite what she was looking for, but that's science."

"A bust?"

"Yup. Drives old Babe crazy, doesn't it? I coated the stick with it."

He shook the can.

"Empty."

He turned quickly on his feet and hooked it toward the metal drum that stood near the little shed.

I watched the aerosol can turn end over end through the air. It seemed to move in slow motion, but it sent my mind racing back to the mess in Allison Carpenter's apartment. Those weren't cans of hair spray I'd seen on the bathroom floor. Those were cans of something that took thirty-five syllables to get halfway through. I knew I'd have dreams about it. Bad dreams, about Allison Carpenter lying up there in the darkness at Grasshopper Glacier, and Margot Fraser already dead, her face thick and runny with some kind of chemical that drove bears crazy.

The can made a sharp ringing sound when it hit the edge of the steel drum and dropped inside.

"Nice shot."

"Yup. Two points for our side."

11

I thought about it all the way down to Hellgate. The long, lonely interstate was empty. The mountains filled up the windshield ahead. Out the side window a couple of dry, withered towns drifted by, on the verge of blowing away, and a couple of Indian trading posts on lease from the Czechs. And then there were none. When I got to a place called Henley, I turned back into the hills on the asphalt, climbing higher and higher with every curve. I reached around, grabbed the sweater from the back seat, and struggled into it without stopping.

The light was already bleeding out of the sky.

Margot Fraser was the lucky one, if you can call dead lucky. She never knew what hit her. It was Allison Carpenter who had had to live with it, and now she was dead, too. It was Allison who had carried all the sad freight—waiting it out in the darkness, afraid to move, afraid to think about the dead girl next to her in the tent and what would come next, hovering on the edge of nothing when the bear finally came over the mountain, and the day broke, and the bear did what it was supposed to do. The whole thing was a charade. Put it in the vernacular. Allison had balls. Why? Why put herself through it? Why kill someone twice? Three times, if Uncle Deadly's suspicions were right. It didn't make sense. Someone had to be with the bear, to turn it loose. Who? There was another question. Why was Allison dead? How do you make someone dead in her own car on a public street without leaving a mark on her?

The road was rough, cracked and heaved by the frost. It didn't shake loose any answers.

On Stellar's Plains the asphalt leveled off. Nobody going the other way, nobody going my way. I was getting close to the edge of the world. A ranch slipped by, back from the road in the scrub trees. I could see the gap in the mountains ahead, the white clouds pouring through, three or four buildings coming up on the flat horizon, and then the metal sign banging in the wind: Hellgate.

It didn't even say slow down.

There are some towns I'd rather live in than visit. Hellgate is one of them. If you lived there, you could stay in the house. You wouldn't have to go out in the wind.

The town was only a block long. Make it a short block. The open prairie widened out behind it, toward the sky. There were three buildings on the north side of the highway, two on the south. Frame. The wood had the life bleached out of it by the wind.

A yellow dog crossed the asphalt ahead of me, head turned, watching.

I slowed down, pulled off the road and onto the concrete shoulder in front of a general store, killed the ignition, and sat for a moment. The wind kept coming from the west. Balls of tumbleweed bounced down the center of the highway past the car. Maybe if there were no buildings you wouldn't hear it, but there were and I did. A low, mournful sound, a whisper, a sudden shiver in the air. Time and the wind was scouring it down to earth again, erasing it, blowing it away. Soon there would be only rock, bone white, and a few brave blades of grass.

I rolled up the window, pushed open the door, and leaned into the wind. Three pickup trucks were parked across the road in front of the saloon. I made my way toward them, head turned away from the wind and the fine abrasive dust, watching.

It was a big saloon but business was nothing to brag about. Four men inside. Three of them turned their heads to look at me when I came through the doors. The other one didn't. He was counting his fingers. I took the stool at the end of the bar and nodded to the regulars, as in friendly. Howdy pardner. They didn't nod back.

"Nice day. A little windy."

It must have been. They didn't argue about it. They didn't say anything.

The bartender broke himself loose from the gathering at the other end of the bar. He walked down toward me on the skids, and before he got to me I let him know what I wanted was a beer. He brought it.

"And Mrs. Fraser," I said. "I'm looking for a Mrs. Fraser. Douglas Fraser."

"Fraser?"

It was nearly a shout, and it came from one of the regulars down at the other end of the bar. He must have been hard of hearing. His voice wasn't too good either.

I stayed put. The bartender's mouth turned downward but it didn't open. He shook his head sourly. I looked down toward the barker.

"Correct. Douglas Fraser. His wife."

The barker turned toward his companions. His voice sounded as though it were strained through gravel.

"Ever hear of Douglas Fraser, his wife?"

"No."

"Bronco. A Mrs. Fraser?"

Bronco shook his head.

"Skippy. Ever hear of Maureen Fraser?"

Skippy didn't answer. Skippy didn't even shake his head. He was still counting his fingers. He was a slow counter.

"You're out of luck, Jack," the barker said to me. "We never heard of her."

I took no for an answer because I didn't have time to work up a yes at those odds, three and a half to one. I finished the beer and went back out into the wind. A Jeep had pulled up behind the Capri across the road, and a kid was getting back into it. I hurried across.

He was slim, maybe fifteen years old, and his blond hair was trimmed closely across the top of his head. He had a large ball of twine in each hand and he was putting them on the floor behind the front seat of the Jeep. He didn't jump.

"I'm looking for Margot Fraser's mother. Where she lives. I was just across the street, you may have seen me coming across. There are three guys in there. You may know them. Curly, Larry, and Moe. The other guy is named Skippy. He's counting his fingers and can't be interrupted. I think he's having trouble with number seven. They never heard of Maureen Fraser. I thought you might."

He looked vacantly past my shoulder at the pickup trucks across the highway and then met my eyes. But only for a second. Cat had his tongue, too. Maybe they didn't learn to talk in Hellgate because the wind wore them out: open your mouth and it cleans your teeth.

The kid stuck out his thumb—west, down the highway. He put his hands on the door and jumped over it into the seat. He backed the Jeep up about three feet. I got out of the way.

"How far?" I hollered. "A mile? Two? Ten?"

He gunned it. It kicked up sand and dust, the wind carried it away, and he squealed onto the asphalt in a wide turn. As he roared past me he grinned—his face was all bones—and he flashed a peace sign with his right hand.

Peace.

I went west, out of town. About a mile out, the road started going up again. At a mile and a half a fence started on the left, and a little further on a gravel lane cut out across the prairie from a house in the distance. I checked it. Two miles. Thanks, kid.

I turned off the road, stopped the car, got out, opened the gate, got back in the car, pulled up, and did it all over again. It was just bunch grass, but the two horses down by the far corner of the fence had their noses in it. The house was long and low, a ranch house. No flowers, no shrubs. Nothing to make it home. I was going to hit the bell but I didn't have to. She was watching. She must have spent a lot of time at the window.

She opened the front door and peered out at me through the storm door.

I said, "Maureen Fraser?"

She had a glass of something in her hand and she raised it. She had the most bittersweet smile I've ever seen.

"Here's looking at me, kid."

She reached for the storm door and opened it, and I stepped inside. Afternoon, and she was already drinking. Alone.

I shook the wind off my back.

"What is it?" I said. "Hemlock?"

"As the wind is, sir, so is mortal life—a moan, a sigh, a sob, a strife."

She waved the glass in the air and it found her lips. She stood there in the doorway, looking me up and looking me down, and when her eyes finally found mine she stayed with them. I returned the favor.

She was thin, a wisp of a woman, with a black sweater and a black skirt that didn't act her age and brown boots that came halfway up her calf. She had nice legs, considering that she'd slipped past forty without bothering to tell anyone. Maybe past forty-five. You could see it in her hands, although her face was still good. Her eyes were steady and alive, bright blue, and if she had any gray anywhere she kept it hidden.

Her laugh was pleasant and I followed it into the big sunken living room. It had some training in it, that was obvious. Today we laugh. Tomorrow we cry. The next day we will laugh and cry.

"What is it?" she said. "Combines? Fertilizer? Tea cups? Heifers?—"

That little laugh had a black border on it.

"Dreams," I answered.

She turned around.

"But I'm collecting, not selling. Have you heard about Allison Carpenter? Allison Carpenter was one of the girls with Margot, up in the mountains—"

She froze, with the drink halfway to her lips.

"They found her last night. Dead."

The drink went the rest of the way. The eyes were a little less steady. She looked away.

"Yes," she said in a small voice. "Of course. I heard it on the radio."

She crossed the room and stood with her back to me, not speaking. She seemed very small against the window and the mountains and the sky outside. Her voice, when she finally found it, was a whisper.

"I don't believe I knew her. I don't believe she attended the—"

"The funeral," I said to myself.

Maureen Fraser lifted her glass to the mountains outside and emptied it and put it down on a small, round table in front of the window. Her heart was as empty as her glass. Her thin black shoulders trembled.

She was weeping.

Her hands hung helplessly at her sides, opening and closing, opening and closing, grasping at nothing.

There are two things you can do. You can get up and go over to them and touch them and turn them around and draw them back from whatever edge they stand on. Or you can leave them alone with it. Neither one is any good. I could hear the wind as it hit the house and swept on past, shuddering down through what they called a town, Hellgate, crying down over the plains and valleys below—cold, heartless, wearing away the flesh and rock, whispering of things that will never be.

I got up and walked to the other side of the room, in front of the fire. Watching the orange flames.

"Well. Forgive me."

Her voice was distant and dry.

I turned, and she was standing with her back to the bright window, looking at me. I took her glass and went into the kitchen. The bottle was on the counter. When I came back she was sitting on the sofa watching the fire, hugging herself to keep warm.

I can't tell you why, maybe it had something to do with the wind coming down from the mountains, or the house that nobody lived in anymore. But she talked. I listened. Her voice was as far away and melancholy as the wind. It drifted with broken dreams, bits and pieces of things that didn't fit together but floated up in her mind because they were there, had been there all along, too long, and needed to come out and break free. The Pierrot she had when she was a little girl. The brother who died in a boating accident. The naked mannequin she saw in the store window. The economics professor at Northampton who looked like John Garfield. The father who had gone to school in New Haven and married in New Haven and had his children in New Haven and made his money in New Haven and went to Florida every summer—Palm Beach, the only place he ever went unless you count Chateau-Thierry—and didn't like it and couldn't wait to get back to New Haven and died in New Haven. Fat and rich and mourned by all who knew him.

And, of course, Douglas Fraser.

She closed her eyes. Her pale cheeks were smooth, somehow younger than the mesh of bone and muscle they masked, or the memories.

"I called him Huck Finn," she said. "He was an engineer, electronics, and he collected Bach. Bach and women. I knew that when I married him."

She looked at her drink, thought about it a moment, and decided yes.

"Douglas had gone to Cornell. He graduated with honors, third in his class, and then came home to New Haven. That's where I met him. A long time ago. I was twenty-one years old then and finishing up at Smith. Douglas had gone to work for the firm, for my father.

He cut a figure. The girls hung all over him, he was quite a catch. I knew that. Father didn't like him. He recognized his genius—I'm sure of that—but they were quite different personalities. Father would say things like—a man without ambition is a man without a future. Work late, grow great. Douglas just sailed before the wind, and Daddy never understood him.

"We were married in the spring. I was twenty-two, and one day Douglas said—let's light out for the territories! So we did. That's why I called him Huck Finn. We moved to Chicago, Douglas gave up a good job, Margot was born there, and he started up his little laboratory there, on the West Side. Father never approved. Bohemians and Poles and Irish and Negroes! Gangsters!"

Her eyes were suddenly warm. She stood up, reached into a big wicker basket for a fresh log, and dropped it over the black screen into the fire. Sparks shot up. She stood there for a moment, watching the flames lick the white sides of the log. Then she turned back to me, arms folded.

"Douglas loved it. Electronics. Those little transistors. He worked on it twelve, fourteen hours a day. It was the theory that interested him. Make everything smaller. They used germanium in those days, a kind of carbon. Douglas had a different idea. Silicon. Those little chips, just like they use today. That's why I say he was a genius. I think he *was*. He was working on silicon, trying to design it. The lab did other things. He had two men working for him, Whitey Millner and Benny Rader, and a woman who did all the paperwork, Florence Cappelman. Flossie, we called her. Future-tronics. That was what they called the lab. He was ahead of his time. Flossie knew something about it. She had gone to technical school. She was the one who told me how close Douglas was to a breakthrough. Instead—"

Her arms floated helplessly at her sides, like the wings of a bird that couldn't fly.

"Instead—the wind. Douglas loved the mountains as much as the lab. We came out here every summer, and when we found this place —right here where the house is—the terrible wind, Douglas fell in love with it. He said the wind sounded like a fugue, like something Bach would write. It helped him to think. That's why he sold his shares to the other two, closed down the lab. They were unhappy, but Douglas wanted to set up here. Alone. He wanted the wind and the mountains and his work. He was so sure he was on the verge of becoming very rich. I think it bothered him, Daddy's money. Instead—"

She lifted her arms again. The glass was empty.

"They were building the house in the summer. Douglas came out alone to supervise it. He never came back. He sent a postcard from Whitefish, that's way north of here, a picture of Grasshopper Glacier. Love, from the yellow brick road, he said. But he didn't come back. Eighteen years, thrown away on the wind."

She had a small smile fixed on her face, but she didn't mean it.

"Eighteen years," she said. "Margot was three. We moved out here and waited. We waited a long time. That's the reason Margot was up there. She couldn't wait any longer. She thought Douglas was dead, of course. She grew up thinking that. Last spring she came home from school and she found me reading his letters. She didn't know what to think. All those letters, those silly little poems, the things he wrote to me when I was at Smith. She read them, too. We had a good cry. She was Douglas's daughter, flesh of his flesh. She couldn't live with questions. She couldn't wait for the wind to bring him back."

"Do you still have the letters? Perhaps he left some clue, unconsciously—"

Maureen Fraser waved a hand listlessly toward the fire and turned away. She'd been fighting it for a long time, never letting go. Now she had. Outside, through the large window, the light had gone out of the air. The line of mountains to the west was dark, a jagged black edge against the coming night. The glass shuddered.

I could have gone. I stayed.

We went out into the kitchen and we talked about other things and she cooked. We listened to the wind, and in a long silence she told me where Margot's room was.

Four or five cardboard packing boxes lined one wall next to the bed. They were unopened. The Pierrot was on the coverlet, a sad stuffed doll from an unhappy pantomime that had gone on too long. The top of the dresser was swept clean. All that remained was a snowy owl, mounted on a heavy branch of oak. It had died long ago, but it looked at me with yellow arctic eyes. It had belonged to Margot Fraser. She had looked into those same dead eyes and asked the same question.

The picture of Douglas Fraser was on the bedstand, a faded photograph in a plain gold frame, all that was left of him. The sun was in his eyes. A shy half smile was on his face. A little dark-haired girl was perched upon his shoulders. She trusted him. Her hands were free. She wasn't holding on.

When I went back to the kitchen, Maureen was nearly done. She had pushed the sleeves up on her sweater. We ate at a little table off in one corner.

She seemed fragile, sitting there dressed in black, laughing now and then to scare away the wind. She had lost more than a husband and more than a daughter. She had lost a dream. She was being carried out by a tide no man could stop, no matter how hard he tried. I tried. We moved to another room, her bedroom, where there were no owls, no photographs in golden frames. But the wind didn't stop. When I finally left, it was very late.

She never even asked my name. She didn't need it.

By the time I got the car past the gate, I was shivering. The wind had knives in it. I looked back once at the dark house on the ridge, sailing out there at the edge of nothing. Not a light was on. It was black as a widow's dreams.

Smooth road, clear night. The wind cried me down through Hellgate, down the long declines of night and into the valley below.

12

Whether it was the mountains or the night or that lonely weeping woman up there on the ridge above Hellgate, I don't know. Maybe it was the wind, or the way the cold stars glittered through the windshield of the car, changing positions every time I turned the wheel to follow the dark road down. Whatever it was, it reminded me of something a lady once said to me at a happy little party that had turned sour and ugly. Something about the human condition, that blind crabbed walk toward oblivion and death. *Let's all fall down and bleed a little and then get up and fight again.*

She wasn't really a lady. But she had it right.

Let's all fall down and bleed a little and then get up and fight again. The more I thought about it, the more sense it made. A long time ago someone had fallen down and bled a little. He had not gotten up.

The little hand was on two when I got back to the motel. In the darkness, the glowing neon pine tree out front looked even more grotesque. Inside, the lobby lights were on low.

"Nick Caine. Messages," I said to the creep behind the counter.

He looked up at the mail slots, stood up, and with two fingers drew out a folded piece of paper.

"Here it is," he said, pushing it across the plastic countertop toward me. " 'Lassie has eaten the grasshopper.' I don't get it. The guy's dog swallowed a bug. He wouldn't even leave his name." His eyes widened. "You an animal doctor?"

"This is it? The only message?"

"Yes, sir."

I folded the memo sheet and put it in my pocket. Then I headed for the room. At the entrance to the hallway, I turned around to see whether the place was as empty as it seemed to be. It was. The clerk had his back to me at the switchboard. The red telephone was cradled between his shoulder and his ear. His finger was doing something to the dial.

The room was dark. I let there be light. The bed looked very inviting. Unfortunately, I didn't have an invitation. Instead I had a message from Pug Collins.

I reached into my pocket and took it out.

"Lassie has eaten the grasshopper."

It had been a long time since I'd seen a message like that. You've already figured it out, so I don't need to explain it. I will anyway. Lassie come home. Pug Collins wanted me up at the Grasshopper Glacier Campground six hours ago. Don't call for reservations, just come.

Whatever he had, it was important. Pug wouldn't dip that far back into the past if all he wanted was good company.

But first things first. Unfinished business.

I checked the room over carefully, from the blue canvas duffel bag on the floor next to the bed to the black and lavender bathroom. The water was still dripping slowly from the sink faucet. The washcloth was still on the floor where I'd hung it.

Which meant it had to be someone other than the maid.

There are a number of ways to do it, but I'd used the simplest trick of all, the old hair-across-the-zipper trick. The hair was from my head. The zipper was on the duffel. I'd pasted the hair across the zipper, about two inches below the pull. You'd never see it, and whoever was curious enough to wonder what I was carrying with me in the duffel, and what caliber it was, hadn't seen it either. It was no longer there.

Except for that, he'd done a nice job.

All of a sudden I wished I had it with me, but it was eight hundred miles away in the second drawer from the top, left-hand side, under a tee shirt that said "Virginia is for Lovers." It wasn't my tee shirt, it was Virginia's, and the fact that I had it proved that she was. I can't remember what she'd worn home.

The reason I wished I had the Margolin Special along for the ride wasn't Allison Carpenter, doubled up behind the wheel of her expensive car with nothing but stoplights ahead. It wasn't that plug ugly John P. Daddano, with a face that would sour milk. It wasn't even the guy who got into my room by mistake and opened the duffel bag by mistake to see what he could see, although obviously he was a pro.

What it was, was the creep on the telephone behind the desk in the lobby. Who do you call at ten after two in the morning?

The kid was still there behind the counter, reading something uplifting. I'm not saying where he was uplifted. His nose took up half his face. His eyes were set so close together that if you slapped him on the cheek they would bounce back and forth for an hour.

When I got close, his eyebrows jumped up to say hello.

I reached across the counter, grabbed him by the collar, and pulled him close. His eyes started to bounce. The book dropped to the floor.

I smiled politely.

"There are twenty-six bones in your left foot. Same number in your right. If each one is broken, that's a hundred and four. Your feet will swell up. They won't fit in your shoes. You'll have to walk on your hands. Get the idea? I don't know how many bones there are in your hands, but they break too. Your mother won't like it. She'll worry about you. You know how mothers are."

He nodded.

He knew what I meant about mothers. His eyes kept telling me he knew.

His tongue worked its way out from behind his teeth. It tried to calm down his lower lip.

"Five minutes ago you made a phone call. You couldn't even wait until I got to my room."

"I-I-I can explain that. Sir."

I released my grip. He sucked in some air. He could see that I was listening. His eyes still had the shakes.

"The arrangements were made by the day clerk," he said. "I'm nights. It wasn't my idea. Honest. A guy came in, he said you were messing around with his wife. You know what I mean? It wasn't my idea."

"What did he look like?"

"I-I-I don't know. I didn't see him. The day man did it. All he gave me was a number—"

"What do they pay for a service like that?"

He wasn't quite looking at me. He was looking over my right shoulder. His fingers were checking out his neck.

"Twenty for me," he gulped. "That's what the day man told me."

I dug into my pocket, found a twenty, and slid it across the counter. It fluttered to the carpet. He didn't look at it.

I said, "It's down there on the floor. By your feet. You've just doubled your end of the deal."

"Yes. Sir. The one I'm supposed to call, his name is Mr. Wolff. He's at the Four Seasons, down the road. Room one-oh-six."

"What does he sound like?"

"He sounds like you. Sir. Unhappy. I think I woke him up—"

"What did Mr. Wolff say?"

"He said thank you. I never saw him. The day man made the arrangements."

I leaned toward him.

"Thank you," I said slowly. "I've had enough messages for tonight."

"Yes. Sir."

I left the kid counting his blessings, twenty-six in each foot. I went down the hall, walked past the door to my room without stopping, and exited by the rear door of the motel. Mr. Wolff was still probably trying to find his pants. He was going to have to wait.

North of town: darkness. As deep as any coming down from Hellgate.

The dashlights in the Capri put a faint green glow on the underside of the windshield. A faint glow, like a bone burning in the night. I kept the window open, the radio off. I suddenly realized where I was going. I finally caught on to what it meant. I was going in and out of the darkness. The same darkness I had tried to get away from once and for all, a long time ago. I was going to go in some time and not come out. Just like Margot Fraser. Or Allison Carpenter. That's the way life works. It doesn't let you get away from the darkness.

The darkness had turned to gray by the time I got across the mountains. Where the asphalt turned off toward Headquarters, I took a right on the gravel. I crossed the Little Spider without looking to either side. Twenty miles more and I saw the sign, slowed down, and took a left down into the little valley.

The lights were on in the ranger's cabin. Pug had company. Three other rangers.

"It's light enough," one of them said. "Let's go."

Instead we sat around the table and killed the coffee. Pug filled me in. His hands played nervously with the leather wallet, sliding it back and forth on the top of the table.

Two of the rangers slipped into packs. We stood up.

"A guy from Sacramento," Pug said at the door. "A tourist. A civilian. He damn near had a heart attack."

We crossed the meadow in the early light. At the far end, we pushed our way through the stiff willow. From there the path went nowhere but up, into the brightening air. It took us nearly two hours. The boys with the packs set the pace, and the packs weren't empty.

"You'd think the fucking government could afford a fucking helicopter," one of the rangers said. He didn't have a pack.

"Or an escalator."

"How about a fucking balloon?"

There was something mean in the air. Something nasty. Something that had to be done and that nobody wanted to do.

We hit a small rise in the trail, saw the ranger's line shack off the path in the rocks, and knew we were almost there.

"Don't you guys keep stuff in the shack?"

"Cleaned out for the winter."

The air was thin and cold. The trail dropped down into a large depression filled with rocks and debris and patches of dirty snow. We went into it.

The sun had come up behind us.

The Grasshopper was dead ahead.

We could see where the ice had fallen away.

I didn't know we'd meet again so soon. You could barely make out his face, but his hand extended out from the glistening ice, the skin stretched tight across the bones.

He didn't look much like his picture at all.

"Ice worms," Pug Collins said.

"Ice worms?"

"He'll be full of ice worms when they finally get him out."

I moved up past the others, for a better look. It didn't do much good.

The milky ice obscured his features. But from where I stood you could look him right in the eyes. The eyes were gone, turned back, looking elsewhere. The jaw was broken—snapped in half. It hung unnaturally down and to the right. Part of it was missing. There was something large and white and swollen in his mouth. His tongue.

He looked like he was screaming—screaming down all the empty years.

"Let 'em get to work." It was Pug, behind me.

A last look: the khaki shirt, the drill pants, the arms upraised, the one hand already reaching out into the decaying air.

The boys in the trail crew made a face and moved in with their saws.

13

The guy from Sacramento was just a guy from Sacramento. He was staying at the lodge down at Headquarters. He drove up to Grasshopper for the day, the day was yesterday, and he hiked himself up to the glacier in the afternoon.

What he found there wasn't in the guidebook.

The slab of ice that had fallen away from the face of the Grasshopper was thirty feet long, maybe eight or ten feet thick. It opened the book on Douglas Fraser.

He was embedded in the fresh ice, after eighteen years that horrible scream was still fixed on his face, one hand was exposed, and the wallet was lying in the mush on the ground. The guy from Sacramento came down fast, and when he got down he had trouble breathing.

But he brought the wallet with him.

The wallet had all his identification, two hundred seventy dollars in U.S. money, a ticket to Chicago (United Flight 111), and a snapshot of the kid sitting on his shoulders just like the one in the gold frame.

The picture wasn't going to do much good. He didn't look like that anymore.

"Eighteen years," I said. "How did he get there? Not like the grasshoppers. The grasshoppers fly into the ice in the summertime and their little feet get stuck. Douglas Fraser went all the way in. I would say through a crevasse, from the top. From the looks of it, with a bullet in his jaw. The wallet? If it was in his hand, I would say he was trying to buy his way out—from whoever had the gun. No sale. Of course, I'm only guessing."

"It might not even be him."

"The cops are downstairs?"

"They will be, when we get there."

"It is."

They were and it was.

So was the photographer from the Associated Press, and that's how my face got on page one. Pug and I had taken over the litter on the last leg coming down; we pushed through the willow, and there was the AP. On the spot. We showed up nice and clear, and the little mound of something under the rubber blanket, and the other guys coming down the trail behind us.

I didn't like it. My picture had never been in the paper before.

The cops were very interested. Not only because it obviously was murder—the slug had taken away half of Douglas Fraser's jaw—but because it was a long drive between the Grasshopper and wherever it was the cops had come from, and it killed a day. It was better than hanging paper on parked cars.

One of the cops decided he should go up to the face of the Grasshopper after all, and the photographer said why not, and a guy from the trail crew shrugged his shoulders and said okay, let's go. He was the guy without a pack. The other two cops sat around in the ranger's cabin with us drinking a fresh pot of coffee and complaining that the Yankees weren't what they used to be.

Neither was Douglas Fraser.

Pug Collins was right. The ice worms had got him.

The ambulance found us and took the remains of Douglas Fraser to Paradise. I didn't bother to wonder what Uncle Deadly would think. I knew he could handle it.

It was late afternoon when the cops cleared out and Pug and I had the place to ourselves. I tried counting the number of hours I'd gone without sleep. I stopped at twenty-four. I could have gone higher, but I was too tired.

Tired. Not sleepy.

You wouldn't be sleepy either, not if everywhere you turned you could feel the cold, silken web of a spider brushing against you, and you couldn't see the spider who put it there, and you wanted to get one good look at him before he came swinging down the web toward you, just to narrow the odds.

"It doesn't explain a thing," Pug said as I was leaving. "But the newspapers will have a wonderful time. Her father was murdered. She was murdered, but they don't know that. Maybe Mono's uncle will get the chatters. Consider it. The Carpenter girl? I don't know. Who is this Mr. Wolff? Obviously, they brought him in from outside. Listen. I'm sorry about it. I had no idea. Some day I'll learn, but from the very beginning I thought it was something . . . do you want me to come down with you? I owe you that."

"No, thanks."

At Hungry Horse I stopped at the Golden Gate for a couple of Big Skyburgers. When I'm on the road, I like to live off the land. Darkness was falling when I got back to Callahan's.

They had plugged in the tree.

I cruised around the parking lot, twice, and didn't see anything that interested me. Maybe he never found his pants. I went into the motel through the back door. No one was around. I locked the door to the room, pushed the dresser and the table up against the door, checked the window, and didn't even bother to pull down the covers.

Before I fell asleep I counted all the items in Allison Carpenter's room. One by one. Over and over. When I woke up, at eight-thirty the next morning, I had it figured out.

Sometimes it's the most obvious thing of all.

It was.

I checked the newspapers on the way out. The newspapers were having a wonderful time. My picture was on page one.

Breakfast is not the specialty of the house at the little coffee shop at the Four Seasons. The orange juice had a tinny taste. The eggs were greasy. The toast was cold. The waitress was all right, except she had something stuck on her tooth, a piece of tobacco, and every time she smiled me another cup of coffee it ruined her face.

She gave me a funny look. Maybe I looked familiar, but she couldn't place me.

It didn't matter. She was big and blonde and western. She did everything with one hand on her hip—there was plenty of room for it. She called everybody honey, and she made you feel she could take care of your problems no matter what they were.

Mine were simple. Somebody had stolen the phone book out of the booth.

She went into the back room and came out with it and put it on the counter in front of me. I found what I wanted and carried it in my head over to the corner.

I looked through the glass. The sun was shining. I hoped he was out there, waiting. I'd made it as easy for him as I could.

It was a sleepy hello.

I said, "Lisa Mueller. With an *s*."

Silence.

"You don't remember me," I added.

The sleep went out of her voice.

"I didn't tell anything."

"Me either. Let's keep it that way. She's dead. You can't do anything for her. However."

"Yes?"

"You *can* do something for me. You're there. I'm here."

"Yes?"

I told her. She hummed a moment, then she agreed. When she said goodbye, there was an edge of excitement in her voice.

I wasn't counting on it. It was a long shot, a real long shot. Maybe it wasn't even there. Maybe they took it. But it was so obvious that it would be very easy to overlook, and if the police had overlooked it, I wanted it.

The blonde behind the counter must have looked in the mirror. The piece of tobacco was gone. She smiled and poured, one hand on her hip.

"A hit," she said. "I can see by your face. She said yes."

"Don't be so sure. She said maybe."

"That's as good as yes."

She laughed. I frowned.

I hadn't forgotten about Mr. Wolff.

I took a look around the shop. The early morning crowd had gone, and what was left were people with nowhere special to go and no reason to get there in a hurry. Four couples in booths, a family with two tables pushed together, three men alone. I ruled everybody out.

He was too slick to get that close. He'd be outside. Waiting.

Somebody cared, there was no way around it, and the way I

figured it they would send the very best. Now that Douglas Fraser had come out of hiding, somebody would care a whole lot more.

The way they found me was easy. I worked it out. Monkey Man was only a bobber on a string, a local boy trying to make good. When I ditched him, he would have to go to confession. He would have to call Mr. Big. Somebody would have to decide where I would go next, and where Monkey Man should go, somebody who knew all the best places to go. They guessed right. Cynthia Farmer. A bee goes for honey just like a bear does.

Monkey Man wasn't the one to handle it. That was as plain as the nose that wasn't on his face. Monkey Man was just holding down the fort at Cynthia Farmer's condominium until somebody better could climb aboard. Somebody with a little slick.

He didn't get there soon enough. Nevertheless, Monkey Man could describe me. Even with a broken jaw. You could count on his making the car outside the condo, and making the license plates. It didn't take a surplus of brains to look the car over, trace the number to the agency, and come up with Nick Caine.

It didn't take a lot of brains for Nick Caine to use his real name, either. But Nick Caine was fishing.

I hoped I'd catch something.

Whoever came into it, came into it with a description of me, a description of the rented car, the license number, and my name. What more did he need? He didn't need a Ouija board. All he had to do was check a few motels, working outward from the condo at Ginger Creek. He didn't need to work outward very far.

She said, "You have nice eyes. No wonder they say maybe."

I pulled out a twenty and put it on the counter.

"I need to make another call," I said. "This one's so young she still rides a bicycle. Maybe she won't make it. Maybe she won't need to make it. I don't want to spend all afternoon doing the crossword puzzle—"

"Hon-EEE!" she whistled.

She took the twenty like she was used to it. She brought it back in dimes, and stacked them neatly in front of me.

"Thanks. You could have made it nickels."

"Why be difficult?"

"I was thinking that myself."

I swept the coins off the counter, went to the booth, and dialed Gallagher. Gallagher took a lot of dimes.

Harry Gallagher's one of a kind. It's hard to say what kind. On his mother's side, he claims to be descended in a direct line from King David. On his father's side, from lyricists and Irish kings. You'd never know it by looking at him. He's a tough, wise bird, an Irish Jew if you can believe his pedigree, and he earns his beer money as a columnist on the *Rocky Mountain Gazette* down in Denver. He hasn't been on the street in years, but he plays the phones like he invented them. He also plays poker, not as well, in an old Victorian house on Delgany Street.

"Where the hell are you?" he snarled.

"Fishing," I said.

"Fishing," he repeated. "I'm stuck in this goddamn office, it's very modern, the windows don't even open, and you're fishing. I'm going to quit this job and go to Florida and serve hot meals to old people. I could use a lot less aggravation."

"It's a lot less money."

"I take it back. The morning edition is on the desk here in front of me. Your handsome puss is on page one. I know you, Al. It's a helluva story. What are you fishing for?"

I explained. I kept it simple, because I didn't want to explain too much. If you sneeze around Harry Gallagher, Harry Gallagher will print it.

The dodge I worked on Professor Reimann, the zookeeper, would work on anyone except a cop. A cop was the only one who would say you and my Aunt Mollie and want to see your press credentials. I didn't have any press credentials. All I had was the names of a few newspapers rattling around in my head.

Harry was another story. Harry could get things out of a cop that the cop didn't know he had to give.

I told him what I wanted. Don't call me, I'll call you. He groused about it. He always does. I ignored it. When you're descended directly from King David, you're entitled.

The phone went back on the hook and I pushed my way out into the sunshine. A red vending machine was planted next to the door. I walked over to it and fed it a dime. When I reached inside to take out a paper, I also turned my head to take in the parking lot.

He was there, all right. He was sitting in a black car, with his left arm resting on the sill. The car was backed up to an eight-foot fence that ran along the rear of the parking lot. On the other side of the fence was the interstate.

He had his share of slick. Not only did he have an unobstructed view of the entrance to the coffee shop, which in this case meant an unobstructed view of me, but he had also parked his car so that the sun hit his windshield in a bright flare of light. I couldn't see his face, which was just what he had in mind.

I let the door to the vending machine bang shut. Then I folded the newspaper under my arm, opened the door to the coffee shop, and stepped back inside.

"Well!" she declared. "Either you are the fastest gun in the West, or—"

I crossed over to the counter, went through the slot, put my hand on her other hip, and was guiding her through the swing door to the back room.

"Wait a minute! Hon-EEE!"

I left her with the cook, who wasn't busy, and tossed the newspaper on a greasy table next to the grill. When I came out the back door I ducked past the garbage cans to a redwood fence and followed the other side of it down to the interstate. There wasn't much traffic. I walked slowly along the back fence, made a good guess, and chinned myself on the fence. Perfect.

I dropped down and went up again, this time all the way up. I balanced for a moment on top of the fence. Then I dropped down to the roof of his car. It was a Ford.

He followed the script. You would have, too. There he was sitting alone in his car doing his job, which was to sit alone in his car doing his job, and all of a sudden something lands on the roof from God knows where.

He opened the car door, put one foot out on the pavement, and twisted himself halfway out to have a better look. It left him off balance.

I caught him just below the throat with my feet. It drove him down to the asphalt. The impact knocked me back against the side of the car, but I landed on my feet and dropped down on him. This time there was nothing between us.

My knee looked for something in his stomach, such as breakfast. It didn't find anything. The air went out of him with a high-pitched squeal. It didn't fit his looks. He was thin and dark and not very tall. He used something powerful on his hair. He had a mustache that wouldn't behave. His eyes came up lemons.

I bounced up, pulled him to his feet, and swung his left arm sharply around behind his back, where it didn't belong. It gave his legs a little something extra to stand on. He tried to make himself taller. His right hand was still free. It dived in his coat, over his heart. Maybe he wanted to recite the Pledge of Allegiance. His mistake. I yanked his arm down, spun him around, and drove him up against the side of the car. His chin made a slight dent in the roof.

Then I said good morning.

14

"Put your hands on the roof of the car and make me feel comfortable," I advised. He took my advice. He made me feel comfortable.

I reached around him and slipped the gun from his chest holster, a snub .38, patted the rest of him down, and encouraged him to get into the car. He slid across the seat and I got in behind the wheel. The .38 kept its eye on him.

By the time we got out into the street, he still hadn't said a word. I wheeled the Ford up the strip, hooked left at the neon pine tree, and parked in the lot behind Callahan's. Not even good morning.

"This way out."

His eyes were back to normal, but they didn't have much to say either.

"It's very simple, so you can handle it," I said. "It goes like this. You walk five feet in front of me. You don't turn around. Try not to call attention to yourself. Try not to say a word. You're doing pretty well so far. These little thirty-eights, I always liked them. And you know what they say. It's not where it goes in, it's where it comes out. Enter the motel. Walk down the hall. Stop at Room One Thirty-two. I will unlock the door. You will open it all the way. Very gently. Now would be a very good time to start."

He started.

I dropped the pistol into my pocket and walked across the parking lot behind him. He wasn't much of a conversationalist, but he sure knew how to follow simple directions.

When we got to the door of my room and I unlocked it, he hesitated a moment. But he decided against it. He pushed the door open gently with his fingers.

I said, "Looks familiar. Right?"

I encouraged him to step forward about three steps into the room. I was right behind him, with the gun back in my hand. I encouraged him again on the back of the head. Not real hard, but hard enough.

He went down softly onto the carpet. This time he didn't even squeal.

I reached back and flipped the "Do Not Disturb" sign from the inside knob. Then I shut the door as gently as he had opened it.

When the cobwebs cleared he was face-down on the bed. He couldn't move his legs because of the way I had them tied down with strips of sheeting. He couldn't move his waist or his neck either. Same reason. He looked comfortable, but you never know. His arms were drawn tightly behind him with the wrists crossed and tied. The towel bar from the bathroom was jammed up between his wrists.

He blinked.

He tried to move and he couldn't. There was sweat on the side of his face. He needed a shave.

He blinked again. It wasn't a dream.

"What do you want?"

His head jerked back toward me, about a quarter of an inch. His voice was thick. His tongue took up too much space in his mouth. He was curious about things. I couldn't blame him. I was kneeling above him on the bed and he probably suspected the worst. A crazy bobo.

I leaned over and looked into his yellow eye.

"When the scientists flipped over the rock and saw you, they had a name for it. What is it? You didn't introduce yourself. I like to know who I'm dealing with. And why. If you're Mr. Wolff, I'm Mr. Bear."

He didn't answer.

He didn't like telling people who they were dealing with. Or why.

He didn't talk to strangers.

I gave the rod half a turn. His body sprang back as far as it could, which was not very far. But I could feel the muscles suddenly harden. His shoulders arched inward, trying to relieve the pressure. That only made it worse.

He began to tremble.

He had stagefright.

"Casanova," he croaked.

The first answer is always the hardest. With the first answer you still believe in mind over matter. You might go one more if you're any good. This guy was fair. I decided he was insolent, and gave the rod another half turn.

The air burst out of his mouth in a hiss. It had sharp edges.

"Holy Christ! Casanova! Sam Casanova!"

Okay. You don't always have a choice.

I said, "Sam, what usually happens is this. The forearms break just above the wrist, they snap right in two, and the bone comes right through the skin. Sometimes the shoulders will pop first, but that's gravy. The forearms always go. With most people it happens after about four complete turns. It all depends on how much milk you drink. You don't look like you drink milk. I've already given you one complete turn and it hurts. I repeat. It hurts. From here on out, it hurts a lot more. They say it feels like someone's driving nails into the back of your head, just behind the ears. I don't know about that. It sounds like an exaggeration. But we can find out. I can sit up here and pretend I'm driving a bumper car at Magic Mountain. Or you can tell me some things."

He told me some things.

He started out with a simple yes and no. By the time I added a half turn more he was into compound sentences. With the rod twisted around in two complete turns he was talking in paragraphs and he didn't need any questions to keep him going.

Forget that a gasoline credit card in his little Gucci wallet said he was Terry Bienvenuta of Brookline, Massachusetts. Forget that his driver's license said he was Lawrence Spooner of Rochester, New York. Forget that his American Express card said he was C. R. Darwin of Atlanta, Georgia, and he never went anywhere without it.

He was just plain old Sam Casanova from Chicago. You can't be lucky all the time.

Sam Casanova did odd jobs. He traveled around a bit. He was in business for himself, a freelance thug, and had been for five years. Ever since he was busted from the Drug Enforcement Administration's strike force. He said the bust was a setup. If I had to guess, I'd guess the other way. He set *them* up. He'd gone to a free school and he'd learned all the tricks the DEA had to teach him and then he started to freelance on the side, trying one trick here and another there, until finally somebody woke up. He was just a dope dog but he drove a Mercedes. Now he was on the other side. He sounded to me like one of those whiz-kid lawyers from Harvard who goes straight to the Justice Department with his sheepskin and his conscience, learns the rules of the road, and then trades it all in for a nice office, a fat salary, a secretary with a very short skirt, and oil paintings on the wall. With the other side.

Two nights earlier Sam had received a telephone call from an old friend in Denver. Name: Martin Bidet. I gave the rod a jiggle.

"Honest to Christ!" he cried. "Bidet! You think I'd make that up?"

Bidet was a former IRS man who was now doing all his auditing from the fancy offices of a high-powered private accounting firm. He had a job for Sam. The job was me.

Casanova was to watch me—where I went, who I saw, what I did. He was not supposed to touch, just look. He didn't know why. He didn't need to know why. That wasn't in the contract. All he needed to know was that Martin Bidet wanted an accounting.

Sam caught the first flight out of Chicago, connected at Denver, flew north, and called back down to Bidet. The idea was to get there first and ask questions afterward. By then Bidet had my name and the license number of the Capri. As stated, it was a piece of cake.

Casanova's first stop was Ginger Creek. But he got there too soon. Three squad cars were still parked near the west tower, the lights were flashing, and the cops were hauling away a big drunk with a funny face. The guy looked like a monkey. When the cops drove away, very slowly, Sam checked out another name Martin Bidet had given him. Cynthia Ann Farmer. She wasn't home, but he'd visited her apartment anyway. She left the dishes in the sink. The bed wasn't made. The building manager liked twenty-dollar bills but he wasn't much help. All he could say was that Cynthia Ann Farmer didn't like living alone.

Sam did the next best thing. He started working the motels. Like I said, it was routine. He made his arrangements and checked into the Four Seasons, down the road. When the desk clerk called at two o'clock in the morning to say that I'd returned, Sam was watching a movie on TV. Something with Margaret Rutherford.

I said, "How long did it take you to get over here?"

"Five minutes."

"Where was I?"

"I don't know. You were gone. The kid at the desk said you were a vet. Somebody's animal was sick. I checked the room again. Then I called Bidet. Woke him up. He was pissed. You got to give me a break on this. I'm telling you what you want to know—"

"How pissed?"

"He was corked. I don't know what he wants with you and I don't want to know. But he seems to be serious about it. He said he was sending someone else up. Someone from Denver."

"Who?"

"Don't know."

"Did he come?"

"Don't know. My job is cover the motels, that's all. I spotted you this morning walking around the parking lot and I followed you down to the coffee shop at the Four Seasons. You were a sitting duck. No offense. But you were easy to make."

"Thanks," I said. "The gentleman from Denver has not gotten in touch with you?"

"No. Give me a break. Loosen that thing up. I've got two kids—"

I could tell you about why Sam Casanova's wife left him, she *was* from Brookline, Massachusetts, and how she was terrific because she liked to cook dinner in the raw, just a little apron with hearts stitched on it, and she wore gold pumps, and how she was a very good cook even though the dinner always got cold, that was before the kids were born, but you don't need it. He wanted to talk, the more the merrier. I guess he figured that the longer his mouth worked, the longer the rest of him would work.

I listened for a while, because I'm a good listener, everybody says that, and then I cut him off.

I said, "Sam. Think about it. I am going to set this thing at two and a half turns. I know it hurts, but you're getting used to it. If you don't fight it, it won't hurt too much. Don't fight it. I'm going to put a rag in your mouth and I'm going to tie your head down on the bed. If you breathe through your nose you're going to be okay. If you catch a cold, you're in trouble. I'm going to be considerate and cover you with a blanket. Your wife sounds terrific and you've probably got a lot of good stories about her. I'll be back."

I did what I said I would do, and when I was done he couldn't move a muscle. Of course I wasn't coming back. How could I? I threw the blanket over him.

He said, "Nnnnngh."

"You'll have to be very quiet," I whispered.

I picked up the blue duffel and moved to the door. From the door, Sam Casanova looked like he was asleep. A late riser.

He didn't look like he wanted to be disturbed.

Sam's .38 went with me. So did the keys to his car. I left the Capri where it was, in the back of the lot, and used the Ford. Ten minutes later I had it parked on a quiet side street in the heart of town. Two minutes after that I was walking in the front door of L'Espresso. I was fifteen minutes late.

But she had waited.

15

She was in a corner booth, and her eyes caught mine as soon as I stepped inside. She was decked out in a blue jumpsuit, which wasn't a bad idea. Her blouse was white silk. Her mouth was a little red pout of worry. She *did* look like Audrey Hepburn. She had a cigarette in her fingers, a Kent 100, and four crushed filter tips in the ashtray on the table in front of her.

I walked past a couple of kids carrying on a conversation with the electronic pinball machines, crossed the room, and put myself in the booth across from Lisa Mueller.

Her eyes were still dark blue.

"I got here early. I thought you weren't coming."

She glanced down nervously at the watch on her pretty wrist. Spiro Agnew was pointing to the seven. I noticed it. She noticed me notice it.

"A collector's item," she said.

"It doesn't go with the jumpsuit."

The little red pout melted away. Her eyes narrowed, and she started nodding her head slowly up and down. She was silent.

"That means you found it," I said.

She leaned toward me. There was a little green in her eyes, but not much. More like aquamarine. She whispered:

"I should give it to the police, shouldn't I? Like, who are you? A policeman? No. Allison was kidnapped. She was murdered. I don't believe those stories about suicide. This could be very, very important—"

"Look at it this way," I advised. "If the police wanted it, they would have taken it. They usually do."

"Really!" she exploded.

Heads turned. She lowered her voice.

"I mean, do you know how dumb the police are? They didn't even ask me about the noise I heard. They asked me about her car. She always parked her car on that street—"

I drummed my fingers on the table.

She opened her floppy leather handbag, it was on the seat next to her, and started talking about it. "Honest to God," she said. "I'm being blackmailed. I can't believe it. I feel like a spy or something. What was her name? Mary Hary?"

"Or something."

She groped around in the bag with her hand, found what she was looking for, and pulled it out. She placed it gingerly on the table and covered it with her hand. She looked around the room. Then she slid it coyly across to me. She really *did* think she was Audrey Hepburn.

"Here's what I think," she was saying. "She had money. She liked thrills. She was going to buy an airplane—"

I looked at it.

It was a small white card, and the cellophane tape had gone brown around the edges. On one side somebody had written: "2A. Allison Carpenter." That wasn't the side I was interested in. It was a business card, all right, and now it was my business.

I turned it over.

I was wrong. If I was betting, I would have bet on Martin Bidet, accountant. Maybe I just wanted to make it easy on myself. But it hadn't belonged to Martin Bidet.

It belonged to Bo.

Under his name was a picture of an airplane, embossed. It looked like a Mooney Ranger. The plane was pulling a telephone number through the sky, and the area code was Denver.

"Who's Bo?"

Lisa shrugged.

That's all, just Bo. He didn't need a last name. He didn't even need the rest of his first name. Bo was enough. He was a cocky sonofabitch. That made him a pilot.

The card went into my pocket. Lisa went on and on.

"And how could I? They didn't really ask me anything. I didn't know anything. Do you think it's important? I could see her car from my window. Through the backyards. It was there all weekend. I'm sure of it. She was dead all the time, that's the scary part. How could they miss it? When you called, I just knew it was there. It was right there in plain sight, on her door, and they never even saw it—"

The waitress made a smile. Sorry to interrupt.

Lisa picked the chili burger and a Coke. I settled for some real coffee and tried to look as though I were listening. I wasn't. I was trying to put things together in my head. If Allison Carpenter went away on weekends, every weekend except one, maybe she flew away. Maybe she flew away to Denver. It wasn't only Bo. It was Martin Bidet. A man who could arrange things—like people to follow you. A man who could arrange more than that.

I suddenly thought of something Sam Casanova said. Something about dishes in the sink and a bed's not being made.

"You'll excuse me," I announced.

I walked across the room to the phone and dialed. She didn't answer. Not even after twenty rings. That was plenty of time to get out of bed and answer the phone, but Cynthia Farmer wasn't having any. Cynthia Farmer wasn't here to have any. The girl who didn't like to live alone.

I thumbed through the phone book, found what I wanted in the yellow pages, and wrote down the address.

When I got back to the booth in the corner, Lisa had talked herself out. She was staring at the table. She was an innocent with creamy skin, a pushover who liked to dress up in mother's clothes. I wished her goodbye, a wish that never comes true.

She looked at me.

Her mouth didn't say anything. Her big blue eyes did. They said: What have I done?

"Bingo!" somebody cried, over by the machines.

I asked myself the same question, except I threw in a negative. Maybe Monkey Man hadn't been alone that morning out at Ginger Creek. Maybe Sam Casanova hadn't hurt enough to tell the truth. Maybe the goons had gone in there and done to Cynthia Farmer what they did to Allison Carpenter.

I thought about it as I drove across town. I thought about it some more when I parked the car in front of TechTronics, Ltd., a low white building, stucco, that helped pay the property taxes in a grimy little industrial park. All those women who lived out their lives on the edge of nothing.

When I pushed my way through the revolving doors and got a look at her sitting there behind the desk in the small lobby, I almost kept right on going around and back outside. But I didn't.

This one was different.

This one looked like she'd gone over the edge. She had a hard time keeping her lips down over her teeth. Her lips must have been painted on, because otherwise she didn't have any. Just that chalky skin sewn and puckered into a mouth that was twice as wide as it should have been. This one sucked milk bottles for a hobby.

Her eyes weren't bad, but when she put her nose up it got in the way of them.

She put her nose up.

"I'm sorry," she said, which made two of us. "I can allow you to see Mr. Sanchez, but not anyone else. Mr. Sanchez handles all the sales and—"

"I'm not selling. I don't want to see Mr. Sanchez."

"I'm sorry," she said. I didn't believe her. Her eyelids fluttered like she was lying. She wasn't really sorry. They were wrinkled with orange something. It probably comes in a tube. Her voice was like a piece of glass being scraped across something it shouldn't have been. Something ugly. Like her teeth.

"Mr. Sanchez handles everything," she whined. "I am authorized to call Mr. Sanchez, but no one else. This is an—"

"I'll see him."

Never argue with a woman whose mouth is that wide and whose nose is up. She's had too much practice.

"Of course," she said. "This is an electronics company. It's not a candy store, sir. We cannot permit people to wander in off the street and look around. We have regulations. We have government—"

"Yes. I'll see him."

Her finger had already found the button. She used purple polish on her nails.

"Sanchez," he said, coming out of his little office.

He stood there with the smile fixed on his face, straightpins in each corner holding it up, and his hand outstretched. I took the hand and nodded at the smile.

I turned to her.

"Pfffht," I said.

"You understand," she said. "We cannot permit people to—"

I turned to him.

"She thinks I'm selling something, which I'm not, or stealing something, which I'm also not, but this is not exactly the place to discuss it."

The smile didn't move. The rest of him did. He stepped backward, swept his palm toward the door to his office—it said "Mr. Sanchez" on the door—and in a soft voice said: "I do have an office."

Olé.

I went in first. He followed, and the door closed behind him.

"It is not much of an office, that is true, but it is an office," he said, taking his place behind his desk. He had a trace of siesta in his English, and he'd never heard of contractions. His smile was very patient.

"I'll get right to the point because I don't want to take up your time. Obviously you're busy. You've got to get *her* back to the zoo before dark." My thumb jabbed the air toward the door.

"She is very useful."

"I'm looking for a girl who works here, Cynthia Farmer."

His smile got a little wider.

"She wasn't home. I thought I'd hunt her up here at work."

And more patient.

It was his turn to shrug. His palm came up and I turned around.

There she was. Not in the flesh, but just about.

It was a large poster, two by three feet, and the subject was Cynthia Farmer. She was dressed in red spangles, if that's the right verb, and I'm not sure it is, and she had her arms raised over her head and she was standing on the tips of her blades in the middle of an ice rink. In the corner of the poster someone had written: "To Sanch. From Sin."

"You have seen her routine, then? Of course. But that is an old poster, is it not?"

I turned back to him.

"You are an old friend," he said.

I shrugged.

"Of course she is not home. Of course she is not here. She is touring. It is the same every fall. The show is called Cermak's Ice Circus, but you must know that. If you are an old friend. The tour began yesterday. Her hours here are very flexible. She is a very good worker, no?"

Yes. Very good.

I made what they call a graceful exit, which means I opened the door before I left.

"If I can be of further assistance to you, you will please be good enough to ask."

His voice came from the little office and he didn't follow it out.

A light rain had started to fall, a mist thick with grief, coming down from the mountains like a shroud.

It wasn't Cynthia Farmer who put me there. Or maybe it was. It wasn't Sam Casanova, either. Although it could have been. On the way out to the airport—I was still driving Casanova's car—I went past Callahan's Motel. The squad car parked at the side door of the motel surprised me a little. The ambulance surprised me a little more. He had come up behind me from nowhere, and he was right on my tail when he let loose with a half gasp on his throaty siren, just for the hell of it. I watched in the rear-view mirror as he turned off silently into the motel parking lot, lights flashing.

You see what I mean about could have been. It was hard to say how much Sam Casanova would find to talk about. Sam didn't feel well. But Sam was a weasel. Sam was slime, and I had the feeling that he'd talk to anyone. It wasn't necessary to tie him down and twist his arm.

If what Sam said was true, Martin Bidet had someone else keeping tabs on me. I hadn't spotted him. Maybe he hadn't spotted me. But I didn't need the cops on my back, too.

I was in good company, a glass of Scotch was on the table in front of me, and I had my back to the wall. The airport restaurant was called Cibola, as in conquistador. The little waitress was related. She had dark hair, full sensual lips, and dark flashing eyes. The dark flashing eyes looked at the glass in front of me. I emptied it, she took it, and when she brought it back it was full again.

The lounge wasn't. But there was still a pretty good crowd for the middle of nowhere. More people than I wanted to see. Some of them were at the bar, the bozos in cowboy boots, but most of them were over near the high windows where they could look out at the runway and see the rain drifting down from the darkness through the lights.

I had a little round table with a fat wax candle in the center of it, and my glass of Scotch, which was half gone, and I decided it wasn't Cynthia Farmer and it wasn't Sam Casanova. It was something else.

It sneaks up on you in different ways, the voice that says: Let it go. Up in the dark mountains at Hellgate the wind was saying that to a lady named Maureen Fraser. Let it go. Her husband had heard the same soft whisper a long time ago. Let it go. For Margot Fraser it had come all too quickly. Click. No chance to say no. Allison Carpenter didn't have a chance either. She had followed her heart and they had snapped it in half. This wasn't just murder; it was theater. It was theater with a very long memory, a memory that lasted eighteen years. If I had one chance to get out, it was now. Otherwise. Otherwise there was only darkness.

The dress was black satin and the little apron on the front was white lace. I looked at her full sensual lips and her dark flashing eyes and I said, "Can I buy you one?" Her eyes turned to heaven. *Mio Dio!* Gracious God, preserve me!

I took no for an answer.

And I put my hand over the top of the glass.

"That's enough for now," I said. "I'll knock the table over if I want another one."

The pay phone was across the lounge, next to the cashier. There was still enough noise in the place to make it private. I had a pocketful of change and used it. Some kid answered. His voice had acne.

"Gallagher," I said.

The line went very quiet. I was on hold. I was on hold in more ways than one. Finally someone got his attention and he came on the line.

"Gallagher," he announced.

"Yes," I said. "Hello, Harry. I'm coming home. The stuff I wanted? Thanks anyway."

He disregarded it.

"Do you read the papers?"

"I do," I confessed. "Something big is going on in Rhodesia and everyone wants to know about it."

He interrupted me. He was all business:

"Okay. Most of it's been in the papers. Some of it hasn't. Cause of death, something called levorphanol tartrate. Five times more potent than morphine. Intravenous. It put her right out, for good. The cops are holding on to that little item because they think they can trace it. She bought the car in Denver three months ago. Cherry Creek. Came in alone, paid with a certified check. Of course they were suspicious, but they also sell cars. She bought the check. That's another thing the cops are holding on to."

"Harry—"

"The rest I'm sure you have. Time of death, Friday evening. No prints in the car. Some kind of charade, sticking that hose in the window. Nobody was fooled. Of course, nobody saw it. The car was there all weekend—I'm just running down the list here. Her room was a mess. She could have been injected there, or in the car. Doesn't matter, the result's the same. The guy they have in custody is—"

"Harry," I said.

"—he's a deaf-mute. They can't get anything out of him. The name is John P. Daddano. Runs some kind of nightclub, and a little airstrip, back in the hills. They can't quite make the connection, but they're holding him on suspicion. On suspicion of being ugly, the cop told me. This guy is a—"

"Harry."

"What?"

"Harry, you're a prince."

"A king. I keep telling you. A king."

He sighed.

By the time I got back to my little table, the señorita had a fresh one waiting for me. I let it down slowly. So Monkey Man had an airstrip. I thought about it, I closed my eyes, and I came up with the same answer. Let it go. There was only one place to go with this one, out in the wind and the darkness. Somewhere out there was the Mad Hatter, laughing up his sleeve.

"Pardon me," she said again, this time with a little more urgency in her voice.

I opened my eyes.

She was blonde unless it was a wig, which it might have been, and she'd been through the wringer.

Her hair stuck out like straw from under her ski cap and she had her hands down on the table in front of me, leaning toward me, looking at me. She was squinting. There were dark circles under her eyes.

"No thanks, sister."

She pulled the newspaper out of the pocket of her jacket and put it down on the table. She didn't look at it. It was open to page one.

"Is that you?" she said.

I looked at it.

It was me. It was me and Pug Collins and a little mound of something under a rubber blanket on the litter.

Her voice was a tired whisper.

She said, "I'm Margot Fraser."

16

I looked for a flicker of emotion—anger, anguish, anxiety, anything. By the time I got to worried or worse, I still hadn't seen any.

Margot Fraser had no emotion left.

She was a sparrow blown off course and into the lights of Cibola by the storm and the darkness outside. Her face was white and lifeless, with just enough resemblance to an old newspaper photograph to let me know she was telling the truth about who she was. She had something blue on her eyelids, something with sparkle, but it didn't.

The dirty olive-green fatigue jacket fit a lot more loosely than the adjectives. It would have been big on her ex-boyfriend, Mononucleosis Oto.

Her body tilted uncertainly toward me.

Across the room, I could see two or three faces turn in our direction. What the hell. It was better than watching the DC-9s.

"You saw him," she whispered. "In the ice. He's really dead."

Her lips barely moved. They didn't want the words to come out.

"It's all over, Margot. He's dead. He's been dead for a very long time."

Her hands started to tremble. She nearly knocked over my drink. Her eyes gave the ceiling the once-over. She was letting herself go.

I moved fast, grabbing her by the arm. It was like holding on to a piece of bone that a dog has given up on.

"Hold on, sister."

I left a little something for the señorita and steered Margot Fraser between the empty tables. We moved toward the door.

It was blocked by a fat man and his wife who were trying to decide whether it was going to snow and how much. We squeezed between them and stepped out into the night.

The rain was still drifting down from the darkness, high above the arc lamps of the parking lot. It fell in shimmering sheets, like sails before the wind. Insubstantial ghost ships coming down over the mountains. The world itself was drifting deeper into darkness.

I dropped my hand down, took her wrist, and tugged her across toward the rented car.

She came after me like a rag doll, a sad Pierrot. Her bones had no marrow and no weight. Her small voice kept saying something over and over, but I couldn't catch it. It was finally drowned out by the whine of a jet overhead.

When I got her settled in the car, I turned to look at her.

Her cheeks glistened, but not from tears. She had no tears left.

She looked straight ahead.

"Then it was all for nothing," she said finally. "He's dead. He's been dead for a very long time—"

"And you. You're supposed to be dead, too."

Something like a laugh came out of that thin throat. But it wasn't a laugh. It was dry and empty and heartless, the rustle of dead leaf-stalks in a dark field, some sort of rodent down there at work where the light would never reach.

"I am," she said.

She cringed and curled deeper into the corner of the seat.

"Nothing matters now. Nothing at all. Daddy's dead. Allie's dead. I'm dead. We're all dead together."

She was talking to herself, to see how it sounded. It didn't sound very good.

"Of course," I said. "It doesn't matter. It was fun while it lasted. It didn't last very long for your mother. She buried someone up there at Hellgate. She thought it was her daughter, but it sure as hell wasn't. It was somebody else. But it doesn't matter. Someone got chewed up by a bear at Grasshopper Glacier and that wasn't you, either. Who was she? Does it matter to her? Of course not. And you? You were busy with the bear. I've had that figured out for a long time now, at least a minute. But of course that doesn't matter."

"My mother?"

Her voice was small and far away.

I let her think about it. She took a long time. It was as though she really weren't there, she was somewhere else, and it didn't matter. Nothing mattered.

"I don't know," she said at last.

"You don't know," I repeated. I wanted to be sure I had it right.

"I don't know who she was. She was just a girl no one knows. Somebody. Nobody. Maybe—maybe it was crazy."

I didn't need to repeat it. I had it right.

Margot Fraser reached into the big pocket of her Army jacket and pulled out a package of cigarettes. She tapped one out and lit it. In the sudden glare of the match behind her trembling hand, I got a better look at her face. Skin too white and chalky. Eyes dark and dry as a bone.

She was turned toward me.

"It was an accident," she said. "I keep telling myself that. Nobody knew who she was. Nobody missed her. She had a bag, a knapsack, with nothing in it. She had the clothes on her back. No purse. No money. No identification. She was about my size, a little shorter. I've seen her around campus but I don't know her name. I don't think she was a student. Somebody would have missed her, and nobody did. Even Allison didn't know her name, and Allison knew everybody. A runaway, maybe. Like me. I don't know. I've gone over it a million times in my head, and I just don't—"

"Allison Carpenter?"

"Yes. Allison Carpenter. I didn't know what to do. There was nothing else I could do. It was an accident, believe me."

She closed her eyes. Tightly. As though the darkness could carry the memories away. It couldn't.

"Nick Caine," she said when she opened her eyes. "That's what it said in the paper."

She was still talking to herself. "Okay. I was working late at the Research Center, going through the motions. I'd been working late for weeks—eight, nine, ten o'clock. One night, Allison called. My roommate's sister. She was at The Tarot and she wanted a lift back to town. I said okay. It was late, past ten, I think, and like I said, I was just going through the motions, not getting anything done. So I drove down. It was a foggy night. It took me a while. I drove around in back, because that's where Allison said she would meet me. There were a lot of cars there, and only one spot open. By the garbage bins. I backed up. As simple as that. I didn't even see her standing there."

"Allison?"

"No. That girl."

"You hit her?"

"Two miles an hour," Margot said softly. "I didn't even see her. I felt the car hit something. I thought it was a bag of garbage or something, and I stopped and got out and looked. She was on the ground. I was sick. I was sick right there. I got back into the car and I turned out the lights and I sat there for a long time. Ten, fifteen minutes. I don't know how long. I couldn't move. I didn't know what to do. I knew I was in trouble. I wanted to get out of there, but I couldn't. How could I?"

"What kind of trouble?"

"I *killed* her!"

I looked at her.

"You don't think it was an accident?"

She took a moment to answer.

"Of course it was an accident," she said deliberately. "But I was drinking. A little. Maybe that's why I didn't see her."

"How much?"

"A little. There's a bottle of Turkey in the office at the Research Center. I didn't have much, but the police can tell. It's all I could think about, that I'd had a drink and I ran over that girl. When Allison came out and got in the car, she could see right away that something was wrong. She went and looked and came back and said the girl was dead. I thought maybe she was a doper, had OD'd or something. Maybe she passed out. I don't know. I thought of everything. But Allie said she'd seen her inside The Tarot and she seemed okay.

"It was like a dream—the fog, The Tarot—and I knew that girl was lying back there on the ground behind the car. Dead. I couldn't believe it. I killed her. I was afraid somebody was going to come out, or the police were going to come, but nobody did. I just couldn't think straight. We sat there and talked for a long time. Then I got the idea—"

"Feed her to the bears."

Margot turned away from me.

"It sounds crazy. Maybe it was. Allie was against it. She tried to talk me out of it. But it was all I could think of. I didn't know if it would work. I was scared. But I was looking for my father on and off all summer, with Allison's sister. I put ads in papers all over the country. We hiked all over the park. I thought—"

"Right," I anticipated. "If you could make it look as though this dead girl was you—if you could arrange it so that she was attacked by a bear up at Grasshopper Glacier—you'd kill two birds with one stone. It would take care of the girl at The Tarot, and the story about the bear would be on page one of every newspaper in the country. If your father was still alive somewhere, how could he miss it? It had everything. Grasshopper Glacier. Margot Fraser. His little girl."

She was silent a moment.

"Crazy doesn't begin to cover it," I added.

"It's all I ever wanted. My father. I never once believed he was dead. He just—went away. I thought he would come back if he only knew—"

"What would you have done if he *had* come back? Then *you* would have been dead. On paper."

"I don't know. He would have—he would have made everything all right. But now—"

"He did come back," I said. "He never went away."

Her cigarette glowed red in the darkness. She ground it out in the ashtray on the dash.

The rain had started to fall harder. It came in gusts, as though the night and the darkness had trapped us in a bad dream that no one was going to wake up from. Not Douglas Fraser. Not Allison Carpenter. Not Margot.

The inside of the windshield had fogged over. I turned on the ignition, slid the lever on the heater across to defrost, and watched the warm air hit the glass.

Two little half-moons began rising from the vents.

"Where'd you get the bear?"

She thought about it for a moment, looked over at me, and then looked away.

"Scarlotti's. Angelo Scarlotti. He has a little animal park north of town, for tourists. And he had a grizzly. An old sow. We knew about it. We almost bought it for the Research Center, but it was too well trained. You couldn't use it. Allison went in and told him she was from the Health Department and he fell for it."

"Allison Carpenter arranged for the bear?"

"Yes. She did—I can't believe she's dead. She did *everything.* She was so—cool about it. Icy. I mean—God! She killed herself? *Everyone* is dead—"

"Who was in on it? You and Allison?"

"And she's dead."

"No one else?"

"No. No one else."

Margot brought her hands up to her face and touched the cold skin.

"And I talked her into it—"

"She was very helpful."

The same something like a laugh came from her throat, and she dropped her hands. I finally recognized it. It was the sound of someone dying, a death rattle, bones shaking loose in a gourd.

"You had to know Allison," Margot said hoarsely.

I considered it.

"It was a nice charade, and Allison Carpenter drew all the tough lines. Think about it," I said. "She was with you at The Tarot. She arranged for the bear. She had to spend the night up there in the mountains with a dead girl. She had to put a bullet in the dead girl's brain. A nice touch. She had to wait until you let go of Angelo Scarlotti's bear, and hope that the bear would do what you said it would do, and not do anything else."

I know there are no lines in a charade, tough or easy. But that didn't matter. Margot Fraser said what I wanted to hear.

Her voice was very small.

"What bullet?"

I stopped considering.

There was nothing more to consider. They'd dug a hole so deep Margot Fraser could never get out. She'd jumped in by herself, but they were waiting for her.

"What are you talking about? What bullet?"

There was a snag of panic in her voice.

Her hand reached out to hold on to the dash. She twisted around in the seat. She didn't know about the bullet. That wasn't in the script.

"The whole thing was a setup, all the way through. The girl in the parking lot? She was dead before you got there. She had to be. That's easy enough to see, unless you've been drinking. A little.

How often did Allison Carpenter call you for a ride home from The Tarot?"

"Allison?"

"Yes."

"That was the—first time."

"Doesn't she have a car? A very nice car?"

Margot looked at me.

I didn't need an answer.

"Okay," I said. "You got scared. That would have been enough for them. It would have given you a lot of explaining to do, let's say reckless homicide. It would have scared the hell out of you and it would have kept you away from Grasshopper Glacier. That's what Allison wanted, she had her instructions and that's why she argued with you."

Margot was listening.

"It didn't work out that way," I continued. "You got fancy. You wanted to bring the bear into it. You wanted headlines. So they went along with you. Why not? You want to hang yourself? Here's the rope. They went along, all right, but they added a touch of their own. Something you didn't know about and you couldn't explain—the bullet. They were counting on the coroner's blowing the whistle. He blows the whistle and your whole masquerade falls apart. All of a sudden you're wanted for murder. Allison? Figure it out. It was *your* idea, *you* came up with the girl, *you* shot her, Allison's a cool number, she proved that. It's her word against yours."

Margot was listening, but she hadn't quite caught up.

"You mean that girl was dead before I got to The Tarot? I didn't run over her? I didn't kill her? Allison did?"

"Allison or Monkey Man or someone. It doesn't matter. If they set you up in the mountains, they set you up down here. The place was jammed. They put her to sleep. They took care of the girl and they blocked off the most obvious parking space and they opened it up before you came over. You walked right into it."

"Monkey Man?"

"John P. Daddano. Montana's answer to the Bearded Lady."

"How? How did they do it?"

"Let me count the ways."

She waited, but why corrupt her?

I continued: "A long time ago, someone wanted your father dead.

Bad enough to take him up on Grasshopper Glacier and blow away half his jaw with a forty-five and lock him up where he'd never be found. In the ice. It's a borrowed solution; murder always is. How long ago was that? Sixteen, seventeen years? You can bet his nerves were shot to hell. Especially after you started making noises about Daddy. You can bet it confused the hell out of him when no one found that bullet in the brain of the dead girl. Maybe he figured Allison Carpenter hadn't had the guts to pull the trigger. If so, he figured wrong. But dead is dead, either way. It saved buying silence from Angelo Scarlotti. It saved buying silence from Allison Carpenter. It made life a lot easier all the way around. For Mr. Big.

"They broke Allison Carpenter in half and threw her away," I said. "She was in the way. You're still in the way, Margot. Twice lucky, third time dead."

Her face was dark. She was silent.

"I can't go home," she finally said.

My eyes took in the window again.

There were three cars parked between us and the access road leading away from the airport. The cars looked empty, even the one with the window rolled down on the driver's side.

"Who saw you come here tonight?"

"No one. I thought—"

"Yeah. You look like a million others. Army surplus. Well, you're one in a million. You're about to be in a war. Do you see that car over there under the lights—the one with the window rolled down?"

She looked.

"Figure it this way," I said. "Whoever's sitting in that car is getting very wet because he has to breathe. If he breathes, the windows fog up. He can't start the car, that's for sure. It would give him away—"

"I don't see anyone."

"So what does he do? It's a nasty business. He's got to open the window to let a little air in. Put both your hands up there on the dash."

"I thought—"

"Don't think."

I threw the car into reverse.

The tires skidded on the wet asphalt of the airport parking lot. The car shuddered crazily backwards. Out of the corner of my eye I saw his lights come on.

Margot Fraser went up against the dashboard. She fell limply back into the seat when I shifted gears.

The car leaped forward.

She was pinned back into a corner—a rag doll filled with sawdust and broken dreams.

17

Sam Casanova hadn't been kidding. They *were* sending someone else in to take over. Not only that, but he had arrived.

I kept the accelerator on the floor where it belonged. We fishtailed a little on the wet pavement, the rear tires finally caught, and we screamed past the other car. I didn't even bother to look at him, except to notice that it was a Ford, the sun visors were down, there was a dent in the rear fender, and a spurt of flame leaped from the open window on the driver's side as we roared past. Whatever caliber he was using, he missed.

But he wasn't kidding either.

By the time we reached the access road leading away from the airport, I had his lights in the rear-view mirror. He was coming at us.

We took the turn onto the access road. The divided highway was a couple of blocks away, an indistinct blur of flashing red lights hanging in the darkness. They said slow down. We didn't.

The rain drove down against the windshield. The wipers couldn't carry it away fast enough. I checked the mirror a second time. He was just straightening out behind us. His headlights did a little shimmy. Then they leaped forward.

We were running out of room.

I hit the brakes. We skidded sideways through the intersection, picking up some gravel, and when I got the car pointed in the right direction it was pointed away from town. He had to see us. He had to know where we were going.

I killed the lights.

The highway was empty and we were a shot in the dark, Margot had slipped halfway off the seat to the floor, and I hoped the cops were playing hearts somewhere out of the rain, where it was warm and dry and safe.

"Stay down there," I said. "The man has a gun."

I was looking for anything.

I found it about a mile down the highway, a roadhouse with red neon over the single gable and half a dozen muddy cars and pickup trucks parked under the tree in front of it. I hit the shoulder and then the gravel of the parking lot and then the brakes, in that order, hoping we were far enough off the road before the brake lights went on.

We spun sideways and came to a stop on the far side of something called The Oasis, in a driveway that led around in back of the place. I turned off the engine and went down on the seat next to my rag doll.

He never saw us.

He was going at least ninety-five when he flashed by, bound for hell and back, and he didn't wave. He must have been in a hurry.

The door to the roadhouse flew open.

We squealed out of the driveway and back onto the highway just as four men stepped into the rain to see what all the commotion was about. There wasn't any commotion. Not any more.

Margot Fraser pulled herself back into the corner and turned sideways in the seat, so she faced me. For a long time she was silent.

The road ahead was dark. The wind was with us, the wind and the rain and the darkness. It carried us south down that long highway that ends in a place where the wind cries through a gap in the mountains and never stops, toward a place Margot Fraser said she didn't want to go. I asked myself a lot of questions. They all started with why. They all had the same answer. There was no going home for either of us.

The night closed its fist around us.

Her voice came out of the silence.

"Nick Caine."

"Yes."

"That's what it said in the newspaper."

"Yes."

"I want to go home."

Okay, she changed her mind.

Maybe it was because she wanted to hear the sound of her own voice, proof that she was still alive. Maybe it was the darkness and the night, and the way they kept the real world at a safe distance. The highway was still empty. Maybe it was true. Maybe she really did want to go home. There was nowhere else to go, and she had to get ready for it, for the black widow up at Hellgate and the wind and all the things that needed to be said but never had been.

This little girl lost. She talked. For whatever the reason.

She knew the woods around Grasshopper Glacier like the back of her own hand. Or the picture of her father's face. Sitting in the darkness behind The Tarot, pinched and crimped by the thought of the dead girl lying on the ground behind the car, she spelled out her plan to Allison Carpenter. Allison, as stated, didn't like it. Allison thought she should call the cops. Face the music.

It was one argument Margot won. Maybe the only one.

Allison left the car and went into The Tarot. She had plenty of time to call Mr. Big. He could roll with the punches. If Margot Fraser wanted a bear, they'd get her one. When Allison came back out, she must have had carte blanche to go along with Margot's crazy scheme. To grease the skids right down to that last little twist of a bullet in the head of a dead girl. She also had an old Army blanket under her arm and a set of keys in her hand. The keys fit a nondescript brown van that was parked off to the side of The Tarot.

They moved fast, bringing the van around to Margot's car, loading the dead girl in the back, and covering her with the blanket. They drove back to town—Allison in the van, Margot in the Renault. On the way they stopped at the Animal Research Center and picked up the spray cans containing Margot's witch's brew of a chemical with thirty-five syllables. Margot could pronounce all of them. What a smart kid.

They left Margot's car in an apartment building parking lot on the west edge of town and headed north. It was a long drive—I know, I've made it—but they got to the road leading down into Grasshopper Campground before the sun did.

Their base was located a half-mile up the road from the ranger's station—a lodge that was boarded up and closed for the season. They carried the dead girl to the cabin farthest from the road, went around behind it, and left her there.

The morning sun caught them at Hungry Horse, an empty van

bouncing down from the mountains, two girls, mummers in a masquerade of death. A couple of hours later they had picked up Margot's car and Allison had worked her magic on Angelo Scarlotti. Margot had stayed outside, because she feared Angelo would recognize her. The bear was no more trouble than the dead girl, and Angelo Scarlotti was easier than both of them. Margot followed Allison back up to the Grasshopper in the Renault.

When they got back to the lodge, they had the woods and the swine smell of the old sow all to themselves. The dead girl was where they'd left her. Down the road, Pug Collins was sitting by himself in the ranger's cabin, feet up on the window sill, smoking Lucky Strikes and thinking pretty thoughts about autumn and the slow draining of life from the forest and the sky, stuff like that, and wondering why John McPhee gets more play in *The New Yorker* than he does. Everyone has his problems, right?

Margot led the bear across the road, followed a little trail along the creek with no name, crossed over a ridge before the ranger's station came into view, and took a hollow deeper into the woods until she was opposite the campground itself. She chained the bear to a tree. That explained something. She climbed the ridge and looked down on the campground. It was empty. Waiting.

Margot and Allison together carried the dead girl, wrapped in the old blanket, into the woods on the other side of the campground. They didn't need to chain her to a tree. She was very cooperative.

That was the setup.

They left the van in the back lot of the lodge, where it couldn't be seen. Margot lined up Emily Carpenter. Allison lined up Cynthia Farmer. The next day they all went up to Grasshopper together in Margot's Renault. The great outdoors.

Long after dark, when Emily and Cynthia were asleep, Margot and Allison went for a walk in the woods. They came back with an Army blanket, a girl nobody knew, the key to their macabre masquerade. It wasn't easy getting her into Margot's sleeping bag, but they did it.

Then Margot took a powder. She had a date with dawn and a bear.

If you think they beat the odds, think again. Margot knew her stuff, and she knew the only thing that could stop them was if Allison lost her nerve. Allison didn't give any sign of losing her nerve. Allison didn't have any nerves.

Now there was nothing left of them.

The dead girl was dead twice, or three times if you want to count Allison's little trick with the .22 after Margot had gone off into the woods by herself, or four times if you count the bear. No matter how you counted it she was buried in a rock-hard grave under a headstone that had it all wrong. Allison? She'd cashed in with Mr. Big. She'd done everything he asked. But she was too dead to appreciate it. Cynthia Farmer? She was out of it. At least, that's the way I figured it. She was a real babe in the woods, with very civilized curves and angles and a heart that didn't like to linger in one place for too long. Emily? A mouse.

That left Margot Fraser.

She sat over in the corner of the seat, huddled against the door. Bone, some cold white flesh, those dark eyes that couldn't tell you anything because there was nothing left to tell. She had too much to remember and too much to forget.

I glanced over at her once or twice as she talked, her voice barely rising above the whine of the tires on the wet pavement and the steady heartbeat of the wipers. Her fingers rested lightly on the door latch, as though she was thinking about stepping out into the darkness forever. Her hand was trembling. I wanted the highway to go on and on, always into darkness, never to stop. What could you do with her? They all think they've gone through hell and not surrendered. This one had. She'd gone through her own hell, one she made herself. She'd surrendered.

Home to what? A mother who had been crushed and kicked by dreams that turned inside out and came at her with knives? A woman who had buried a daughter and a husband and who was already far beyond mourning?

My mind raced on ahead, to that house sailing out on a rocky rise above Hellgate.

The road was dark. And empty.

Several cars had gone by the other way, headed for town on the other side of the divided highway. Maybe he was one of them. Maybe not. Maybe he was still ahead of us, foot slammed down to the floor, knuckles white around the steering wheel, the gun out on the seat next to him.

She was still talking.

She'd waited alone in the woods that morning, until the sun rose and the bear had gone its way like a mechanical toy, following the trail she'd laid, and at last the silence was broken by the sound of distant screams and the heartless cry of the automobile horn in the middle of nowhere. The bear was the only one who got away scot-free. Margot watched from the ridge as Pug Collins came out of the ranger's shack and then she turned and walked the other way along the ridge—past the ranger's station and down to the access road and into the back lot of the boarded-up lodge to where they'd left the van.

Somewhere along the line she picked up the straw-colored wig and the fatigue jacket. As a disguise, it was close to perfect. It made her look like anybody, or nobody. She stayed in an isolated cabin back up in the hills above the Research Center, out of sight if not out of mind, living on food she'd stashed there. At night, when no one was around, she'd sneak down for the newspapers in the Professor's office. She followed everything in the papers. Allison's death threw her for a loop. She figured it for a suicide, like anyone else who read the papers, and it didn't add up for her. Not after all Allison had done. When her father came out of the ice, it knocked her off her pins again. It meant one thing—the whole charade was for nothing. She counted her money and went to the airport, thinking to go anywhere. Where didn't matter. Just get away, from all that had happened and all that hadn't happened. She had been at the terminal for three hours, wandering around, when she spotted me.

She was still talking, but I was listening to something else. The night. The darkness.

The goon who picked us up in the airport parking lot and used us for target practice had done almost everything right. Except lose us. But maybe he hadn't lost us. It was a big world out there, with plenty of places to hide. He had disappeared into the night and the darkness, and he was waiting for us.

I didn't like it.

In the distance a glow of lights made a yellow smudge against the low sky. I knew what it was. Conover—a crossroads on the way to nowhere in particular, a strip of lights and all-night joints where the log-rollers and ore-carriers pulled their rigs off the highway and stoked up on black coffee served in white mugs, and Big Skyburgers, and peroxided waitresses who reminded them of what home wasn't like.

We came up slowly. I watched the traffic light slip into something yellow, then snap to red. It must have been meant for someone else.

I turned to the right without stopping, checked the mirrors, and gunned the car. We shot west into the darkness, leaving the lights behind us.

"Where are we going?"

"This is the short way home, is it not? Comes up on the other side of Hellgate? Unless the guy who drew the map was smoking something funny."

"This is the way to The Tarot," Margot said softly.

We were in darkness again, rolling country, on a road that dipped back and forth between the fences. I opened the window. The air was cold and wet. The rain had diminished to a thin curling mist that kept trying to get out of the way of the headlights. The fences stayed close to the road.

The Tarot came looming up out of the darkness and mist, on the right side of the road. It was a big, two-story roadhouse, old and square. A giant yardarm extended out from the center of the building and supported a neon champagne glass, cocked at an angle, with neon bubbles rising up the rusty chain. The neon was dead. The champagne had lost its fizz.

But the vapor lights in the parking lot were still burning. They cast an eerie orange glow. The parking lot was empty. The Tarot was dead.

I slowed down and took in what I could: a large Tarot card mounted to the front of the building over the entrance. Smaller cards swinging from brackets over the darkened windows on the ground floor, being toyed with by the wind. From a distance, the sound of barking dogs.

"I call him Monkey Man. Do you know him? He's the missing link, in more ways than one. John P. Daddano."

"No."

The orange glow fell behind. Off to the right, I could see the level airstrip.

"He runs The Tarot. He knew Allison. He's got an airstrip and it's out of the way and Allison took off every weekend and right back there next to The Tarot is where she took off from. It adds up, with no remainder. When you pulled off your little stunt in the mountains, and it didn't work the way they wanted it to work, they turned Monkey Man loose. They gave him a job to do. It confused him. He's the link, but he's not Mr. Big. Was Allison an animal lover? No. She did what she had to do. It would take an animal lover to like Monkey Man. Who was Allison's boyfriend, Margot? She had a boyfriend, that's obvious."

"Everyone knew she had a boyfriend. He bought her clothes. That fancy car. Emily hated him."

"Emily Carpenter knows him?"

"No. That's why she hated him. Allison would never talk about him."

"She did what she had to do. And they snapped her in half. Allison was his eyes and ears. She kept tabs on you. She filled him in on your every move, the hunt for your father, and that's why they set you up. They set you up with the dead girl. They made it easy to get the bear. They set you up all the way down the line. Now they want to set you down. About six feet down, Margot."

I glanced across at her. She was still huddled in the corner of the seat, pinned there by the weight of bad circumstance. I wondered if she would ever squirm free.

"Mr. Big," I said. "He operates with a small army, and he keeps his pretty hands clean. He pulls the strings and Monkey Man's one of his puppets. So is Sam Casanova, whom you've never heard of, and Martin Bidet, whom you've also never heard of, and Allison Carpenter, who is dead and it doesn't matter. Not even Monkey Man knows who's pulling those strings, Margot. But there's one person who does know. And who doesn't know she knows."

"Who?"

"You do," I answered.

"Me?"

She turned toward me. My eyes were on the road.

"How else did it start? How else did he find you? He murdered your father and kept his eye on you and somewhere along the line he started pulling strings. Maybe you've met him. Maybe you know him. Maybe you don't and he thinks you do. Either way you're the key to it, Margot. That's why we've got to keep you alive."

Darkness. Silence. No answer.

We'd driven for an hour when the road quit kidding around with us and curved up onto a flat and straightened out. The rain and the mist had been swept away by the wind. It pushed and shoved at the car, nudging us toward the shoulder. The moon sailed in the black sky behind us.

I slowed down when we got near the house. The wind had shifted. It slammed into us from behind, tried to push us on past, down through Hellgate and the valley and on toward a place with a little light and warmth and safety. Anywhere but where we were. It tried to do us a favor.

The gate was open.

The house was completely dark.

I stopped the car just inside the gate and killed the engine. It made an ominous machine tick, an insect sound, a death beetle gnawing in the night.

The wind shook the car.

Margot Fraser had both hands on the dashboard. Her face was a white mask. All roads lead somewhere, even if it's nowhere.

I reached behind her and locked the door.

"I'll go," I said. "Stay here."

I opened my door and locked it and slammed it shut. The wind carried the sound away. I moved around the front of the car and crossed the gravel driveway and worked my way up toward the house along the fence.

I had Sam Casanova's .38 in my hand, in case I needed to unlock any doors that didn't want to open or answer any questions. It didn't matter. The kitchen door was unlocked. The questions had all been answered.

Inside, the moonlight showed me broken glass all over the kitchen floor. Every window in the room had been shattered from the outside. It was the same in Margot's bedroom, and Maureen's.

The house had been taken over by darkness.

The wind cried in through the shattered windows, the wind and the darkness and the night rasping past the teeth of glass that grinned in the wooden frames.

I found her in the living room, sitting before a fire that had gone out years ago.

"Maureen."

She didn't answer.

Her hands had fallen limply in her lap, next to Margot's sad Pierrot.

Her head was turned toward me, fallen back against the chair, and her eyes were wide open. Dark, wasted eyes just like her daughter's. Eyes that could tell you nothing.

The bullet hole was a small dark circle in her right temple.

He had taken his sweet time. Her cheeks glistened.

She had been weeping.

18

We didn't hang around for the funeral.

Funerals are one of the niceties. Assuage the grief, salute the fallen hero, reflect on the impermanence of life. We didn't have time for the niceties.

There was nothing fancy about this one. No tricks, no sleight of hand, no subtleties. No more charades. They had finally closed the curtains on the costume ball. They'd thrown away all the props but one—my guess was a .38 caliber special—and they'd used it. It couldn't have made much difference to Maureen Fraser. Those tears were for all that was lost and would never come back.

Never speak for the dead.

Those broken windows, the shattered glass, the way that house had been opened to the cold and the darkness and the wind—those things weren't meant for the dead.

They were meant for the living.

They were meant for Margot Fraser.

Call him Mr. Big. He was in a panic. He didn't have time for niceties, either. Not any more. He was going to wipe out anyone who could connect him with Douglas Fraser. He was going to obliterate the past.

Whatever Margot Fraser knew, whatever she didn't know she knew, was part of it. It made her vulnerable. There was only one thing that could keep her alive. With no guarantees. After all, I was a little rusty.

I had realized too late where the goon had gone after we ditched him. Straight to Hellgate and a house on a hill, to leave us a little reminder of the impermanence of life.

When I got back to the car, Margot hadn't moved.

Her knuckles were white. Her face had no expression. Her eyes were large and brown. Whatever it was—the moonlight, the wind, some faded music in the air, take your pick—it had told her all she needed to know.

She was letting go. She was being carried away by that same deadly wind, into the darkness.

It was a little after midnight when we got back down to the airport. Cibola was closed. The seven cities of gold were undiscovered. Margot was silent. A little pressure on the arm, she moved. A little pressure on the arm, she stopped.

A small knot of us stood out on the tarmac of the runway when the plane was finally ready for boarding. The last plane out. The fat man was there and his wife. A middle-aged woman who was traveling alone and looked like she was used to it. A couple of kids with knapsacks. A tall blond man who stood off to the side with his Qantas bag, an exotic, a movie star. Except for the deep red scars under his eyes. It looked like someone slugged him and didn't want him to forget it.

We all have our troubles.

The fat man was drunk. He looked up at me like his chins hurt and he said, "Snow. I predict snow. Snow up to your ass."

"You want your face fixed, right here on the runway?"

"No, sir. I was just saying, I think it will snow."

The clouds had blown away.

Someone had thrown stars all over the sky.

The stewardess was about forty and wasn't happy about it. She figured she was good for about ten more years and nobody would ever have the chance to know it. The skin around her eyes was dark and she wore a brown wool coat that came down below her knees. She needed it. Forty years old and still flying through the stars in the middle of the night in the middle of nowhere.

The coffee was black and just as bitter.

I was still looking out the window a half-hour later. Dark mountains, dark plains; dark towns below, dark skies above. Death everywhere. Things you could not see and wouldn't want to see if you could.

I felt Margot's weight against my shoulder, a sparrow's weight, as though all the marrow had gone from her bones. Her eyes were closed.

The fat man looked at me across the aisle and smiled. He still didn't want his face fixed. He probably thought it was pretty. There was spittle on his chin. His wife was already asleep. I would bet his wife was always already asleep. The two kids were on the port side in front. They were sharing a blanket and looked like they were getting their act together. The middle-aged woman who was traveling alone and looked like she was used to it had changed her seat, moving a few rows behind us to join the movie star with the kangaroo case. They were carrying on a quiet conversation.

I turned back to the window.

All I could see was the reflection of a face in the glass, a face that had no past and no future. A face that was used to being on the edge of nothing but had been away from it too long, two years too long, and now was doing everything wrong. I'd laid Monkey Man out in the lobby of a condo that looked like a rocket to the moon, but I hadn't laid him out flat enough. He had come back to earth. I'd hog-tied another guy, a little slick named Sam Casanova, but I hadn't tied him tightly enough. He could still talk. I'd let Cynthia Farmer go her own way—a tough, frightened dream of a girl who didn't like to say goodbye. She'd said goodbye anyway, as though it didn't matter. I'd taken a poor wounded bird under my wing, to carry her home.

I'd left my calling card everywhere—Mononucleosis Oto, Uncle Deadly, Hoe Norse, the punk with the computer in the university offices, Audrey Hepburn, the widow Fraser, a daffy duck of a professor. I never used to work that way. Not halfway. Any one of them could connect the dots. Any one of them could call the cops. I didn't want them. Neither did the face in the window glass.

A few hours earlier I had been sitting in an airport lounge, ready to walk away from it. Ready to say goodbye to the face in the mirror.

Now I couldn't.

Halfway wasn't good enough anymore.

"You have something stronger than coffee," I suggested.

"Not on this flight, sir," she answered. "I'm sure you'll find something at Denver."

She pulled her coat closer around her stringy body. She didn't smile.

I put my head back on the seat and closed my eyes and tried to focus on the man I didn't know. The man who made his mistake a long time ago.

Mr. Big. The top banana. Mr. Magic.

What did I know about him? One word floated up out of the darkness. Power. He was a powerful man. Lift a finger and the mummers go to work. Monkey Man. Sam Casanova. The guy who took care of things up on a pass in the mountains and smashed a few windows so the darkness could come in, and you couldn't fail to get the message. A guy so good you didn't even know he was there.

Mr. Big. When his nose itches, twenty people gladly sneeze. All I could see was plush carpeting and a big walnut desk and a little man sitting behind it with a quizzical half-smile. A man to whom pain was amusing. A man who liked charades.

He came out of the past of Douglas Fraser—electronics, brains, big money, that yellow brick road that took a wrong turn and led up to the mountain wind and silent ice of Grasshopper Glacier. He had put a slug in Fraser's jaw and then he'd put Fraser into a crevasse, forgetting that all things move. Even ice and stone.

Now time was running out on him. He couldn't stop because he didn't know where to stop. Eighteen years of silence had come down on his head with a roar, and he was the one who heard it best. He couldn't cut his losses and run, because he had too much to lose, sitting there behind his big desk and his half-smile. Life must have changed plenty for him in the past eighteen years. He didn't want to lose it. Whatever was in his way would have to go.

That meant Margot Fraser.

That meant me.

The key to it was power. Immense power. I thought of Martin Bidet, sitting down in his office in Denver—a front man, he had to be—calling Sam Casanova in the middle of the night and asking for a little favor, for old time's sake. I thought of a little white card that was tacked to the door of Allison Carpenter's room and that the cops hadn't bothered to notice. Bo. A flyboy. Out of Denver. I thought of that little item Harry Gallagher had dug up on Allison's fancy car: purchased in Denver. I thought of a weedy airstrip out in the middle of nowhere.

I could connect dots, too.

I stopped thinking.

I had my head back on the seat and I had my eyes closed and I listened to the strong, steady surge of the engines as the plane raced southward through the night. They were trying to tell me something. And I listened. And at last I heard it, over and over again. The steady, droning sound of power at the one point it bore in on the life of Margot Fraser:

Augerman, Morgan, Rashad. Augerman, Morgan, Rashad. Augerman, Morgan, Rashad. . . .

The cabbie dropped us off at the corner.

I paid him, threw my duffel over my shoulder, and walked the last block in the predawn darkness. Margot drifted along beside me, holding tight to my arm.

The street was very empty.

In a couple of hours it would be filled with CPAs and government word processors taking the shortcut to work in their Toyotas and CVCCs and Tonkas, figuring their gasoline consumption down to the tenth of a mile on their silver pocket calculators, happy to shake a free finger at the rest of us.

We walked past Facettes, the disco run by everybody's pal, Michael Moro, home for the young pretties who go there every night to pose for the future. Across the street was another country, the Down Home, where the good old boys go for ten-cent beer on Tuesdays and the Dolly Parton look-alike contest on Thursdays and just raising hell the rest of the week.

Someone was sitting on the curb over there, a neighborhood regular, a dark lump of a ragman sniffling his bottle of wine and hoping morning would come sooner rather than later.

My place was down at the end of the block where it belonged, three stories of what I call home. We crossed over.

Margot saw them first—a bundle of red roses on the doorstep, wrapped in green paper. She let out a little moan. It was the first I'd heard from her in some time.

I picked them up and handed them to her. Then I got out the key. It still worked.

I put the duffel down on the floor in the hallway and listened. What I heard was my own breathing. Twice as fast as it should have been.

Augerman, Morgan, Rashad.

Flowers for the living. Silence for the dead. Someone was letting us know they knew we were home.

I slid my hand along the wall and turned on the lights.

19

It wasn't what you'd call a beauty sleep. Four hours. We were sitting at the table in the kitchen. I made the coffee. She was wearing one of my shirts. That took care of her down to the knees.

"There are some rules," I said. "Your room will be on the third floor to the left of the landing. Next to mine. The same place you slept this morning. The door between the rooms opens from either side. Let's pretend it doesn't. The drapes are drawn. Let's leave them that way. The view isn't spectacular, unless you're on the outside with a rifle. Stay away from the window. Don't answer the door. It's a big house, you can roam around, but don't get lost. I want to know where you are. I don't want to have to worry about it."

She looked at me with those sad brown eyes. She was listening.

I continued: "You'll find clothes in the dresser. You'll find something that fits. I used to know a girl about your size and she left her stuff all over. The shower's down the hall. You don't go outside. I think we understand that. They're looking for you. Everyone thinks you're dead. Except you. And me. And someone else. I wish you'd think about that. You may have the key to whoever's behind this. Even if you don't, they think you do. They've already taken one shot at you. All it took was one shot up at Hellgate. I don't like leaving you alone, but we don't have much of a choice. The house is safe. I can't make any guarantees about the street. Or the rest of the world. One other thing. There's a woman who comes in once a week to clean. I'm not perfect, but I do pick up after myself. I don't wear pajamas. So it's easy work. Her name is Xuan. You can trust her. She won't ring the bell. She has her own key. And she knows how not to speak English. Can you make chicken *zatsivi?"*

"Chicken what?"

"Forget it. I'll make it. Tonight or tomorrow night or sometime. Do you know how to open a can of soup?"

She smiled. A thin, wry smile. It wasn't much, but it was something.

"Okay," I said. "I'm going to be gone most of the day. You're going to entertain yourself."

"About the flowers."

I was waiting for it.

"Yes?"

"I got a bunch of flowers like that not too long ago. A dozen roses. I've been thinking about it. Three men came up to school. They help fund the Professor's lab and they gave him some money —they gave the check to me—and after they left the florist delivered a dozen roses to my room. They were—"

"Augerman, Morgan, and Rashad," I stated.

She looked at me like I knew something she didn't. I did. After I'd got her tucked in, I'd walked down the street to the Down Home and found the guy who was holding the curb down and helped him wake up. Then I'd asked him whether he'd seen the delivery boy drop the roses on my doorstep. He had. It was the longest, blackest Cadillac he'd ever seen. Not your usual horse-drawn wagon.

"Forget it," I told her. "Whoever sent the roses didn't include a card. Maybe they were for me. It's my house. Who are these guys? Augerman, Morgan—"

"Businessmen," she said.

"Did any of them seem especially interested in you? Or were they just being polite? Businessmen are very polite."

"Yes," she said softly. "Like I said, I've been thinking about it. Mr. Morgan couldn't keep his eyes off me. They had a little ceremony, they presented the check to the school, and Mr. Morgan kept working his way around so he could stand next to me. He looks like what's-his-name. That old movie star. Does it mean anything?"

"The world's full of movie stars," I said. "You understand the rules?"

She shook her head. She understood the rules.

I pushed myself away from the table and went into the library.

The messages were still there, where Xuan had left them: Harry Gallagher, Michael Moro, Dr. Lew Diamond ("wants to borrow your book by Weston LaBarre"), Gallagher again, Virginia ("wouldn't leave last name"), Gallagher again.

I got the message. I dialed a number, none of the above, and then I called Gallagher. We shot the breeze and when the wind died down I told him we could get together at seven o'clock, I had some things to do, and he suggested the place. Then I asked him for another favor. I had the names of three guys, all I had was the names, and I wanted the rest of the goods. The chicken *zatsivi* would have to wait.

Back upstairs in my bedroom, the drapes were still drawn. I like it that way. I could hear Margot Fraser down the hall, in the shower. The plumbing is old. It makes a hell of a racket. I went over to my dresser and pulled open the second drawer from the top, left-hand side.

It was waiting for me.

The Margolin Special—nickel-plated, semiautomatic. A limited edition, you might say, from the bad old days. It packs the punch of a Webley RIC, weighs two ounces less, and has one other virtue that suits my fancy. It was designed by a blind man. A gun designed by a blind man better be a little bit better.

I dropped Sam Casanova's .38 into the drawer, strapped on the Margolin Special, and went downstairs.

Then I went out into what was left of a gray day to look for a guy who didn't fly to Montana anymore. The roses, in the blue vase on the table next to the front door, were already wilting.

They were a message I couldn't ignore.

20

He was standing on the lower wing next to the cockpit of the rebuilt Fokker D-7. It was a beauty—bright red and yellow. The plane was making so much noise that we could hardly hear each other.

"Who is it you're looking for?" he asked. There was impatience on his face.

I looked up at him.

The pencil-thin mustache on his lip curled upward. He squinted at me with his teeth while the backwash from the single propeller sent shivers down his long silk scarf. He was wearing a steerhide jacket and a scuffed leather bonnet and yellow goggles pushed up on his wide forehead.

He looked like Ronald Colman, bound for Bombay.

"Needle in a haystack," I hollered. "A guy who doesn't fly to Montana anymore. His name is Bo. Bo Something."

"Montana," he shouted.

He tried to place it, but he didn't try very hard. One elegant booted foot went into the cockpit. He swiveled around to show me his britches, and he sank up to his shoulder in World War I.

"Guy who used to fly to Montana," I called after him. "Weekends. Nice-looking girl with him. Redhead."

"Redhead," he shouted.

He was shaking his head. He pulled the goggles down over his eyes and he let his mustache drop about an inch. His chin went up in the air. The sun was a small white circle behind the bank of pearl-gray clouds. Who knew what ghosts and dangers lurked up there, Gothas or SPADs or Sopwith Camels screaming out of the sun?

He looked back down at me and shook his head more vigorously than before. The engine growled at me. I took the hint and let him go. He bounced down the dirt toward the end of the runway and his rendezvous with destiny.

That made six for six. Six airfields, six strikeouts. I'd been to Stapleton, Adams County, Sky-Hi, Westminster, Clearwater, and now the Circle-K. No one had heard of a guy who used to fly to Montana on the weekends to bring a redhead home for fun and games, and who didn't fly to Montana anymore. Of course, it was no Fokker that shuttled Allison Carpenter back and forth for the pleasure of Mr. Big. But it would have been appropriate.

I found the car where I parked it, in the long yellow grass behind the hangar, got in, and didn't turn the key. Instead I pulled the map over onto my lap and held it there with both hands.

The wind wanted it.

I heard the drone of the Fokker overhead.

My finger traced an invisible circle around the city. Okay, let's say I was too close. Mr. Big was too smart to bring her in too close, where people might remember a redheaded regular. Better to bring her in farther out, to an airport that was closed, or a private field like the one up north, or a no-radio airport. Anyone who could bring a plane down on that dirt strip next to The Tarot could land blindfolded and in darkness down here.

That left anywhere.

I checked my watch.

The day was shot. I had two hours left. That meant I could get up to the Winged "C" west of Fort Lupton and back to town by seven. One haystack was as good as the next, and the more I thought about the Winged "C" the more I liked the looks of it, even though I'd never seen it. I didn't know anyone who flew from there, which meant maybe nobody did. The last I'd heard, the place was up for sale. And it was far enough away to be very, very private.

"What's the big rush?" she said in my ear.

I turned to look at her.

She was standing right next to the car, with one hand resting lightly on her hip. The other hand was resting lightly on my arm.

She had stringy blonde hair and aviator's goggles holding it back off her face, which was nice enough to make your day if you were feeling bad enough, and a pair of soft leather boots that came all the way up to the top of her thighs over the jeans. Everyone at the Circle-K was into leather. This one was very much into leather. I'd seen her in the hangar office, on her hands and knees behind the counter looking for something in the pigeonholes back there, and she looked even better on her hands and knees than she did with one hand resting lightly on her hip and the other resting lightly on my arm.

I pulled my arm in.

"Is this your car?" she asked.

The Fokker sounded like a fly, at a great distance above us.

I reached out and patted the side of the car. It's a beat-up Chevy of undetermined age, and I picked it up for a hundred bucks from a kid who didn't want it anymore. She shifted her hips and patted the side of the car.

"I think I saw it in a movie," she said.

"Some other time," I said.

She drew her hand back. In the rear-view mirror I saw her give me the finger. She was very chic.

I pointed the car north, stretched my neck, and glanced at the face in the mirror. If the superior man persists, misfortune comes. A prophecy that didn't want to go away. I thought about it.

I'd already called the number on Bo's card, before I left the house. Disconnected. So I called another number that I know and a lady answered and I told her the number I had. She read me back an address. It was across town. I went there first. Notathome Answering Service, second floor. I climbed the steps. I knocked. She said come in. It was a good trick. She had five sticks of gum in her mouth. She weighed 210 pounds, and that's just counting the parts I saw. She was sitting behind a desk, next to a switchboard, and she didn't move. She pulled open a drawer and checked the records. She had no order for Bo Something. She had no record for Bo Anything. Yes, that was one of their numbers. No, it wasn't being used. Hadn't been used for months.

My luck wasn't any better at the airports. No one had heard of Bo Something.

The road was empty. It carried me a little distance into the foothills and then back out onto the prairie again. Finally, in the distance, I could see the big fuel tanks of the Winged "C" far off across the fields. The sheet-metal hangar looked abandoned.

It wasn't.

In the back, in the furnace room, I found a stick-figure of a man in blue overalls. He was monkeying with the furnace.

"It's gonna snow," he announced, when he eventually noticed me standing at the doorway to the furnace room. "Goodbye summer. I'm Forsythe."

"So I've heard."

I stuck out my hand, but he didn't take it. He only had three fingers. They were all greasy.

"You've heard of me?" He sounded hopeful.

"No. I heard it was going to snow."

He looked disappointed.

"Won the Tri-Corner Rally in 'sixty-two," he said. "American Eagle, with a Kenner K-5 radial. Grand Champion. Of course, that was a long time ago, wasn't it. Rolled that bird into a ball."

He wiped his hands on a large rag and finished the job on his overalls. We walked out through the mouth of the empty hangar into the afternoon.

"Trying to sell this place." His hands worked each other over vigorously. "Goddamn white elephant. Forty miles to nowhere." He looked up at the flat horizon. Then he looked up into the empty sky. "Good for sugar beets. Maybe."

He was a pleasant little man who lived and died for airplanes. He was mostly dying at the present moment, and when I told him that I'd seen a Fokker D-7 that afternoon he licked his lips and let out a thin whistle.

"Not original," he said. "Built from scratch. Plenty of scratch."

He lived in town with his wife. The town was Fort Lupton and the wife was unnamed. She was too large for anything except a four-seater. Forsythe often bedded down in the hangar. He didn't dream about blondes in boots on their hands and knees. Only silver Tiger Moths and Luscombe Phantoms and a certain Monocoupe he bought for a song down in Fort Collins with a Velie M-5. They were all gone now, gone the way of flesh and fabric and thin stretched metal.

"I'm looking for a friend of mine."

"Yep. That's for sure. We'll never see the likes of those babies again."

He was stuffing the rag back into the pocket of his overalls.

I said, "This friend of mine is flying something very nice, although I can't tell you what it is, and he's got a soft spot in his heart for redheads. In fact, he used to have a young lady up north. Montana. And he'd move her around every weekend. Back and forth."

The little man's eyes lit up.

"Back and forth," he said, shaking his head as though he understood what I was saying.

"He may not have her anymore. You know redheads. They can pretty much pick and choose—"

"He don't."

"No?"

"You're not speaking of Bosack?"

"Old Bo," I said.

"Mooney Ranger. An M20C," Forsythe said quickly. He knew everybody by what kind of wings they had. "Beauty of a plane. Not as fast as the 20E, but more range. Hell, I could never afford it. Bosack. He used to fly a redhead in and out of here on Friday night and Sunday afternoon, regular as a clock. In on Friday night, out on Sunday afternoon. But I don't know. He's missed the past couple weeks. So I don't know."

"That sounds like Old Bo. He's a fussy devil."

"Rich blood," he corrected me. "Mr. Bosack had himself picked up and delivered in one of them stretch Caddies."

I shrugged, as though it happens every day.

"He can afford it. You saw them coming in or going out?"

"Going out, mostly. Sunday afternoons. He'd come in after dark on Fridays, and I'd find the Mooney down there by the storage tanks on Saturday morning. Saw him once or twice on Friday, damn near midnight. Once I was out here late and the driver was down the road waiting. Parked down there by the tanks. I didn't talk to him and he didn't talk to me. Just stood there leaning against that black Caddie smoking one cigarette after another. Right next to the fuel tanks. I figured it was his business. And I got insurance, if you know what I mean. I put the glasses on him and watched him for a while, but I was long gone before the Mooney came in that night, and the light's not good down there—"

"What did he look like?"

"Jesus! All white, with a red stripe down the fuselage. A double stripe. A real beauty! The wingtips were red—"

"The driver."

"Drivers! What the hell do they look like? You can't tell them apart."

He laughed to himself.

"They're either young or they're old. They have light hair or dark hair. Take your pick. Five-ten. Average height. You know. They all look like child molesters."

"The Caddie had plates. Do you remember the number?"

The little man looked at me like I was out of my mind.

"Shit, I don't pay much attention to automobiles. They can't *fly,* can they?"

He delivered himself of another one of his long, drawn-out cackles and spit into the dirt.

"But, hell, you can ask Bosack yourself. He lives down by Carson at that trailer camp. Sunshine Acres." He thought about it a second. "Can't beat those eggs, can you?" he laughed. "Sunshine Acres! Flying a Mooney Ranger and getting his ass hauled around in a stretch Cadillac, and he lives in a tin can!"

This time he was laughing to himself.

"Hey!" he called after me. "You find him, ask him why he don't come around anymore. Ask him where the hell he's keeping that Mooney. This is a good place for him. No one out here to bother him—"

I left him looking up at the empty sky.

Twenty minutes later I was standing in front of a large white house trailer in Sunshine Acres. The dogs knew I was there. They were telling everyone about it.

The sign next to the door said "Office," and the door was open. The old lady peered out at me suspiciously through the screen.

She still had her housecoat on.

"Bosack," I said politely. "You got one around?"

"You play the French horn?" she said.

She sucked on a tooth and looked at me. Now both of us were suspicious.

"No, ma'm."

"Mr. Bosack did. Played that French horn night and day. Disturbed a lot of residents, I can tell you. Way in the back. Third one this side of the fence. Look it over from the outside and if you're still interested I'll come out and let you in. I'm making biscuits."

I knew I smelled something funny.

"It's for sale?" I asked.

"Sure is," she said emphatically. "Your Mr. Bosack left here owing. I'm within my rights. He missed two months before he left, and he'll soon owe another."

"When did he go?"

"Well! It's only been two weeks. He thinks he's pretty sharp, but he can think again. You a friend of his?" Her nose was touching the screen.

I shrugged.

"He's got another think coming, taking off like that!" she said sharply. The tip of her nose got wider. "Cleared everything out! Didn't say a word!" Her voice dropped. Her eyes narrowed. "I talked to the mailman. I found out where he went. I'll catch up with him!"

She was delighted with herself.

"I'd like to catch him myself. It's been a long time—"

"Hold it," she said.

She disappeared back into the trailer, and when she returned to the screen door she had a slip of paper in her hand. She had her spectacles on.

"That's it," she said, peering closely at the paper. "Martin Bidet. Thirteen-thirteen Colfax. Down in Denver."

She looked up at me triumphantly.

"That's where the mail's going," she declared, "and that's where he is. He owes me two months. Tell him that if you see him. Going on three. I'm going to get it, mister, one way or another!"

I backed up a couple of steps and nodded. She sounded like she meant it.

"I hope you do," I said.

21

Lucciano's is a little Italian place with plenty of atmosphere. When you walk in off the street all you see is darkness and shadows and floating red candles in the center of each table. The noise tells you the place is open for business. Harry Gallagher's on the tab as a regular.

It's not quite downtown. I was there not quite at seven and not quite straight from Sunshine Acres. On the way in, I'd stopped at a gas station and called the house on Delgany Street. The phone rang fourteen times and nobody bothered to answer it.

It was enough to take me out of my way.

I found Margot Fraser sitting alone at the kitchen table, working on her third pack of cigarettes. She was also having dinner. She knew how to open a can of soup.

"I knew it was you," she said when I filled the doorway.

She looked up at me. Her eyes were brown and bright. She was still wearing my shirt.

"I followed your rules. Except for once. I looked out the window in your library. I saw a man get out of a taxi at the corner. The phone rang four times. Three times this morning and once about twenty minutes ago. But I didn't answer it."

"Good."

"I've been thinking a lot about it, Nick. Augerman's a creep. He looked, you know, rotten around the edges. Do you think he's the one who—"

I walked over to her and gave her a paternal kiss on the forehead. It had been a long time since she had a paternal kiss on the forehead.

"You stay here. That's in the contract. Try not to think about it. Watch television. Maybe there's a good movie on. There are plenty of books in the other room. How's the soup?"

"Cold."

She managed one of her tentative smiles. Her eyes watched me as I went out the door.

There was nothing tentative about the girl standing at the register in Lucciano's. She wasn't a kitten; she was a tiger. The black badge on the front of her blouse said "M. Garner."

I gave it a try.

"Marie? Mabel? Matilda? Mahalia?"

"Get serious," she advised. "Marilou."

She put on a smile, which helped her face a little. Then she led me through the darkness like she knew what she was doing. I followed her perfume.

We stopped when we got to the Naked Lady, Harry's favorite work of modern art, and I helped myself to a chair.

"Something from the bar," M. Garner insisted.

I agreed.

Harry Gallagher still wasn't there.

I was nursing my second Scotch forty-five minutes later, and it brought back memories, when I heard him at the front register. I couldn't see him, but I heard him. Cackle, cackle, like a crow that's found something dead in the middle of the road. "Hey! Harry!" a couple of voices shouted out from the darkness. They probably could see him. He took long enough to make his way across the crowded dining room, zigging and zagging to pinch a cheek here or slap a back there. He always takes the longest distance between two points, because that way more people will see him. A fluorescent white face floated after him like a little ghost. The ghost didn't pinch any cheeks and didn't slap any backs.

"Emmett Crouse," Harry said when he found me and did the introductions. He reached across the table and pinched my cheek. Then he leaned down, took my tie in his hand, and pretended to blow his nose. An old trick.

He scraped up a chair of his own.

"You always sit with your back to the wall," he said. "You're crazy. Somebody going to put a knife in your back?" Cackle, cackle. "Nice to see you. How was the fishing?"

Even in the dark I could see his black eyes flashing.

"The oddest thing, Harry," M. Garner was saying. She was leaning between us, and almost had her head on Harry's shoulder. "I had a gentleman last night with two imaginary friends. Invisible. He ordered for them. He ate their food. He ordered from the bar. Whisky sours. Three of them. He drank them all. He talked to his imaginary friends for an hour, and I even had the cook come out to look—"

"Did he leave a tip, darling? That's the question."

"They all left a tip," she said. "All three of them."

"It's an item!" Harry snapped. He pinched her on the hip.

I looked across the table at Emmett Crouse. Thin blade of a nose, very aristocratic. Pale watery eyes. I couldn't make out the color. His mouth was a tight line that went down at the corners, and I knew what he was thinking. He was thinking that Harry Gallagher might reach out and pinch his cheek, or pretend to blow his nose in his tie, and then where would he be? Eight years at Princeton shot to hell.

Emmett Crouse looked like a drama critic. Very thin wrists. But he wasn't. He was the top financial and business editor on Harry's newspaper, a computer, Harry told me, and it only took one look to see that Harry had him pegged right.

"Are you hungry?" Harry asked.

I said, "Sure. Do they serve Scotch here?"

Emmett Crouse opened his mouth a crack, but he didn't quite have an answer. M. Garner returned with a little something for Harry and a little something for his pal, and then she went bye-bye again.

"This guy here—" Harry began. He interrupted himself to wave at someone at a nearby table. He blew a kiss. "This guy here," he resumed, "is the answer to your prayers. He is the best in the world. He knows everything there is to know about—" Harry broke it off. "Ah! My dear! How are you, darling?" he said loudly to a lady who was passing our table. His head bobbed up and down. He may have Japanese blood, too.

Emmett Crouse carefully placed his drink off to the side. Then he reached down by the side of his chair and brought up a thin black leather briefcase, which he placed on the table in front of him.

The corners of his mouth turned upward.

He looked at me as though it were just the two of us, a very private transaction, and Harry Gallagher didn't even exist.

"Hey! Harry!" someone cried out.

"May I ask what your interest is?" Crouse asked.

"You may. Earlier this year, February, March, I'm not sure, all three were up north. In Montana. Augerman, Morgan, and Rashad. They have a lot of largesse, apparently—you would know—and they were giving some of it away to the university up there. They also happened to—"

"I understand you precisely. The question of corporate support for universities is one we have not dealt with for quite some time. An interesting question. Not since the nineteen sixties, I believe, when there was such a fuss with Dow." He turned to Harry. "Or did we do something with Chase Manhattan? We must have. Not merely interesting, is it? It's an *important* question. The influence of the military, of corporations, or foreign governments, acting through—"

"You understand me precisely," I shrugged.

"Hey! Harry!" came another voice from the darkness. Harry waved. "They love me," he whispered.

Emmett Crouse's eyes had turned yellow. A very private transaction. Someone had switched the lights on inside his head. When he closed his briefcase again, one corner of his mouth was curled up, the other down. A thin, malicious smile.

He placed three manila folders on top of his briefcase. His fingers drifted over them like they were sable or ermine.

Harry: "Listen to what this guy has to say, Nick. I'm not kidding. He's a sweetheart, the real goods. Gets off on net gains and gross income. Isn't that right, Crouse? I mean, really gross income. I've been trying to get him to look into the porno shops, rubber ducks."

The wince was almost imperceptible, just a slight tightening of the skin around Crouse's eyes. Maybe he had to work with Harry Gallagher, but he didn't have to like it. He opened one of the folders, carefully extracted an eight-by-ten-inch glossy photograph, and slid it across the table to me.

"The Emperor," he said thinly. "Never to his face, of course. But that's how he's known. The Emperor. It fits like a—like the—"

"Like the skin on a snake," Harry helped.

"He's president and chairman of Empire Industries, Inc.," Crouse continued. "The largest land-holding outfit in the entire intermountain region. The state's single largest taxpayer. Last year, assets amounted to—"

I looked down at the photograph of Martin Augerman.

"Hey! Harry! Hey! Harry!"

"I'm busy, pal! Give me a minute."

A large bony head. Hair nearly white and cropped close to the skull. Large ears. Eyes sharp little points of light, focused directly on the camera lens. A very small mouth, as though he had just swallowed something that wasn't what it was purported to be. Such as a nickel. The line of his jaw let you know just how fixed and rigid the rest of him was.

"—in the business of going out of business," Crouse was saying. "It makes a very good rate of return for the investors, and Augerman is the chief investor. His brother-in-law has ten percent. The procedure is simple. They get their hands on land that's good for nothing except grasshoppers. Large amounts. Sometimes they option it. Sometimes there's not even a paper connection. But they promote the hell out of it—orange trees, flowing streams, minerals. You get the idea. He's got hundreds of salespeople, high-powered boys who are moving up into the big time from used cars and encyclopedias. They work the Northeast and the South. Door to door, mass mailings, that sort of thing. There's a lot of money out there. It grows on trees. There's a lot of people who think the grass is always greener somewhere else. So the money comes in. It goes into paper corporations, box numbers, and it's bled off just as quickly as it comes in. There's no trick to going into bankruptcy, and that's where these corporations go."

He looked down at a sheet of paper that was still in the open folder in front of him.

"Listen to these names. Leisureland. Mountain View. Eden. Can you believe that one? Eden. Apple River. Golden Lake. Western Highlands. The Moors. Every one of them bankrupt."

"He's never been nailed?"

"He doesn't keep it all for himself," Crouse said.

His eyes burned brighter than ever. The old power plant inside his skull was starting to heat up.

"Harry said you were interested in personal information."

I nodded.

"Married," he said quickly. "Four children. Two of each. The boys are dopers, University of Arizona. The girls are very talented musically. The wife is a drunk. Birmingham, Alabama. She's known as—we call her Southern Comfort. Augerman has a couple of other ladies on the side. One of them is Shirley Anne Smith, the actress. Augerman tried to set her up on Broadway. *All Day Sucker,* do you remember that one? A musical. He tried to cash in on the *Oh, Calcutta!* thing. Wrong time, wrong place. It's the only time Martin Augerman was in the wrong place at the wrong time. It closed in Parma, Ohio. Never made it to Broadway."

He opened another folder with his thumbnail and slipped a photograph across to me.

"Herbert Lehmann Morgan," Crouse said. "New York. You can tell by the tilt of his nose. Straight up."

"You don't like New York?"

"I don't like Morgan."

It was true. Crouse didn't like any of these guys very much. That was as obvious as the tilt of Morgan's nose. Sour grapes? Maybe. The poor guy was scraping along on five hundred a week on a beat where five hundred a week didn't matter.

I gave Herbert Lehmann Morgan the once-over.

None of these birds had changed since the day they went up to Montana and turned over a check to Margot Fraser and got immortalized for the Professor's wall, between the hawk and the timber wolf. They weren't endangered species. Margot Fraser was.

Morgan was a nice-looking chap. Freckles across the bridge of his nose. Boyish. Calm, light-colored eyes. The trace of a smile just above a rock-hard jaw. He looked like a politician. He looked like the sort of man you could trust not to trust.

He also looked faintly familiar, and the little bell wasn't ringing in the back of my head because of the picture on Reimann's wall. It was something else.

I tried to place him, but I couldn't.

"Doesn't like cameras," Crouse said. "No press conferences, no public appearances. He was named man of the year by the American Hospital Association a couple of years ago and never even showed up for the award. Sent a flunky. He's overloaded with flunkies."

I gave him another look. He still looked familiar.

"Maybe I've seen him before."

"Not unless you work for him."

"You've seen a lot of people before," Harry said. "They all look familiar."

I slid the photograph across the table to Crouse. Then I asked for it back. I didn't want to give up.

"He looks like Van Johnson," I said.

"The movie star?"

"Used to be."

"What a memory."

"He watches television, that's all," Harry explained to Crouse.

I ignored it.

"What's his racket?"

"Everything," Crouse said. "He's into everything. His subsidiaries have subsidiaries. And he makes the other two guys look like storm-door salesmen from Syracuse. All he had to begin with was the name. Came up the hard way—Louisville, Indianapolis, Chicago, St. Louis. Never stayed long, but he rolled everything over. He's a master at it, and now he's found a home. Been out here eleven or twelve years, a shooting star who isn't going to burn out. American Laboratories is his baby. He took it over and built it up from nothing. They make drugs, the kind of stuff your wife takes when she's got a cramp or thinks she's going to itch herself to death like a dog or can't get to sleep or has that bloated feeling. You have a wife?"

Harry cackled.

"No?" Crouse looked surprised. "Maybe you have hay fever then? Your sneeze puts money into Morgan's pocket. He's got big pockets. Body-Tone Health Spas, fitness franchises. He takes forty percent of the gross. Renewal Clinics, another plum on the money. It's all good for his health. He bought out one of the biggest hospital supply outfits in the country. Beds, sheets, and mops to wipe up the blood. Four or five years ago he took over Piser Beer and made it into what it is today. Lousy beer for the upwardly mobile. 'My adviser drinks Piser.' You heard of it? Of course. His bank is Cosmo National, and when I say his bank I mean it. He's the chief stockholder. There was talk last year that he was going to take over HospiTech, Rashad's outfit. Nothing ever came of it. The government put up a red flag, restraint of trade and all that. But that's how he works. He takes over. Usually, big fish eat little fish, right? Morgan eats big fish. He's quite a fisherman, by the way—Argentina, Yugoslavia. You want personal?"

Crouse worked on his drink a moment. Herbert Lehmann Morgan was making him thirsty.

"There is no personal," he answered himself. He wasn't happy about it. "We've tried to set up interviews with him, do feature stories, all that. The public likes to read about people in his position. His position is on top of the heap. But he won't sit still. He's a moving target."

Harry Gallagher grabbed my arm.

"We sent a guy over to do an interview on him, to his office, and Morgan personally threw the guy out. Personally!" Harry said. "Thank God he's got class. Class and a four-inch carpet. Our guy could have broken his arm in six places."

He turned toward Crouse.

"It wasn't like that in the old days."

Crouse continued, "Of course that doesn't stop us, just because someone's uncooperative. We've looked around. Unfortunately, we haven't found much. Except for his wife."

"His wife?"

"She moved to Idaho."

"What?"

"She killed herself. Six years ago."

"Overdose," Harry explained. "She probably thought she was going to itch herself to death and swallowed the whole bottle, just to be on the safe side."

"Morgan," Crouse added. "He's got a heart of gold. Real easy to live with."

He closed the book on Herbert Lehmann Morgan and opened the folder on Muhammad Rashad.

"An American success story," he said, sliding the photograph across the table to me.

"Hey! Harry!" someone cried from the darkness.

For an American success story, Rashad didn't look at all like Augerman or Morgan. He had a thin, dark face and his nose took up most of it, spreading out east and west. An Arab. Or Assyrian, coming down on the fold. His eyes had scimitars in them, cruel hooks of light. There was a cruel twist to his mouth as well, as though he had tasted torture and blood. And liked it. He had coarse black hair combed straight back from a low forehead. He was wearing a dark suit, probably blue, with just a trace of pinstriping.

"The company bio lists him at five feet seven," Crouse was saying.

"I'd make it five-three. But he thinks big. Likes a fight. You know what these little guys say, last to get rained on, first to drown. He's ready for anything. Not as diversified as Morgan, but he's got a few things going for him. Land, for instance. Something like a million and a half acres with shale oil and coal rights. Getaway Car Rental? That's his. He's got a piece of the Territorial Terrors, the soccer team. An ad agency, CommuniTech. He set it up to handle—"

"CommuniTech?"

"Right. Capital *c,* capital *t.* He set it up to handle Rashad Enterprises, the corporate umbrella. Their biggest account is HospiTech. Rashad's the sole owner. It's his biggest money-maker."

"Capital *h,* capital *t?*"

"Right. Hospital supply. There's a little friendly competition with Morgan's outfit, but in this case Rashad has the edge. He's smaller. That's why the government stepped in and said no-no when Morgan started price-cutting and lining up captive suppliers and then made noises about a takeover. It's not how big a piece of the market you have. It's how you get it. The government smelled a rat. My own opinion is that Morgan was angling for Fun & Games, Inc., which Rashad also owns. Pinball machines, pocket calculators, talking toys. They're moving into home computers, the new frontier. It's going to be a real jackpot, and when Morgan started making takeover noises last year, Rashad beat him off for old time's sake."

"Old time's sake?"

"You said it. I told you he's an American success story. He started out with a storefront lab in New Jersey about fifteen years ago. Solid-state stuff, diffused transistors. He's a real wizard. Unlike Augerman, he was in the right place at the right time. Came up with big improvements over the original transistors, germanium. Don't worry, I don't know what I'm talking about, but I did a story on it. I'm an instant expert, just add a little vermouth." He smiled weakly. "I think Rashad was one of the first guys to start working with silicon, and I know for a fact he's got a dozen patents in his back pocket. If you want to figure out what those patents were worth to him on the way up, you'll need more than a pocket calculator. It bankrolled all that land. HospiTech is his money-maker, but his main game is electronics. This is the electronic generation—he's a quiet guy, but he had quite a lot to do with it. In a very quiet way."

I had my glass to my lips. A sliver of ice slid onto my tongue, cold as a glacier.

"When it comes to brains, he's got plenty," Crouse went on. "And a good image, unlike the other two. Very big on charity—that university up in Montana, for instance. Goes up every year to make a drop. He used to go alone. Now he drags Augerman and Morgan with him. You know how they feel about it. You've heard of Open Heart, the big Christmas charity for the less fortunate—such as financial writers? Rashad personally dropped five hundred thousand into the tin cup, and then he twisted Augerman's arm until The Emperor coughed up half a million, too. He's got a place up in the mountains, corporate headquarters and his own little digs combined. He calls it Mecca. He likes it enough that he doesn't leave it very often, and I don't blame him. I was up there once for a party, and it knocked me out. He's good with the press, by the way."

"Wait a minute," Harry interrupted. "He *used* to be good with the press. Odd thing, about a year ago he turned it off. Went into a shell. Rarely seen anymore. Even Emmett here has a hard time—"

"That's true," Crouse said. "My personal view is that he pulled in his horns when Morgan started talking takeover. Those guys used to be thick as thieves. Birds of a feather. Now it's hard to say."

Crouse nodded his head, confirming something to himself.

"Used to have a very active social life," he continued. "He's got a wife, but she's part of the background. The word is, he slaps her around a little bit. But he's got a good deal up in the mountains. No neighbors to complain about cries in the night. So, who knows?"

"He's not the sort to get in trouble," I said.

Crouse took me seriously.

"We had a rumor he had money in the U. S. Investment Fund with Keith Barish. If he did, he got out as quietly as he got in. They never touched him, and we couldn't nail it down. So he slaps his wife around. That's trouble? Depends on the wife. You've got to understand one thing. These guys all have money. Plenty of it. They have power. And they're bastards, when you get right down to it. They have to be. So a lot of people get their toes stepped on, right? We get a lot of letters with no name at the bottom. You know what I mean? Sometimes they pan out, sometimes they don't. Even when they do, it might not be a story."

"Langostini," Harry Gallagher said suddenly.

Hc must have waved and I didn't see him. The waitress was standing at his shoulder again. This time she went around making a list and checking it twice.

Emmett Crouse was refastening his briefcase when Harry reached over and tried to pinch my cheek.

"That's okay, baby. Don't thank me. A short course in modern economics. For free. But don't thank me."

I ignored him and looked across the table at Crouse.

"You sound like you work for the government."

He managed a wan smile.

"The government works for me."

We passed the time talking about baseball and fishing and a night-club act Harry had caught the week before, some guy who blew into a milk bottle and made pretty music. "A freebie," he explained, shoveling some more salad into his mouth.

It wasn't until we were halfway through the langostino that I popped the question.

"Let me draw a name out of the hat," I announced. "Maybe it will ring a bell."

"Shoot," Crouse said.

"Martin Bidet."

It rang a bell.

Harry Gallagher dropped his fork. The lights inside Crouse's head went back on.

"Martin Bidet," he said quickly. "A big outfit. He has a whole floor of the Builder's Building. Accountants. They're the biggest in the city. The mayor called him in to check the taxicabs when we were making noises about collusion in the fare hikes. He found nothing. Very slick. He's paid well to find nothing."

Harry Gallagher had picked up his fork and was waving it in my direction. He was about to change the subject. Maybe not.

"Leaper," he said. "Just before we left the office we had a report of a leaper." His mouth was stuffed full. "Somebody said it was a dago lion tamer, circus people or something. Sailed right off the top floor of the Builder's Building and clipped a sailor from the French navy on the way down. I keep telling people, this is a goddamn cosmopolitan town."

His fork went back for more.

"An unfortunate combination of numbers," Crouse said.

I glanced at him.

"The Builder's Building. Thirteen-thirteen Colfax."

"Don't worry," Harry said. "The sailor's okay, just a broken collarbone, and they won't have to raise taxes very much to cover the lawsuit. Maybe ten percent. But the dago's dead. That's why we were late. In this business your life isn't your own. What a racket! Deadline every minute."

He had cheese on his chin.

"Hey! Harry!" someone cried.

But Harry wasn't listening. His eyes were fixed on me.

22

Harry Gallagher didn't call until eight o'clock the next morning. He sounded like he'd been up all night.

"You awake?"

"Almost."

"Have you read the paper this morning?"

"Not that awake."

"Well, wise guy, they found that dead girl's mother up in Montana. Dead. She was murdered. Her name was Maureen Fraser. First the girl gets it. Then they dig her old man out of an ice cube. Now her mother winds up with a stopper in her head. Of course, you're not surprised by that because you're not surprised by anything. But it's a hell of a story. It's *my* story because this is my town and you're telling me that Augerman or Rashad or Herbert Lehmann Morgan had something to do with it. I've checked it out, Nick. Augerman's in Tortola. I've never even heard of it. Morgan's in New York. I've heard of it. Rashad's up at Mecca. He never leaves there. You owe me one. I want to know the connection."

Harry Gallagher paused a moment, but it wasn't for an answer. He was only catching his breath.

"Am I going too fast for you? Because if I am, I can start over. You mentioned Martin Bidet. I looked into it. He's on the board of Empire Industries; that's Augerman's outfit. He's the registered agent for American Lab; that's Morgan's outfit. He's civic-minded, right? Bidet and Rashad? Nothing there. No connection. That's why

I'm calling. I want to know what the connection is. I want to know why you're interested in these bozos, because whenever you're around I smell smoke. I know there's a fire. You owe me one, and I don't mind reminding you."

"Angelo Scarlotti."

This time Harry Gallagher paused for more than a moment. Then he began to sputter. It was either Gaelic or Yiddish, I'm not sure. Finally he got the right language.

"You lousy son of a bitch! I didn't even tell you his name. We didn't even *know* his name last night. Angelo Scarlotti!"

Maybe it was Italian. Or Calabrian. There are a lot of things about Harry Gallagher that I don't know.

"Fifty-seven years old," Harry sputtered. "Of course there's a connection. You're not telling me a thing. The guy's from Montana by way of Prague. They found the clippings in his wallet, some kind of Czech circus I also never heard of. He probably played Tortola, right? For the past eight years he ran something called Animal House, a goddamn petting zoo. His last act was terrific. No net. He sailed out of a window on the eleventh floor of the same building where Martin Bidet has his offices, but what does it tell me? Nothing. That's why I'm calling you. The whole floor was vacant, the cops found the window open and they figure he went out head-first. Maybe it surprised him, a window that actually opened up. Don't forget, it's an old building—"

"Harry?"

"I'm all ears."

"Why was he there?"

Harry laughed. "That's a good question. But guess what? I'm not looking for good questions. I'm looking for answers. I've got two guys on the way up to Montana. They're going to get me some answers. I don't want to wait. I want to know now. The boss is on my back. Those pretty little bastards on TV are out there with their pretty little cameras taking pretty little pictures. They're throwing dummies out of the window on the eleventh floor of the Builder's Building just to see what it looks like. It doesn't look good. Not for me."

"What do the cops say?"

"Come off it. The cops say go away. You know what a prick Lew Diamond is."

"Dr. Lew Diamond," I said. "A tourist surprises himself because a window actually opens up and he lands on the street and they give the case to the chief of detectives."

"The son of a bitch won't return my calls. I always told you he was a bastard. We sent a kid over there and they let him cool his heels in an empty office for an hour and then Diamond comes out and says no comment. That's why I'm calling you. Have I stated my reason? You owe me. You owe me a big one. I checked out that other broad for you, Allison Carpenter, and she's also dead. I dragged Emmett Crouse to Lucciano's so you could pick his brain. I give, you take. Pretty soon the old man's going to come out here and throw a dummy out of *our* window. Me."

Harry Gallagher's voice dropped to a hoarse whisper.

"Listen, pal, I'm descended from Irish kings. I deserve to die in bed. With a blonde on each side. All I need is a nudge in the right direction and when the ice show opens tomorrow night I've got a bell-ringer. It'll make those bastards on TV look like they never left Peoria—"

I was listening, pal.

"The ice show?"

"Cermak's Ice Circus," Harry whispered. "At the Arena. I've already talked to Michael Moro and he's setting things up. Now *there's* a friend. There's a skater in that show by the name of Cynthia Farmer, this is between you and me, and I don't suppose I'm telling you a goddamn thing. She was up in the mountains with that Fraser girl and your friend, Allison Carpenter. Both of whom are dead. I don't need to remind you because you know more about it than I do and you're not talking. But like I say, it's a bell-ringer. You follow? Moro says Cermak wants to keep her out of the papers. Maybe he's hot for her. Cermak's crazy. Keep her out of the papers? Is that any way to run a railroad? This broad knows the connection, Nick, I'll bet my hat. She can blow the lid off the whole thing and I'm going to be ready for her. If they don't get her first."

His whisper faded away to an ominous croak.

"If who doesn't get her?" I asked.

"For Christ's sake," he sputtered. "Whoever's behind an unnatural number of unnatural deaths. Save a life, baby. Who is it? Rashad? Morgan? Augerman? That little weasel Martin Bidet? You owe me."

I considered it.

"Harry?"

"I'm all ears."

"Maybe Scarlotti was an accident."

He laughed so loud it bounced the phone off my ear. Something was caught in his throat and he washed it down with a swig of coffee.

I heard him gasping for breath.

"I'll make you a deal," I said.

"I'm listening."

"Tomorrow night, at the ice show. We'll talk."

"Forget it. I can't wait until tomorrow night."

"In the meantime, have your delivery boys find out whether Angelo Scarlotti had a cookie jar and what he has in it. If he has money in it, find out where it came from. If it's only cookies, you're in trouble."

"I'm listening."

"Check the Porsche. Allison Carpenter's car. It's a fast car for a fast crowd, and she didn't have that kind of money. You said it was purchased down here."

"I'm still listening."

"That's it, Harry."

"That's it?"

"That's it."

"You bastard!"

He hung up.

I was on my way to the refrigerator when the phone rang again.

"Nick?"

"I'm all ears," I said.

"Lew Diamond's not the chief of detectives," Harry Gallagher rasped. "He's the chief of homicide. As in murder. It wasn't an accident."

He hung up again.

I was eating my breakfast, a cheese sandwich on rye, and looking over the airline schedule when Margot Fraser found her way downstairs. Not that she was lost. She was behaving very well. She was following the rules.

She was dressed in her own clothes and she was even wearing the old Army fatigue jacket that would have been big on Mononucleosis Oto.

"Going somewhere?" I asked.

She walked over to the window and drew back the drape. She was following most of the rules, not all of them.

"Maybe," she said softly.

I looked at her. She was holding up. Maybe it was a good sign that she'd gotten out of my shirt and into her own pants.

She'd been asleep when I came home from Lucciano's. Either that or she'd been faking it. She's a very modern young woman so the odds are she was faking it, but give her the benefit of the doubt. She was asleep. She was still asleep when I got up. I'd walked down the hall and looked in on her. She had the comforter pulled up to her chin and it made a soft line along her hip and waist and shoulder, like a range of morning hills far away. I stood there a long time. It reminded me of a woman who used to live in hills like those, desolate hills, and what she had told me.

I realized then what I had to do.

For Maureen Fraser, the past had been too much to bear. It had crushed her long before a stranger showed up in the night and ended her exile from all her sad dreams. Now she was part of the past. That's where the answer was, in the past. She had known what it was without telling me. She had told me without knowing it.

The past had swallowed up everyone except Margot and the man who wanted her dead.

Margot walked across the room and sat down at the table opposite me. I pushed my coffee toward her, but she put her head down on her arms.

"I'm tired," she said.

"Look at me."

She lifted her head.

"What do you *do?*" she asked.

"I work at it."

"You don't look like you're working at anything."

"Did you ever try to have a cheese sandwich for breakfast?"

A faint smile flashed across her face. Maybe she was going to be okay.

"I'll be gone today, back tonight," I added. "If you need anything—"

Her brown eyes widened. She sat up straight.

"It's almost over, Margot. He plays with shadows and marionettes. He's not easy and I'm out of practice. I was wrong about him."

"Wrong?"

I shook my head. "It's not that business up at school when they came up with money for the lab and you were picked to take it. That's not what worries him. What do you remember about Chicago?"

"Nothing," she said after a moment.

"Nothing at all?"

"I was too young. My parents lived there when I was very small. Too young to remember anything about it."

"How would he know?" I asked myself aloud. "How would he know you were too young to remember? He figures that somewhere along the line you're going to remember, and what you're going to remember is the way he was."

"Who?" she said suddenly. "I would tell you. I want to *do* something." She leaned across the table.

"Whitey Millner. Benny Rader. The two men your father was in business with before he broke it off."

Her face showed no expression. She was trying to remember.

I pushed myself away from the table and gave her the rules again. I don't even know if she was listening. She was trying to remember and she couldn't.

"You'll stay put?"

"Yes."

"You won't go outside?"

"No."

"You want company, I'll call Xuan. Otherwise I'll be back tonight."

She brushed the hair back from her face.

"I'll be okay. I just wish there was something I could do—"

An hour and a half later I was looking out the window of a 727 at the brown plains below and the Platte River and noticing something about the way the river lay like a brown snake on the brown earth.

It was coiling to strike.

23

Chicago is one of those places where once you land you're still not there. It was thirty minutes from the time the wheels hit the runway until they found a place for us at the terminal. I don't want you to think I'm complaining. Some drunk in a Volvo had wandered out onto one of the runways and was leading the cops on a merry chase and that tied things up. Human error. Getting a cab was easy, only twenty minutes. I could have made it in less except for the old lady and the very large dog. It took another hour to get downtown. Of course I'm not complaining. It would have taken even longer if the yokel who dumped his tanker truck on the expressway had fallen on his left side, not his right. As it was, he only blocked two lanes and the shoulder. He was carrying corn syrup.

There's a reason for all this. They don't want you there.

They call it smog, just so they can keep up with the Joneses. But it isn't. It's bits of flesh and steel and concrete floating in the air. The city's cannibalizing itself, tearing up its streets and buildings and people so they can make new streets and buildings and people to tear up. It's like a game. Progress.

It's not pretty and they don't want you watching.

The cabbie let me out downtown, in front of the telephone company headquarters.

"Good luck," he observed. "You call that a tip? For Christ's sake."

It was a nice sentiment.

Seventy-two degrees and the sunlight barely made it to the street. It was a toss-up as to whether there was more noise or more people, and the odd thing is the noise didn't come from the people. I'd seen people like that before. The noise came from the elevated trains and the dump trucks and the air hammers. There was a war on out there in the streets and the people were losing. They were keeping very quiet about it. Maybe they didn't want anybody to know they were there.

When I pushed my way through the revolving doors into the lobby of the telephone company the noise went away.

So did the people, except for a sweet young thing who sat on a stool behind the counter.

She was having gum for lunch.

Everyone else had stuffed cotton in their ears and gone outside.

The girl dug up an old directory and slapped it on the counter. I checked the date on the cover. Nineteen years ago. A window on the past.

I looked at the girl and smiled.

"Where were you nineteen years ago?"

"Don't ask."

They were all there in black and white, just as Maureen Fraser had described them. The Frasers, Florence Cappelman on the North Side. Future-tronics, Inc., on the West Side. Benjamin T. Rader, Hyde Park. Whitey Millner? There were a lot of Millners, he had plenty of brothers and sisters and uncles and aunts and second cousins, but none of them was named Whitey.

The current phone book was down at the other end of the counter, chained to the Formica top. I went down to pay it a visit.

I told you, progress. They were all gone, except one. F. Cappelman. It was a different address from the one she had twenty years before, but it was still on the North Side. I noted it and hoped it wasn't Fred or Frank or Fannie.

"Hell, the worst of it's over with," the cabbie said, turning his head to look back over his shoulder at me. "But wait until three o'clock."

We were cruising northward along the lakefront and we were moving pretty well. The lake is the one thing they haven't monkeyed with. Maybe some day the water level will rise a hundred feet or so and give the aldermen and architects something else to think about.

The driver took a shortcut through a park and we entered a neighborhood of dull gray streets and old apartment buildings that must have been something special once upon a time.

The one we stopped at said "Altamont" on it.

The lobby was dark, and so was the fat man in a red monkey suit who sat next to the marble-topped desk examining his fingernails. His fingernails were pink.

I gave him my name.

I told him whom I was looking for.

He dialed a number on the house phone, and when he hung it up he showed off his gold teeth.

"Yassir. Room seven-eleven. You may goan up, Mr. Rader."

She was waiting in the hallway next to the half-opened door to her apartment, a white lump of an old woman in a shapeless house dress. She was wearing fuzzy house slippers and hair to match.

I gave her the smile I reserve for old women in shapeless house dresses.

I introduced myself and told her I wanted to talk about Benny Rader. I didn't know if the doorman got it right.

"Yes," she said softly. "Benny Rader."

Her brown eyes had widened, so that some of the white skin showed between her eyes and the dark circles underneath them. She opened the door a little wider and invited me through.

The room was a mess, and that's all she had. One room and a mess. The ironing board was set up, clothes were everywhere, magazines were piled knee-high on the floor, and the ashtrays were all full. The sound was turned down on the big color television set in the corner but the people still looked out from the screen and moved their mouths, like fish trapped behind a glass. Their faces were bright orange, sort of a Day-glo. It must have taken her a long time to get just the right color. The single window in the apartment was covered with grime and scum, some on the outside and some not. I peered through it, trying to see what kind of a view her Social Security check entitled her to, and when I saw it I realized the grime and the scum were there on purpose.

"A lady over there was arrested this morning, about five o'clock," Flossie said from behind me. "Right over the cleaners. Can you see her porch? The policeman chased her right out onto the porch."

So this is where they wind up—all those sweet young things in their high heels and stockings with straight black seams and short skirts, sitting behind counters and chewing gum, typing and filing and crossing and uncrossing their legs until someone comes along and turns out the lights and says it's Christmas, Miss Jones, go home.

Flossie wanted to know if I wanted a cup of hot Ovaltine. I didn't.

"Do you remember Douglas Fraser?" I asked.

"Douglas Fraser," she repeated slowly.

"He's dead."

"I suppose so," she agreed. "Yes, I suppose so. I didn't know that." Her eyes didn't change expression.

"You don't read the papers?"

She shook her head sadly.

"I saw his picture on television some time ago," she said. "A day or two ago. So I suppose it's true then. Douglas is dead." Her face brightened a little.

"They didn't say anything about it on television?"

"Oh!" she laughed. A faint, weak laugh. "I *never* turn the sound up. I don't like the way they talk. So smutty! They even had an abortion on some time ago. A day or two ago. Where are you from?"

She looked at me with wide, quizzical eyes.

I swung my grip up onto the ironing board and took out the three glossy photographs that Emmett Crouse had given me and turned them face up so she could see them. It was a shell game without the shells and she went straight for the pea.

"My!" she said with a rush of surprise. "Doesn't he look well? I haven't thought about him for ages. Such a nice boy. And so smart!"

She clucked her tongue.

"We always called him Benny. The nicest young man—"

"Benny Rader. That's why I'm here."

"Oh, my!" she gasped. "He's hitting her!"

Her eyes were wider than ever, large vacant pools of light staring past me at the silent television screen. Her hand flew up to her mouth and fluttered there.

It was hard to get her attention and even harder to keep it. Time had not been kind to Florence Cappelman. I thought about going over and turning the television off, maybe it would have been easier, but I didn't. It was her fix, her close encounter of the first, second, and third kinds, the only thing still alive and moving in that desolate little gray room. I left it on. And I cast out my questions like barbed flies on the Little Spider, letting them drift lazily down with the slow current of her mind until they quivered over that deep, empty pool that was the past.

She sat stiffly facing the television in an old armchair. Her feet were flat on the floor, her arms were rigid, and her head nodded up and down and smiled vacantly.

Whitey Millner was dead.

After Douglas Fraser shut down Future-tronics and headed west, Millner had set himself up as a radio and television repairman, operating out of a little storefront in the suburbs. One day he got up early, went to Mass as usual, and dropped dead of a heart attack on the front steps of the church. He was dead before he hit the ground, which is more than can be said for most of us.

All I really had needed to know was whether Benny Rader and Muhammad Rashad were one and the same. Flossie had settled it. They were one and the same. But she surprised me.

She couldn't tell you what she had for breakfast that morning, but she remembered every brick of that little laboratory on the West Side where dreams were made and where the motto was "Smaller is Better."

Douglas Fraser was one of those men who worked eighteen hours a day. There are a lot of women in the suburbs who know men like that. He had no time clock to punch, no boss watching over him. All he had was his own haste and conviction that the work he was doing was going to pay off in big bucks. Flossie worked at a battered old desk in a back room. She remembered that Fraser often came into that room alone and sat on the edge of the desk and talked to her as though he were Albert Einstein. He was talking to himself, of course, bouncing his ideas off another warm body. Flossie didn't have the first hint as to what he was talking about. But it must have sounded good to Fraser, because he kept talking about the electronics revolution and a payoff that was going to be worth millions.

It was one big happy family until the day that Fraser lined them up against the wall and told them he was closing down the company, the future was now, and he was moving out west with his family to carry the ball the rest of the way by himself. He didn't say anything about Benny Rader's or Whitey Millner's or Flossie Cappelman's coming along for the ride. They had a little party, Douglas got drunk on bad champagne, and Benny Rader spit in his face. It was ugly, but that was the only unpleasantness Flossie could remember about the entire association. It led to halfhearted apologies all the way around.

Flossie landed on her feet. She found a job with a loan company, underwriting churches and television sets for Ukranians in babushkas, and she finished out her working days with them. Typing and filing and crossing and uncrossing her legs. Millner had kept in touch, sending her a Christmas card every year. Always the same, a picture of the Madonna. She never heard from Douglas Fraser. And she lost track of Benny Rader a couple of weeks after they closed down the laboratory for good.

"It's *so* nice to see him," she said. "Isn't it curious?"

"It sure is. Isn't what curious?"

"That Benny asked *me* to mail all those postcards and letters for him. Why! *He* knew where the mailbox was! Right next to the fire station!" She looked at me very confidentially and started nodding her head. "God planned it that way. One of the postcards was a picture of Milwaukee Avenue, and *that's* where the loan company was!"

She started to laugh, an aimless titter.

"It's funny?"

"That man fell off his chair!" she said loudly.

Her eyes had drifted past me and were fixed on the television screen. I turned to look. A man with an orange face was sitting on the floor in a purple room. His chair was overturned beside him. He had an incredibly stunned look on his face.

I pulled in the line and cast again, drawing her back, spinning the questions out over the slow movement of her memory and hoping something would come up from the depths of that dark pool. What letters? What cards? What did it mean?

"That's what's so curious," she said suddenly, looking straight at me. "I used to work for a man named Douglas Fraser. Did you know him? His picture was on the television some time ago." She picked up the photograph of Muhammad Rashad and looked at it closely. She smiled at it. Her mouth dropped open slightly.

"The poor thing," she said. "Benny took it hard. When Douglas went away, Benny came to me in my old apartment. He brought his mail. My! All those letters and postcards. Wish you were here! Having a wonderful time!" She looked up at me, laughing silently. "He wanted me to mail them the next week, and I did it, poor thing. He didn't have time. Don't you see? God planned it that way. The postcards were all pictures of Milwaukee Avenue! And *that's* where the loan company was!"

"You read the postcards?"

"Yes! Wish you were here! Having a wonderful time! *He* didn't have a job yet, and *I* didn't have a job, but he was *such* a nice boy!"

I looked at her.

"And you put them in the mail? The week after he brought them to you?"

"Of course. I still worked for him."

She began to rock back and forth in the armchair.

It was my turn to smile. It was my turn to laugh silently. Time hadn't changed Benny Rader. He was just as shrewd then as he was now. Keep those cards and letters coming—all the time he was off in the mountains hunting down Douglas Fraser, stealing all his secrets, putting the genius on ice forever. It was a setup. It was the alibi Benny Rader never had to use.

"There she is!" Flossie cried. "Dinah!"

She slumped to her left, so I could see better.

"Doesn't she look terrible?" she said to herself.

The cabbie was right. The traffic got worse. Much worse. It took more than an hour to get out to the airport. I killed two hours waiting for the plane. After we boarded, we sat for thirty minutes while the boys in the tower thought it over. I don't want you to think I'm complaining. I had what I came for. Even more.

When the plane finally got up in the air and sliced out over the lake and then swung around again, I looked down past the wing at the gray streets of the city. They were empty of all the people who mattered. Douglas Fraser was dead. He'd been dead a long time. Whitey Millner was dead, too. Flossie Cappelman was well on her way. And Benny Rader?

I pulled the grip out from under the seat and put it on my lap and opened it up and looked at him. He looked back. Those eyes. Those thin, sharp hooks of light. He didn't blink.

The plane banked and shifted.

The horizon tilted away from us and then straightened out, swinging into view through the window. The sun was just touching the rim of the world, a clot of blood that seemed to grow larger and larger as it descended.

The plane shifted again.

We flew toward it.

24

This time she wasn't sleeping. She wasn't even faking it. She was gone.

The house had an empty, dangerous air when I opened the front door. It took me a moment but I finally identified it. Faded roses, dead flowers. Somebody's funeral.

I closed the door and went upstairs.

Her bed was made. Her jeans and khaki fatigue jacket were on the bed. The closet door was open. She had found something to wear. I went back downstairs, two at a time, and checked the street. It was dark and empty. Down the block, on the sidewalk in front of Facettes, a small group of people had gathered. They were either trying to get in or they had been kicked out. Either way, they were having a good time.

It wasn't until I went back into the library that I found Margot's note. Her handwriting was strong and firm.

Dear Nick:

I followed your rules. Almost. An hour after you left, a man came to the door. He wouldn't go away so I let him in. His name was Martin Bidet. At least that's what he told me. He said he was an attorney—I looked him up in the book, he is—and he said Mr. Rashad wanted to see me. Something about setting up a scholarship in my father's name. How did he know I was here? How did he know who I am? How did Mr. Rashad know I was alive? There's only one way they could know.

I'm okay. I didn't even have time to faint. A friend of yours showed up right behind Bidet. Lew Diamond. It was like open house. Sorry about not following the rules, but it's just as well. Bidet took off when your friend showed up. He said he'd get back in touch with me, but he hasn't. Your friend didn't stay long either. He wants to talk to you. Who is he? There's no Lew Diamond in the phone book.

I'm okay. I mean it. You've been terrific. People have been protecting me all my life, and what do they get for it? Nothing. Join the crowd. I thought about it all afternoon—my father, my mother, Allie, the whole crazy idea. I started the whole thing. I don't know what I think. I don't know whether I'm doing this for you or for me. It scares me a little, but goodbye. Thanks. I've got to do something. Does it matter?

Two pages, lucky you. Believe me, I'm okay. You owe me a *zatsivi.* What is a *zatsivi?*

She didn't sign it. She didn't have to.

I reached for the bottle of Scotch and the phone, in that order, and I said hello to two women and a sergeant before they put me through to Dr. Lew Diamond.

"Caine."

He wasn't surprised.

"Yeah, Nick, I was looking for you. Didn't know you were back in town. Who is she? Looks good in that sweater."

"The question is Martin Bidet. You were tailing him. Where is he?"

"Yeah, Nick. I notice he stopped by your place, too. You know him?"

"You're going to be cute."

"No, no, no," he protested. "I've got a little look-see going, guy fell out of a window on Colfax. It's routine, Nick, a garbage job. Who's the girl, by the way? She's a little young—"

I hung up.

I wasn't going to get anything out of Dr. Lew Diamond. The guy's a cop and he carries a purse. You can't expect him to shoot straight. He never has. Funny that the chief of homicide should be in his office at five minutes to midnight.

I was trying to figure out how long Margot had been gone—seven hours? eight hours?—when the phone rang.

"Why'd you do that?" Diamond asked.

I didn't answer.

"Yeah, well, we lost him," Diamond said. "I'm ashamed to admit it. He's not at home. He's not at his office. We ran down his secretary. She doesn't know where he is either. It was just an idea. Doesn't matter. Although I'm curious about why he showed up on Delgany Street. Was he going to see you or the girl? I've just been running that through my head, a little question without an answer. Probably means nothing. I went back to your place around five and she wasn't there. You weren't there either. I don't know. She still awake? I'd like to talk to her."

"Out like a light. Do me a favor."

"Anything."

"Altamont Hotel. Chicago. You got friends there? Send them over. Florence Cappelman. Room seven-eleven."

There was a slight pause before Diamond said: "Thanks, Nick."

I was working on my second Scotch and looking out the window onto Delgany Street when the phone rang again. I was getting used to it.

"Nick? Lew Diamond. I'm coming over."

It was his turn to hang up and he did.

Fifteen minutes later he was sitting in the library, his long legs stretched out in front of him and his brown musette bag sitting on the floor beside the chair.

They had found Flossie Cappelman a few hours after I left her. She was watching the ceiling. The television was still on, with the sound turned all the way down, but she was watching the ceiling because of the way her head was tilted back in the chair. Her head was tilted back because of the way her throat had been slit through.

"Plenty of blood," Diamond said. "I'm glad I wasn't there. I hate blood. They found spiders on the ceiling. Her eyes were open. She was watching the spiders. I think there's something in Camus about that."

He lifted his glass toward the overhead light and gazed at it.

"Any leads?"

"No prints. Nothing. The place was a mess. They figure she was burgled and she put up a fight and the lights went out. Then he tore the place up a little. She was retired, secretary for some loan company. She couldn't have had much. The police are a little better off. She had a visitor early in the afternoon, and she never had visitors. They've got a description of him from the deskman."

His eyes drifted down from the glass to me and stayed there.

"Okay," I said. "Sam Casanova. Have your friends hunt him up. He's a local. Ex-DEA. They'll know about him. His wife fries liver in the raw."

Dr. Lew Diamond's eyes closed.

"You've been away."

"Yeah."

"Montana."

"Yeah."

"Saw your picture in the paper. Grasshopper Glacier."

"My picture?"

Diamond smiled.

"Scarlotti was from Montana," he said. "The leaper."

"Um," I said.

"I'm tired, Nick. Give me that again. Scallopini?"

"Casanova."

"She's gone, right?"

"Yup."

"Who is she?"

"Didn't leave her name."

Diamond was silent a moment.

"Maybe I can do something," he said.

"Find Bidet."

"Right."

He finished his drink.

"The little bastard," he added.

We were two hounds, working around a bone. We understood each other perfectly well. Neither of us was going to get it.

Not tonight.

I stood at the front door for a long time after Lew Diamond left, looking down the darkness of Delgany Street.

Cut and drift. I'd never find her. It's a big city, filled with kids and accountants and bright young engineers who used to live in Houston or Boston or Atlanta. They talk to each other in tongues—COBOL and FORTRAN. Their bedrooms are always dark. It's a good city to get lost in because everyone's a stranger. Everyone's passing through. You have to keep moving. The concrete for the streets is mixed with radioactive waste. They store the nerve gas out by the airport, they make a game out of it, and the coppers all carry the antidote under the seat of their squad cars in case the pilot of some 727 goes bingo. We're all very safe.

Even Margot Fraser.

I had the roses in my hand.

On the way out, Lew Diamond had observed that they needed water. He needn't have.

The stalks broke off in my fist like sticks of straw.

25

The next evening I was sitting in the mezzanine at the Arena, section 2, seat H-10, looking at the clean white oval of ice far below me, waiting for the orchestra to stop practicing, and trying to clear my head.

I hadn't heard from Margot Fraser.

Neither had Dr. Lew Diamond. He didn't know her name but he knew enough to look. Abandoned cars. Warehouses. Hangouts where the kids lay around inhaling dreams. All he got for his trouble was nothing.

It didn't take much to figure out where Margot was most likely to have gone. After all, she looked him up in the phone book. She'd put two and two together.

Diamond had a plainclothesman stationed somewhere around Martin Bidet's office twenty-four hours a day. Bidet wasn't making any public appearances. I even put through a call to Bidet myself, but all I got was Joan Crawford's voice:

"Mr. Bidet is out of town. I'm very sorry. He'll be back next week. May I take a message?"

"Tortola?"

"Who?"

Diamond also had a plainclothesman standing somewhere in a shadow near Bidet's fashionable apartment. Bidet wasn't making any private appearances either.

Maybe she didn't go to see Bidet. Maybe she went straight to Rashad.

I spent the afternoon with the bottle of Scotch and a headful of bad thoughts. Benny Rader and Muhammad Rashad—the snake that shed its skin. You didn't need to be a genius to figure it out. One day he's brown-bagging it to work in a rundown factory on Chicago's West Side, second fiddle in a one-man band. The next day he's an entrepreneur in New Jersey laying the foundations of an empire. With Douglas Fraser on ice, and all of Fraser's work in his hip pocket, Rashad had clear sailing. It's the land of opportunity.

I didn't know Douglas Fraser. Maybe he deserved it.

I knew more than I wanted to about Muhammad Rashad. He was sitting pretty in the mountains, in a little fortress called Mecca, with a lot to lose. And a lot to fight for.

He had his troubles, but they didn't stop him. He just killed. You sit in the boss's chair long enough, you get like that. Rashad had his net out, and now he was drawing it closed. He was picking up anyone who knew who he was and sending them goodbye forever. Flossie Cappelman, that old bag of gray bones and flesh propped up in front of the television in her grimy apartment, knew who he was. But not anymore. Maureen Fraser, who had those cold winds whistling through her soul long before Rashad's thug showed up, could have said who he was. Not anymore. Margot had no way to know who he was, no remembrance of those bitter days in Chicago. But Rashad couldn't take a chance. Not anymore.

Scarlotti was a big mistake, and it told me something. There was nothing discreet about sending a guy head-first out of an eleventh-floor window in the heart of town and having him land on a French sailor. Someone was bound to ask questions, even if it was only the street cleaner.

It told me Rashad was getting desperate.

No more shadow shows. He was holed up at Mecca pulling the strings on his little puppets like crazy. Monkey Man. Sam Casanova. Martin Bidet. The goon who finished off Maureen Fraser. Cut the strings and it didn't matter. You still had Benny Rader pretending he was boss, going straight for the jugular.

I made chicken *zatsivi* for dinner, with walnut sauce. It didn't work. She didn't show up.

I tried to figure out who still made him vulnerable. By the time I got to a woman who didn't like to say goodbye, the orchestra was playing something to lift my spirits and the lights were going down.

"Right after duh show," Michael Moro was saying. "Duh old man guarantees it. He don't want yuh interfering wit their concentration right before duh curtain. It's like show business. And listen. Yuh oughta catch dat little midget while you're at it."

He rolled a Cuban cigar through his fat little fingers.

Michael Moro handles publicity for Cermak's Ice Circus and any other show that happens to breeze through Denver. He spends half his time strutting around newspaper offices and the rest of it managing Facettes, the discotheque on Delgany Street. He was sitting to my right and leaning across my lap to talk to Harry Gallagher.

At least he *said* it was a Cuban cigar. It smelled more like New Jersey.

Harry was wearing his gold lamé jacket.

"I don't give a shit about midgets," he said.

He turned to me and pointed a finger at the photograph on page four of your program. It was a photograph of Cynthia Farmer, doing the splits in midair. She looked just about as good as ever.

"You know who this is?" Harry croaked.

"Eleanor Roosevelt?"

"He's a class act," Michael Moro insisted, grabbing Harry's arm. "Dis little midget, Tiny Tim. He skates under everybody's legs. I seen him before."

He blew a smoke ring.

"Why don't you get us some popcorn?" Harry said.

"Popcorn?"

"Yeah."

"You mean popcorn?"

Harry cracked a smile. Michael Moro got to his feet and moved sideways down the row, away from us.

"Hey! Harry!" someone cried from a few rows behind us.

"Nice and private," I observed.

"Eleanor Roosevelt is dead. Relax. I'm not telling you anything, and I know it. They should be promoting the hell out of it, but they're ignoring it. They think nobody reads the papers? They think everybody's home watching the New York Philharmonic from Lincoln Center? It's a two-bit operation."

Harry Gallagher folded the program in half.

"You were right," he said hoarsely. "Scarlotti had plenty of money."

"How much?"

"Two grand. My guys talked to his daughter. She no speaka da

English very good, but they got through to her. They found the dough in his dresser this morning, under his socks. Screw the cookie jar. That went out with the three bears. He had bears, too. One was picked up by the health department two days before Margot Fraser caught her lunch."

He looked at me out of the corner of his eye.

"You follow?"

I frowned.

"The daughter said the old man never had money like that laying around. They don't know where it came from. And when he left to come down here, he didn't tell anybody where he was going."

A self-satisfied grin spread slowly across Gallagher's face—a pretty good trick, considering Gallagher's face.

"I got a lot of questions for this girl, if she doesn't fall on her ass out there," he said.

She didn't.

The orchestra suddenly started a two-step and I wasn't ready for it. Nobody was. She came flying out of the chute to our left. The crowd gasped.

She looked even better than ever.

She was what we were waiting for.

She was wearing a little red something that looked more like Florida than Colorado. She liked red. Little tufts of red feathers were attached to her ankles, just above her flashing skates. Her arms were spread back, her breasts were bon vivant. Her hair even had an aureole of honey. Of course, it could have been my imagination.

She swept around the ice alone, forward and then backward, and the spotlight had a hard time keeping up with her. She cut into figure eights and then flew into a series of waltz jumps, turning herself around in the air. She seemed to hang above the ice, and you could hear something wonderful in the crowd's throat. The feather wings stood straight out from her heels, her hair streamed out behind her, and even from section 2, seat H-10, you could see that she was oblivious to the audience.

She was tracking it in her head, dancing on the ice at the edge of darkness. There was something free about her and she couldn't hide it, yet she kept it under control, spinning around and around the rink in time to the music, staying just inside the rim of white light. She had everybody's attention.

When she came flying down the side of the rink for the finale—

body curled forward, arms reaching back, gathering more and more speed around her—you knew something good was going to happen.

It did.

The lights were coming up, blue and green and red. The orchestra was going crazy. She turned diagonally across the ice, did something fantastic in the air, and came down in a spin so fast that she was just a blur of feathers and flesh.

Everyone was tickled.

"Double lutz," Michael Moro shouted into my ear. "Want some popcorn?"

The audience screamed for more, but she sashayed backward across the ice, blowing kisses to the crowd. She disappeared into the chute.

"Long legs," Harry said.

"You gotta see dis midget. Don't you want dis popcorn?"

We saw Tiny Tim, the midget. We saw a chorus line in top hats, and a skating mouse who kept tripping over his tail, and a duet that went by the name of Marabel & Morgan and made every move together.

When the show was over and they all came back out on the ice for their bows, I looked for her. I saw a line of pretties in top hats and a midget and a mouse and Marabel & Morgan.

What I didn't see was a girl who didn't like to say goodbye.

"She does one number?" I hollered at Harry. "Where the hell is she?"

"Let's go."

The crowd carried us downstairs, pushing and shoving. Michael Moro didn't catch up with us until we were on the narrow staircase to the lower level, where the dressing rooms are and the public isn't. He pushed past us. The cop at the door said, "Hey! Harry!" We breezed through. Michael Moro followed the end of his cigar down the hallway and we followed Michael Moro.

When he ducked into an open doorway, we did likewise.

The fat man behind the desk looked at Harry first. Maybe he'd never seen a gold lamé coat. He looked at me. Then he looked at Michael Moro. He had a cigar, too, and it shifted from one corner of his mouth to the other. His eyes were half-closed. It appeared to be a chronic condition.

Michael Moro actually bowed. He's got very continental manners.

"Mr. Cermak, dis here's Harry Gallagher, who I was telling yuh about. He wants to do a wonderful story about dis show, and especially about dis girl here, Cynthia Farmer—"

Cermak shook his head slowly.

"Farmer I can't do. I can give you a mouse or a midget. You the photographer?"

His voice was as fat as the rest of him. He was looking at me and trying to smile, but his lips kept getting in the way.

"Can't do?" Harry exploded.

"He wants tuh interview dis Cynthia Farmer, a wonderful act," Michael Moro was explaining. "I tried tuh tell him about duh midget, but yuh got tuh understand. Dis broad's got something—" He tried snapping his fingers. "Cheesecake sells, too. Especially in dis town—"

Moro blew another smoke ring.

"I agree, a wonderful act," Cermak said softly. "But I'm afraid it's impossible. Cynthia has gone back to the hotel. I'm told she's ill."

His eyes drifted to the doorway, and he suddenly bellowed:

"Maria!"

An elderly, white-haired woman poked her head into the office.

"What is the problem with Farmer?"

"Duh crowd loved her," Michael Moro said.

"She's not feeling well," the woman said. "Did you notice her mohawks? Very shaky. I sent her back to the hotel so that she can rest—"

Cermak lifted his ponderous hands from the desk.

"Tim's a good interview," he said to us. "He's short, but he's a damned good interview."

Harry Gallagher didn't let him finish.

"Tell it to those creeps with their TV cameras," he snarled and turned on his heel.

He turned a little too far, so I was out of the room ahead of him.

26

Cynthia Farmer had disappeared, but I couldn't get her out of my mind's eye. That blur of flesh and flashing skates, a figure with forty arms reaching out to me at the edge of darkness. Those gold-flecked eyes and that faint, crooked smile.

Who were they meant for?

What lay behind them?

The guy at the door downstairs told us he hailed a cab for Cynthia an hour before the show ended. She left alone. At the time, we were eating Michael Moro's popcorn.

Michael Moro was apologetic. Michael Moro has a lot to be apologetic about. He followed us outside like a puppy looking for a treat.

"I talked tuh her myself before duh show," he whined. "I give her your name, Harry. She never heard of you. I give her your name, Nick. Her eyes light up. She says, *'Nick Caine? Here?'* You in show business or something, and I don't know it? Duh old man came along then and tells me tuh get upstairs. Maybe she don't want tuh talk, he says. Maybe she don't like duh newspapers. Yuh know what I mean? He's sitting on something, Harry. He knows something. But don't forget, dis a two-bit outfit. I noticed that myself. Duh broad's mohawks ain't that good—"

"Thanks," Harry snarled.

"Anyway," I added.

Michael Moro went his way. We went ours. Even a dog knows when there're no treats left.

Our way took us through the false daylight of the parking lot to the car, then down into the darkness of the street. We headed downtown.

"She knows you," Harry said. "There's nothing like a nice quiet life. Naps in the afternoon, all that crap."

"The cab should be easy enough to trace."

"I'm ahead of you. I'll check when I get back to the office. But I've got a hunch. Let's try the Lamplighter. That's where all the shows stay when they're in town."

I kept the speed down to within ten miles an hour over the limit. We still hit every stoplight on the way in. Harry kept his mouth shut. I know what he was thinking. He was thinking that I wasn't playing fair with him. He was thinking that he was right about me all along. Maybe he was.

Harry also handled things at the Lamplighter, fishing his press card out of his wallet and announcing to the desk clerk that he had an appointment to interview Miss Cynthia Farmer of Cermak's Ice Circus and he was sorry he was ten minutes late. But you know how the newspaper business is. And would he please ring her on the house phone.

The press card made a big difference. The desk clerk stopped saying "sir" at the end of his sentences.

"No answer," he said sullenly, thirty seconds after he stuck an old-fashioned white and gold phone in his ear.

"What do you mean, no answer? She's expecting me. What the hell room is she in?"

"Four fifty-two."

The clerk extracted the phone.

"I'll go up," Harry announced. He was good at making announcements.

"I'm sorry, that's against the rules," the clerk announced. He also was good at making announcements.

An old man sitting by himself in the lobby folded his copy of the *Gazette* neatly in half and looked over at us. He knitted his brows. "Hey! Harry!" he said.

Harry turned and waved. Then he turned back to the desk clerk.

"Confidentially, she may be in the powder room," he rasped. "Working on her mohawks in front of the mirror. Her mohawks need a lot of work. I'll wait. You can try her again in a couple minutes."

"Very well."

Harry drifted over to talk to his fan club, the clerk got busy, and I wandered around the corner of the lobby like I was killing time. I headed for the elevators. The brass doors opened silently and closed around me. When they opened again, I was on the fourth floor.

The hallway was empty.

I found room 452 halfway down the hall and tapped lightly on the door. I got the same answer as the desk clerk. No answer. She was still working on her mohawks.

I did something to the lock and the door swung inward. The room was dark. I slipped inside, shut the door smoothly behind me, and put myself flat against the wall on my left. I reached my hand into my coat and took something out of its holster.

"Cynthia," I said.

She didn't want any.

My other hand went for the light switch and found it. As I flipped the switch, the rest of me moved across to the other side of the door.

The room was empty.

Two double beds, three bags of clothes hanging from a metal rack, a television set, and a long dresser with a mirror that showed me the bathroom door was open because nobody was busy.

Wherever Cynthia Farmer had gone, it wasn't here.

The phone on the little stand between the beds started to ring. The clerk was trying again. I went out the door, took the stairs down, and used a side door to get out on the street. I was waiting in the car when Harry showed up.

"Nothing?" he asked.

"I'm way ahead of you," I said.

He opened the door and got in.

"Look at it this way," he said. "It was a mistake to have Moro handle it. Her mohawks were shaky because she recognized your name. That means she knows you. That means you've met. That means she doesn't want to see you. Don't ask me why. I find you irresistible. You've only got one fault. You play by funny rules. Maybe she's normal. Maybe she doesn't like funny rules. She went for a walk. She needed fresh air. She doesn't like reporters. Take your pick. You can't make a federal case out of an ice skater who misses the finale. As soon as I get back to the office, I'll call Diamond at homicide."

"Don't bother."

We were silent all the way back to the *Gazette* office. Every light in the place was on; it looked a beacon of truth and responsibility.

"The least I can do is check the cab," he said when he got out of the car. "She went somewhere."

"Good night, Harry."

"Hey!" he cried as I pulled away.

I didn't have far to drive, and when I got there I parked the car on a side street about a block away and walked on down.

The Builder's Building was big and dark, a cloud against the night sky, except for the lobby and a few lighted windows on the second floor. I stood on the sidewalk in front of the place and looked up in the night toward the eleventh floor.

It was a long way to fall.

I pushed my way through the revolving doors and nodded to the rent-a-cop. He was sitting on a stool next to the elevators, modeling the uniform. He looked like a lifer.

"Yes, sir," he said.

He was grinding out a cigarette in a glass ashtray.

"Martin Bidet. I know it's late, but he said he would meet me here."

"Second floor. Bidet and Marek. Someone is still up there. You'll have to sign in."

He pointed to the register on a little stand next to his stool. He watched me sign it.

I looked past him at the black signboard on the lobby wall. They still had a soap company listed on eleven.

"I'm going to walk. It's only one floor, right? Good for the old ticker."

"Yes, sir. I'd never make it myself."

He shifted a little on his stool. There was quite a bit of overhang where his body hit the wood. He lit another cigarette. That was his exercise for the evening.

"Pretty quiet?"

"Yes, sir."

I walked across the lobby, opened the door to the stairwell, and started up. When I reached the landing on the ninth floor I stopped for a moment to rest, hands on my knees. Too many naps in the afternoon. I persevered. When I got to eleven, nothing was left but a narrow metal walkway to the roof. I listened very carefully at the door.

Then I opened it.

Don't get me wrong. I knew where the trail ran. The trail ran straight down to the second floor and Martin Bidet, the accountant who accounted for a lot. I was going to follow it. But first I wanted to see how Angelo Scarlotti managed to do it.

My mistake.

The foyer was empty. The elevator doors were on my left, and a line of dim lights extended to my right toward the front of the building. The gilt lettering on the two large glass doors straight ahead of me said "Handmaiden Soaps."

They didn't make a sound when I opened them and stepped inside.

Once it had been a big office. It still was, but it was empty now. Handmaiden Soaps had moved out along with Angelo Scarlotti.

The only light came from the big windows at the front of the building.

I moved toward them.

The whole city was spread out below me—the glitter and flash of lights, cars moving slowly down the streets, signs blinking silently on and off in the distance. It was an eagle's roost, a place to dream of other things. It was a nice view if you weren't falling through it.

I lifted one of the windows.

It came up smoothly from the sill, and a sharp blast of air hit my face. It was cold.

From far below came the soft, strangulated sounds of the city. Business as usual. Mice being stepped on. Animals coughing and dying in the night. Necks being broken. Whispers. The sound of a snake, dark and sinuous, slithering through the streets.

It came in waves, softly: Rashad. Rashad. Rashad.

Whispers.

"It's a beautiful view, but I'm afraid you can't enjoy it," said a man's voice from behind me. He sounded sympathetic. "It's already been tried. With unfortunate results."

I turned around slowly and put my back to the window.

That would be Martin Bidet. He was tall and thin, and his head was a shade too small to support the Fu Manchu that dragged his upper lip down over his teeth. The way he stood, you could tell he thought it was sexy.

His arms were folded across his chest. He was wearing a dark suit and his white shirt had French cuffs. I couldn't make out the monogram, but give me credit. I hardly glanced at him.

What caught my eye was the dish standing next to him. She'd look good in any light, or no light at all. But the soft light from the windows made her look even better. That perky little turned-up nose. Those flashing eyes. That faint, crooked smile.

Her hair was an aureole of honey.

She had a shiny little .38 in her hand and it was pointed straight at my heart.

27

Cynthia Farmer took two baby steps to her right and gave the gun a little shimmy. She didn't look like a killer, but sometimes it's hard to tell. The light wasn't very good.

Her voice was husky.

"Be careful," she said.

The warning might have been for me, it might have been for Bidet. If it was for Bidet, it wasn't necessary. Bidet was already being careful. One of his eyes was on the gun and the other one was on me.

It did something uncomfortable to his face.

His mustache twitched. It was nervous.

He came over to me and started patting me all over. He'd seen a lot of television. When he got to the Margolin Special, his breath came a little faster. He lifted the gun gingerly from its holster, looked at it carefully in the dim light, and then slipped it into his suitcoat pocket.

He stepped back quickly.

Maybe he thought I would explode. Maybe he'd heard about me somewhere.

From the open window I could hear the slow, curling cry of an ambulance far in the distance. It was faint and grew fainter, like a heart that was running out of time.

"Never seen a gun like that," he said.

"Want to buy it? It'll cost you plenty."

"Listen, wise guy—"

His voice went up an octave, like somebody goosed it. He stepped back another step, just to be on the safe side.

I'd seen his kind before. There was nothing behind that Fu Manchu. He was all atmosphere, a slicker trying to pretend he was a gangster and taking orders from a dame. Behind that Fu Manchu he was naked and afraid. He'd sold himself to the highest bidder, Muhammad Rashad, and now he was down to nothing. A feint would put him down in a pool of tears.

As for her kind, another story. She was too pretty to knock around.

She said, "Don't get him excited. He might do something foolish."

She waved the gun toward the hallway and I did as it suggested. Inside the elevator I watched the luminous numbers count down the floors on the lighted panel above the sliding door. I could feel the .38 watching me from behind.

The numbers stopped at two. The doors hissed open.

"What else could I do?" Bidet asked suddenly. "He knew too much. He was wild. *He* was the one who got excited. I *had* to hit him with the board."

He'd been thinking about the circus all the way down from eleven. He'd been thinking about Angelo Scarlotti.

If he was looking for sympathy, he didn't get it.

I stepped out of the elevator and followed Bidet down the brightly lighted hallway toward the front of the building. We went by one dark office after another. When we reached the little anteroom just before his own corner office, he waved me inside.

"Sit down," he ordered. "Make yourself very comfortable. You won't be comfortable for long. Not when Helmut Nasenklammer gets his hands on you."

Something like a smile struggled to get out from under his mustache.

"I'll call the Boss and let him know what a nice fish we've caught."

He went through the connecting door into his office. Cynthia Farmer was right behind me in the hall doorway. The faint, crooked smile was gone. The .38 wasn't. It was still pointed straight at my heart.

I heard Bidet dialing a telephone in the other room.

I made myself very comfortable. There was a *Forbes* magazine on the glass-topped table in front of me, but I didn't feel like reading about grain deals. I didn't feel like anything, not after seeing Cynthia Farmer on the other end of a gun.

When Bidet reappeared in the anteroom, his face was blanched white. His mustache was doing a little dance.

"You've got to keep that gun on him for forty-five minutes," he said to Cynthia. "Don't let him move. Noseplug is coming down in the car, but it'll take that long. It's snowing."

He turned to me:

"Sit still, wise guy."

He couldn't sit still. He paced back and forth, like a ferret in a cage that's too small. Then he went back into his office. I could see him sitting behind his desk, watching. His mustache was still doing a jig.

I looked at Cynthia.

"I know it's not easy, but you handle it pretty well," I said. "Something I should have expected—your handling it well. The way you hold that gun, I can see it's not the first time. With you there is no first time."

"Shut up!" Bidet said from the other room.

"Let him talk," Cynthia answered. "That way he doesn't do anything foolish."

She wiggled the gun at me, like she was trying to tell me something. But I had something to tell her.

"Sure," I said. "My mistake. You were in on it from the top. You're one of Muhammad Rashad's little amateur acts. You're in this up to your pretty neck, and that's as far as it's worth going. Why? I don't know. Greed. Boredom. Take your pick. You were the connection. Monkey Man didn't go to your apartment that night because he figured I'd be there. Hell, no. I gave him too much credit. He's too slow. Put him in a ketchup bottle and he'd never come out. What he wanted was instructions, and he got them. From you. Because you were in on it from the beginning. You and Benny Rader—"

"Who?" Bidet asked sharply.

Cynthia was shaking her head. "You've got it wrong, Nick, all wrong."

I was watching her eyes. There was something there—a remembrance, a bond that wasn't ready to be broken. I wanted to work on it.

But Bidet interrupted.

"Wait'll Noseplug gets here, wise guy. You won't feel like talking then."

Cynthia was wiggling the .38 at me again. But I wasn't done with her.

"I've figured it out," I said. "I know what it is, because I see it everywhere I look. Boredom. When the wind blows, you go with it. They could make one of you in Benny Rader's little laboratory. Tie a few nerve endings together, touch it, and watch it skitter off. Like something that lives in the dark at the bottom of the ocean. There's nothing inside, baby. You should have been an actress. Not an ice skater. Your mohawks are lousy—"

I was trying anything and it worked. It worked her up.

For a brief moment the old brightness came back into Cynthia Farmer's eyes, the brightness I remembered on the morning after, when it was just her and me and a world that didn't give a damn outside the huge windows of her apartment at Ginger Creek. She didn't like it. I could see that.

Then suddenly those beautiful eyes were misty.

I stood up.

"Don't move! You're going nowhere!" Bidet squealed. I heard his chair move back. But I was looking at Cynthia. Sin for short.

"You have it all wrong," she said. "You don't understand."

It sounded like someone was squeezing the air out of her.

It was a bad situation, holed up in an empty building at night with a couple of amateurs who figured somebody else could do it better, somebody named Noseplug, but there's always a catch. This time I couldn't miss it. Not the way she was waving the .38 at me.

She had the gun in her hand and she obviously knew now to use it. She could do anything with it that she wanted to.

The catch was she didn't want to.

I finally caught on. She was right. I didn't understand. She didn't have to tell me anything because the gun told me everything.

"Sit down! Sit down!" Bidet ordered, rushing into the anteroom.

He looked from Cynthia to me and back to Cynthia. His eyes never quite caught up with his head.

"What's the matter with you?"

Cynthia didn't answer.

"Give me that."

"I'm okay," Cynthia said.

Bidet backed himself up to the doorway of his office. He was trying to be in charge without getting too close. He must have known what happened to Sam Casanova.

Cynthia breathed in sharply.

An awkward silence filled the little anteroom, but it was broken a moment later by the hiss of the elevator doors opening and then closing out in the hallway.

Bidet looked down at his watch. When his head came up again, he was wearing a frown.

The rent-a-cop filled the doorway behind Cynthia. Fat as a moose, and he moved like a cat. With one hand he tried to rub his face awake.

Cynthia didn't turn around. She knew it was too soon for Helmut Nasenklammer. Her hand was in the pocket of her coat. So was the gun.

"Good evening," the rent-a-cop said pleasantly. "Mr. Bidet," he nodded. "Everything all right?"

"Sure is, Hank. Thanks for checking." Bidet's head was bobbing up and down. But the rent-a-cop was just warming up.

He looked at me.

"I see you found him."

"Yes," Bidet said sharply. "He walked up past our floor, but we got together. We're—uh—negotiating, you know. Everything's fine. Thanks for checking."

The cop sighed. He scratched his chest.

"Everything's fine now," he said, "but by morning everything's going to be dead. It's really coming down out there."

"Snow?" I said. I tried to put a little surprise around the edges of it.

I heard the rent-a-cop agree. "They been predicting it for a week." But I was already on my way into Bidet's big office. By the time I got to the big glass window over the street, Bidet was at my side.

He was making a strange rasping sound in his throat.

I smiled at his reflection in the window.

"There are two things you can do," I said softly. "You can hand me my gun—that would be good manners—or you can make a fuss. A fuss would be bad manners. You remember what happened to your friend Sam. He still hurts. And when Angelo Scarlotti hit the sidewalk down there, I'm sure Rashad didn't appreciate it. You're on bad paper, Bidet. You wouldn't want another fuss at the same address. Jesus. It really is snowing."

Bidet's cheeks twitched upward and he squinted at me. It took him a moment to decide, but his manners weren't so bad. I slipped the Margolin Special back into the holster under my coat.

"Of course you've never seen one like this," I said. "Only three were made."

Bidet's eyes were yellow with emotion. All losers get that way.

"You're not home free," he hissed, under his breath. "When Nasenklammer gets his hands on you—"

I walked away from him.

The rent-a-cop smiled back at me. He was still scratching his chest. "You're right. Snow," I said. He followed me down the hall to the elevator.

I didn't tell Cynthia Farmer goodbye. She doesn't like to say goodbye. She never did turn around.

"It's lucky Mr. Bidet found you," the old man said on the way down in the elevator. "You'd just gone upstairs when he and the woman came down. It's a darn good thing I mentioned it."

"You said it."

The rent-a-cop stopped at his stool—the elevator ride took a lot out of him—but I went straight for the doors.

The night was cold and dark. The street was deserted. The snow was coming down in big flakes. It wouldn't last. Not down here. But up in the mountains, up where a little man named Muhammad Rashad was holed up in a fortress called Mecca, the snow would stick. It would cover everything like a shroud.

Something was over with, and they were pulling a white sheet up over its face. When daylight came the snow would be cold and white and hard. It would hold the tracks of the hunter and the hunted, a few feathers, a little blood. It would all be over.

I was in the shadowed doorway of a shoe store, three doors down from the Builder's Building, when the car turned the corner at the end of the block. It cruised slowly down the street and stopped before it got to me.

It was the longest Cadillac I'd ever seen, big enough for a very little man. I could hear the wipers swishing away the wet snow, and the low throaty hum of the engine in idle.

There was nothing little about the sweetheart who opened the door on the driver's side and stepped out into the little patch of light on the walk. He came off the same assembly line as the limo. He was big and he looked expensive.

His blond hair was in curls, carefully. There were muscles under his brown silk shirt. He didn't bother with a coat. The black leather driving gloves on his paws were special order, and he had a neck that looked like he used it to lift weights.

He did use it to lift weights. His head.

His head certainly belonged to a Helmut Nasenklammer. Life imitated art. He had a square jaw, a wide brow, high cheeks, broad nose, and solid bones. They wouldn't break easily. He was part Mongol, part Prussian, and the rest of him had been borrowed from a very large dog. He'd be out of place anywhere except in a war movie. Or up at Aspen or Steamboat Springs, with the ladies spread out at his feet like bearskin rugs.

But that wasn't the kicker.

When he lifted his chin to look up at the second floor of the Builder's Building, the light from the lobby caught him full in the face.

He had deep red circular scars under his eyes. Somewhere along the line he'd made a mistake and the mistake had stayed with him, carved into his flesh as a little reminder that would never go away.

It was a comforting thought. We're all human.

Of course I recognized him. We'd taken a plane ride together once, down through the long night of Montana. He was the goon who finished off Maureen Fraser and then kept a friendly eye on me all the way home.

Cynthia Farmer and Martin Bidet met him on the sidewalk in front of the building before he had a chance to try his muscles on the revolving doors.

They argued for a moment and looked up and down the street. There was nothing to see. I was well back in the shadows of the doorway. The snow had melted off the sidewalk. Nothing as simple as tracks.

I couldn't pick up what they were saying, but I could see them easily enough through the plate glass windows of the shoe store, and Helmut Nasenklammer was saying most of it. In a voice that sounded like a dog who knew there was a bone on the counter and couldn't get to it.

When he finally put himself into gear, it was to snap the back of his hand around so hard against the side of Fu Manchu's head that the little accountant caved right in. He crumpled against the side of the car and slid down to the bottom of column one, carry two.

Helmut bent over, picked up a handful of expensive suitcoat, brushed the snow off Bidet's face, and stuffed him into the back seat.

Then he turned toward Cynthia Farmer.

She stood facing him with her long legs slightly spread and a faint smile on her lips. There were tears in her eyes. She had her hands halfway up, as though she were going to resist. I knew that body. I hadn't unlocked the heart, that's for sure, but I knew that body. It was smooth and taut and it didn't resist.

Helmut's lip curled upward in the middle. Maybe he knew something I knew.

He reached out and opened the door to the Caddie. Cynthia put herself in.

They sped past me.

Helmut Nasenklammer was behind the wheel. He drove with both hands. He was not happy. Muhammad Rashad wouldn't be happy, either. Not when they told him they had me with my back up against the wall but forgot to close the door. I caught a glimpse of Cynthia's face in the rear of the car as they went by. Chin up, lips tightly closed, eyes straight ahead. Not happy.

Martin Bidet still didn't know what hit him. His pasty face was pressed against the side window. His eyes were puffed shut. His mustache was trying to climb back up his nose.

I suddenly realized the power of the blow that had put him in the gutter.

He couldn't help the silly grin.

He was happy.

He was dead.

28

Nasenklammer had a nice cargo. Death and a dame who talked out of both sides of her heart.

They left the street empty, except for the old Plymouth taking up the curb in a no-parking zone straight across from the Builder's Building.

Inside was Dr. Lew Diamond's stake-out.

There was nothing silly about the grin on his face. He didn't have a grin on his face. His head rested gently against the window on the driver's side. He slept with his mouth wide open.

The way I had it figured, it would take Nasenklammer at least an hour to get back up to Mecca. With the snow, maybe longer. He wouldn't want to get stopped for speeding and have to explain away the funny look on Martin Bidet's face. Once he got to Mecca they would move fast. All they had to do was pick up the telephone to put someone on the street where I live. Someone to watch over me.

The way I had it figured, I had it figured wrong.

That was obvious as soon as I turned onto Delgany Street and cruised past Facettes. Someone had picked up the telephone as soon as they heard from Martin Bidet. Someone thought less of Martin Bidet than I did. I'd thought pretty highly of Martin Bidet. He didn't know it, he didn't know anything anymore, but he'd let me know just how wrong I had it figured.

All of a sudden it was a new ballgame.

The problem at hand was a blue van, and on the side of the van it said: "Dozer's Sweet Juices." A lousy job of lettering. I didn't believe it. It was parked down the block from Facettes with a clear view across Delgany Street.

The clear view was of my front door.

I drove past him, turned the corner, parked the car on the other side of the block, and used my legs the rest of the way. I came up on him from behind. His attention was elsewhere—across Delgany Street, my front door.

"You're lost," I declared.

His head turned very slowly.

He looked at me with blank brown eyes. His window was rolled down, and we were very close. He had a pork-pie face. Round and soft and flat.

"You got a license for that?" he asked.

"Not only that," I stated. "You'll notice that my finger is on the trigger. It's a very sensitive mechanism."

He noticed.

What he noticed was the steel-blue barrel of the Margolin Special pointed straight at his little yellow teeth. He tried to smile but he was out of practice.

His eyes came up and memorized my face.

He was big and he was young and he looked to me like a cop trying to pick up a little beer money on the side. It's either that or shovel snow off the roofs in the winter. He needed the money. Maybe he was on a bowling team.

"I was waiting for my girl."

"Goodbye."

"She's in there dancing. Loves to dance—"

"Here's what you do," I said. "I'll go slow because I see you have very small ears. You turn the key in the ignition. You put this tin can into gear. And you go away."

He winced. Then his face puckered into a frown. His head turned and he glanced across the street. He didn't like to give up easy.

"Are you Caine?"

"Welby," I said. "Marcus Welby. And I'm going to operate in about ten seconds."

"Someone ought to call the cops," he muttered.

My eyes had followed his.

"I think someone did."

He forgot his manners. He rolled up the window, started the van, and didn't bother to say goodbye. He was going for a phone, but not to call the cops.

My attention was already across the street, where a lanky figure had folded a newspaper in half and was sitting on it on my front steps. His musette bag was on the step next to him.

I walked on up the stairs without bothering to say hello.

"Her name is Margot Fraser," he said quietly.

I whirled around.

"Look, Diamond, you can—you can—"

You can fill in the blanks.

"She's supposed to be dead," he continued. "But isn't. Or wasn't. I'll have to take it up with the Mad Hatter. Not in the files, of course. Found her picture in the newspaper. Wonderful thing, a free press. Otherwise you get piles."

He shifted a little on his newspaper.

"They picked her up in Portland."

"Where?"

"Portland, Maine. Trying to get to Ireland. No money. No luggage. No passport."

I backed down a step.

"She's all right?"

"She didn't put up a fight. Due back in the morning. We'll have to get together. By the way, I think I told you there's nothing doing at Bidet's. There isn't, is there?"

I looked at him.

"You've got nothing better to do than follow me around. Why don't you stake out your stake-outs?"

"You don't tell me much, Nick. That's the problem. And besides, it's a nice night. I like the snow." He put his palms upward, an honored practice among police. "It's stopped."

I backed all the way down the steps and bent over to look him squarely in the eye.

"Have I stayed out of your way for two years?"

"Yes."

"Have I offered my opinion about your lousy police department?"

"Not lately."

"Have I made any rude comments about your purse?"

"Not in my hearing."

"Did I teach you how to do the Texas tommy, which you never heard of?"

"Yes."

"I hate to do this."

"You hate to do what?"

He never saw it coming. He landed in a heap against the railing. I picked him up, threw him over my shoulder—a stringbean like Dr. Lew Diamond weighs about as much as a stringbean—reached for his purse, which was plenty heavy, unlocked the front door, and threw him on the couch.

"Yankees in five," he said thickly.

Five minutes later I had what I needed and was on my way out the front door. The timers were set. Lights would be going on and off all night, all through the house. Not that it mattered anymore.

Lew Diamond was still laying odds on the Series. I shut the door quietly. He had no takers.

I crossed the street, went down the alley, and entered Facettes by the back entrance. I found Michael Moro three flights up, in his office. The music reached all the way upstairs. They call it music.

Michael Moro threw his arms around me. He has short arms and an even shorter memory.

"I need your office. Ten minutes."

"For you, Nick, anything. Didn't I tell yuh?"

He beamed.

"Ever hear of Greta Garbo?" I asked.

He stopped beaming.

His lips made a little pink rose near the middle of his face. It didn't go with the rest of him.

Finally he shrugged.

"Okay. I'll go down and, uh, count the house."

"Send Tony up."

The door closed behind him. I pulled a packet of maps out of my pocket and spread them out on Michael Moro's desk. First I had to push away the junk mail. Michael Moro gets a lot of junk mail. All the vineyards in California know about him.

I studied the maps until every creek and contour of Tennessee Mountain was fixed in my head. They showed a single habitation on a high spur running west. Mecca. By the time I finished, I didn't need the maps anymore. I used a gold pen from Michael Morro's desk to mark the route I was going to take. Then I folded the maps and stuck them in the bottom drawer of the desk, under Michael

Moro's old *Playboys* and *Penthouses*, in case anyone went looking for me. Eventually.

I pulled out the Margolin Special and unsnapped the trigger guard so I could use it with my gloves on, in case I needed to use it with my gloves on. It was only a little thing, but it reminded me of how far back I'd come. Back to the world of darkness and strange rooms and people who were ciphers of darkness. Impossible jobs. A world where you remembered only one rule and could forget about all the others. The one rule you remembered was: survive.

Michael Moro knocked on the door because he was polite. After all, it was his office.

"Can't find him," he said through the door.

"Thanks," I said as I walked past him.

"Anyway," I added about half a flight down.

I went all the way down, to the basement. Tony's the janitor. I found him in a storeroom smoking something that smelled funny. He didn't want to interrupt himself, but five dollars changed his mind. He went out to get my car and bring it around to the alley in back.

"Around the block, Tony. Not down Delgany. Into the alley. Pretend there's dope in the hubcaps."

He nodded out the door and I went back upstairs.

"Hey! Can I use my office? What's going on?"

I killed the lights and shut the door. Michael Moro's field glasses were on the edge of his desk. I took them to the window with me.

Terrific view. Parking lots. Factories. Warehouses. About a block and a half up Delgany, a blue van was parked just out of reach of the street light. The juice man was back for more.

I raised the glasses and looked at the mountains. They were dark. Somewhere up there was Mecca and a girl who never said goodbye. Somewhere up there was a man who had tasted blood and liked it.

It seemed like a long time ago. I'd tried to stay away from it, the memory of that last bright morning up on the Little Spider two years earlier when the two thugs came after me and made a big mistake and all that was left was the sound of a car horn out in the middle of nowhere and the soft hissing of flames.

Maybe there are some things you can't walk away from, no matter how hard you try. Things catch up with you. Or they're waiting for you around the corner. Things were catching up with Muhammad Rashad. Things were catching up with me.

"You're a friend of Mr. Moro's, no?" Tony asked when he got out of the car.

"Right."

"Here's the fin." A sheepish smile stuttered around the corners of his mouth. "You know, man, live and let live."

"Keep it."

It didn't take long to get out of town. I worked my way up through the hogbacks with the window wide open, because that's the way I like it. The air was a sharp razor scraping my neck. I was looking at the bare hills, the shoulders of the mountains, the pools of almost luminescent snow far up on their flanks. The wind jolted the car. The darkness rushed around me.

The snow started to fall when I left the highway and headed north. It came in sharp, stinging pellets, splattering against the car. I left the window halfway open. The air was cold as death. The snow continued to spill out of the dark sky. Up there it was harder to be human. Up there in the mountains everything extra was blown away by the wind and burned off by the stars. All that was left were basics. Breathe in. Breathe out. Repeat until dead.

The turn-off road was just where the map in my head said it would be. By the time I reached it the snow had started to thin out. The headlights picked up a faint mist curling down through the trees.

I pulled off onto the shoulder and sat there for a moment. The wind shuddered against the car. The road was empty. The snow slid in globs off a small metal sign that said: "Rashad Enterprises. Private. Check at Gate."

My watch told me that Nasenklammer had already been there for two hours—Nasenklammer and a dead man and a girl who was in over her head. A girl who didn't want to hurt anybody, except maybe herself.

I started up and counted thirteen switchbacks in two miles. What I wanted was the last one, the one running out to the western ridge. I was almost there when I noticed a thick white light bleeding across the low sky ahead of me.

But then the road turned and dipped down into darkness again. I passed the guardhouse. The gate was up and the guardhouse was empty. Maybe they weren't expecting company.

The road curved to the left and angled upward again. I followed it until it leveled out. Then I hit the brakes and killed the lights.

I was almost upon it.

Straight ahead of me on the level mountain ridge a huge building of pale green glass and steel soared into the white air. It was all pyramids and angles, three stories high, and bathed in brilliant white floodlights. The soft insistent hum of the power generators came from somewhere in the darkness.

I was wrong about expecting company.

The parking lot was filled with cars—forty or fifty of them, parked in neat rows. Under a wide canopy in front of the building stood a very small man, trying to light a cigarette in the wind.

I recognized him. Even without his skates.

Tiny Tim.

The snow fell silently between me and Mecca.

29

I drove around to the back of the building and parked between a multicolored van that advertised itself as belonging to St. Vitus and the Vixens and a car that didn't need to advertise itself at all. It was the longest Cadillac I'd ever seen, and I'd seen it somewhere before.

Except for one or two lights upstairs, the top two floors of Mecca were dark. The action was downstairs, in the big glass-enclosed lobby that encircled the ground floor. Even there, it was lights-out in the back of the building. On the way in I'd noticed dark figures moving around behind the green glass of the front lobby. A lot of them. Let's say they were dancing. I could hear the half-strangled sound of music coming from within.

For a man who liked to be alone, Muhammad Rashad had plenty of company.

He was having a party.

No wonder Tiny Tim was standing outside by himself under the canopy, trying to light a cigarette in the wind. There wasn't a woman alive who would trust him on the dance floor.

The music got louder, not better, when I opened the side door to Mecca. I'd already pulled my hand out from the inside of my jacket. It came out empty.

I saluted.

"Invitation?" he squinted.

He was only a doorman, but he was beautiful people. Green jacket, blue slacks, maroon shoes, a rope tie with a silver longhorn steer for a clip. He had flunky written all over him, flunky for Rashad Enterprises.

The rectangular badge on his lapel said:

"Hello! I'm ———."

Where it said "———," someone had printed in there for him: "Col. Hunker."

I looked him over. He did likewise.

He was an old guy and his thin dark hair was greased straight back from his forehead. He didn't have much of a forehead. He was wearing thick glasses and they were smudged, so his fingers must have been as greasy as his hair. I reminded myself not to shake hands.

Col. Hunker squinted again.

"You've got an invitation? I have to see it."

"Sorry," I answered quickly. "I'm from the Arena. Tiny Tim told me to drop up and join the party if I had time. I had time. But if you've run dry—"

Col. Hunker nodded his head gravely and welcomed me inside.

"No problem," he said.

His eyebrows made a sudden leap for his hairline, and almost made it.

"The Arena?" He dropped his voice and it broke. The result was a gravelly whisper. "Between you and me. This Marabel and Morgan. They *really* do everything together?"

"Between you and me, Hunker—"

"Yes? Yes?"

"No."

The corners of his mouth headed for his earlobes.

"Nice couple anyway, real nice. I didn't think so." He waved a paw toward the front of the building.

"Bar's down there around the corner," he explained. "Mr. Rashad has already been down and gone back upstairs. You missed a wonderful speech. He did real nice."

"He's not coming back down?"

"You know how he is. But those lady musicians are pretty good. You'll enjoy yourself."

His eyes tried to focus on the dancers at the end of the hall, where it opened up into the front lobby. That's how he spotted the two women, bottle blondes, with the tag ends of their Calvin Klein jeans up against the wall about twenty feet away from us. It was a toss-up, them or me, and they won.

It was pretty clear what Col. Hunker's job was: watch the door, keep the curious away from the back of the building where the lights were out. But you can't keep a good man down.

"Have you heard my riddle, ladies?" he said loudly, waddling toward the blondes. "What planet do you see when you put your head between your legs? Ha?"

He was the life of the party.

Not me. I didn't come to dance. I turned and walked the other way, toward the back of the building, taking in the floor plan as I went. The lobby went around the outside of the main floor—tinted glass on one side and the guts of Mecca holding things up in the middle. Closed doors, conference rooms, the bank of elevators. The elevators would go down as well as up. Mecca would be only the tip of the iceberg.

An open office area extended across the back of the building—desks, the square shapes of VDTs, darkness. All the light was outside. I went for the windows and gave the top of the mountain a going over. There was no way down. The floor trembled, somewhere beneath my feet an underground garage door was rumbling open, and in a moment I saw two Cats with snowplows grinding up a ramp into the parking lot. They dropped their blades and went to work. Rashad didn't want any overnight guests.

I slid my hand back into my jacket and felt the cold metal over my heart.

Then I laughed.

I didn't even have to turn around.

She was standing alone in the darkness behind me. Flimsy red chiffon dress—she looked good in red—black spike heels that were no good for dancing or skating or anything except kicking off and tossing under the bed. The aureole of honey. I could see her reflection in the window.

Her mouth made a little motion of surprise.

"Okay," I asked the window. "Do I put my hands up now, or do I wait until later?"

She grabbed my wrist. Her fingers were like ice.

"Don't go up front," she whispered. "Nasenklammer's up there, working the bar. They're expecting you, Nick. Somebody called. They know you're coming."

"The party's for you," I told the window. "Star of the show. Rashad bought the Ice Circus, just like he bought everything else, and that's the only way I can figure it. All these years of skating. It's your big chance."

Her fingers let go of my wrist, and she moved up alongside of me. I still hadn't turned to look at her.

"I wouldn't have used it," she said. "I didn't know what to do."

"Of course not. It was obvious you knew how to use a gun, the way you handled it. But you don't keep the safety on if you intend to use it, and that was the catch. Don't worry about it."

She turned toward me.

"I didn't know who to trust. I never met Rashad before. Bidet handled everything with Cermak, all the arrangements. When I found out you were at the show tonight—I just couldn't go on, Nick. I was supposed to do three numbers and barely made it through one. I went to Bidet and told him all about it—Margot Fraser, Monkey Man, bad times. He already *knew* about it. He said nothing was accidental. That you were in on it. That you killed Margot Fraser, that her mother was murdered, that you killed Allison Carpenter. He said they were looking for you, trying to stop you. I couldn't believe it. But he handed me the gun—"

"Bidet's dead."

A sudden chill went into her voice.

"Yes," she said. "They brought me all the way up here with a dead man."

I watched her face in the glass.

"I heard them talking about it upstairs," she said finally. "Rashad, Nasenklammer, someone else. They're going to take him out in the morning and drop him in the mountains. A helicopter, I think. And they know you're coming—"

"Where's Rashad?"

"Upstairs. Third floor. He has a suite up there. He lives there. That's where they took me. They put Bidet in the garage, underground, and they took me upstairs. I heard them arguing—"

"Have you heard my riddle?" boomed a gravelly voice behind us.

I spun around and watched Hunker feel his way across the darkened lobby toward us. He squinted from Cynthia to me and back again.

"What planet do you see when you put your head between your legs?" he chuckled.

"Take care of her, Hunker."

I was halfway across the lobby when I heard her say it:

"Goodbye."

I kept going. It takes some people a long time to find out what it is they don't want.

The hallway was dark. I moved down toward the colored lights and the beautiful music of St. Vitus and the Vixens. When I got to the elevators I hit the button. The doors opened immediately.

The elevator took me upstairs and when the doors opened again, I saw her.

She was sitting at a bare table in the foyer, facing the elevator, and her mother never taught her how to cross her legs. She didn't shave them either. She was wearing a starched white dress and thick black shoes and it would have been stretching things to call her a woman. Not with those arms. Not with that bristly black hair combed straight back.

She glanced at the Margolin Special in my hand and then took in the rest of me. Slowly. She wasn't impressed.

"The Boss," I said. "You're not it."

She smiled. At least I think it was a smile. I heard the elevator doors hiss closed behind me. She scraped back her chair and stood up. The overhead light didn't do much for her complexion. It did one thing, though. It brought out the highlights in her mustache.

The gun nodded at her and she nodded back.

"This way," she said.

I followed her. We took a right and walked down to the end of the hall. She stopped before a closed door and rapped on it with her knuckles. I noticed she had thick knuckles.

The voice from inside was very pleasant.

"Yes?"

She opened the door, stepped inside, and then moved out of the way.

It was a big office with a big walnut desk and a big man sitting behind it, with his back to the windows. Nice-looking chap. Freckles across the bridge of his nose. Calm, light-colored eyes. The trace of a smile just above a rock-hard jaw. He looked like he could be president of anything. Even Rashad Enterprises.

The walls were hung with fishing tackle—a greenheart Castle Connell and some other vintage rods. There were photographs of big catches in Iceland and Patagonia. There was even an old-fashioned coat rack in the corner behind the desk. But there was no coat hanging from the peg.

Instead there was an Eddie Bauer crusher hat and an Eddie Bauer vest, the one with 427 pockets, and an Eddie Bauer chamois shirt just in case the wind came up and darkness came early.

Herbert Lehmann Morgan was ready for action.

I won't say it didn't surprise me. It did. It surprised me a little, even though I already had it figured.

After all, Muhammad Rashad and Martin Augerman were self-made men—one by blood and the other by a fast mouth. Morgan was the only one who specialized in take-overs. What he had taken over was Muhammad Rashad. Emmett Crouse had suggested as much, at dinner in Lucciano's: Rashad's profile was getting lower and lower. Now it had disappeared. Crouse had given me another piece to the puzzle; Morgan was a fisherman. Martin Bidet tied the knot when he mentioned to Cynthia that he was going to call the Boss and tell him about the big catch they'd made. Bidet wasn't the type to talk in sports terms. He didn't strike me as a fisherman. No patience.

More than that, Martin Bidet had never heard of Benny Rader. You'd think that a guy up to his neck in the soup pot would know something about his boss. I'd bet that Morgan had heard of Benny Rader—I'd put money on it. My own money. He'd clawed his way up through Chicago years ago. He probably knew Douglas Fraser, too, and wondered what had happened to him. Until he figured it out.

It surprised me a little. But it surprised him even more.

"Yes," he said slowly. "I believe we've met."

The Little Spider, on a nice September day before Pug Collins came thrashing up through the underbrush to tell me he had something that I'd find interesting.

Morgan's placid eyes drifted upward from the Margolin Special to my throat, or to my right shoulder, or to the open doorway behind me.

Take your pick. It didn't matter.

I felt the gun drop from my hand. I heard someone—the woman—try to say something. I finally sensed the pain shoot down the length of my spine as though someone had closed the jaws of a vise around my head.

Then I said hello to the carpet.

30

"Exemplary," Herbert Lehmann Morgan said. "I didn't think you had it in you. More of a man there than meets the eye."

He was looking directly at Muhammad Rashad, but Muhammad Rashad wasn't returning the favor. Rashad was giving the carpet the once-over. He kept his mouth shut.

A thin veil of irritation flickered across Morgan's face and then disappeared.

There was no doubt about it. He was the Boss. Mr. Big. His hands were folded in front of him, beneath his chin. His cuff links glittered in the light from the overhead fixtures. His pudgy fingers were interlocked. He looked very comfortable.

Rashad was another story.

He sat in a plastic chair against the wall, a terribly shrunken little man. His thin lips were stretched tightly over his teeth. His hair was combed straight back from his low forehead, it seemed to be the style at Mecca, and his hooded eyelids hovered over the wine-colored circles beneath those tiny mahogany eyes.

His hands lay limply in his lap.

Every so often his eyelids jerked back a fraction of an inch, as though he couldn't control them. For instance, every time Morgan opened his mouth.

Rashad wasn't the puppeteer anymore. He was the puppet. But Morgan's eyes smiled at me.

"It must have been the angle at which he struck you," Morgan said. "It seems unlikely that such a small man could so easily dispatch a person of your tenacious character. But with an iron pipe, all things are possible. I'm assured that no bones have been broken. Better yet, the iron pipe is intact."

He smiled again. His tongue played a little with his lower lip.

"Rashad belongs to you?"

"Certainly," Morgan answered. "A marriage of convenience, and pregnant with possibilities. Although perhaps more convenient for me than it is for him, and with more possibilities for me as well. Yet it saves him from the gas chamber or the electric chair—"

"And Nasenklammer?"

"He will be here in a moment. He anticipates renewing his acquaintance with you."

"Sam Casanova."

"Indeed. Poor thing."

"And Martin Bidet?"

Morgan did a toothpaste ad.

"Your tenacious character," he said cheerfully. "Of course I didn't realize at the time that you would prove to be so persistent. To all appearances you were merely a fisherman like myself. If I had known, I would have shot you then and there. Your body would never have been found. A very nice stream, by the way, the Little Spider. I don't get up there as often as I'd like. When I do, I prefer to have it all to myself."

Morgan's eyes darted over toward Rashad, and he smiled.

"There are many things I prefer to have all to myself," he added.

Rashad wasn't watching. He was still counting the threads in the carpet.

"You sent for Nasenklammer?" Morgan snapped. He looked at his watch.

"Yes," Rashad mumbled as he looked up.

It was the first time I'd seen him look at Morgan, and I liked what I saw. A dull brown glaze of hatred in those tiny eyes that were once as sharp as scimitars.

It was Morgan's turn not to notice. He was talking to me.

"I have made all the usual inquiries, of course, and some slightly more than usual. They were fruitless. There is nothing to be learned about Nick Caine except for the most obvious things. I have the greatest respect for that. You're a man without a past, which is a very useful thing to be without. A man floating on the surface of society, and a man of great potential. I recognize that. And I regret the circumstances, Caine. They make you a man without a future."

Morgan smiled, but this time he was smiling to himself. He liked his style. It was a big smile, the smile of a man who is very satisfied with himself, and it opened the door to his office.

Helmut Nasenklammer filled the doorway.

He didn't look any prettier than the last time I'd seen him.

"Sit down," Morgan ordered. He dropped the smile. He was all business. "What about the girl?"

"Yes, sir," Nasenklammer said in a drawl that was strictly Southern—slow but tough. "I spoke to her before I came up. There'll be no problem."

"Exemplary. I'm sure she'll cooperate. She's a very modern young woman. Wants to be a star. We'll make her a star. There's no need to muddy our hands with her. She plans on going back with the other members of the ice show?"

"No, sir. You wanted her here."

"Of course. Better that she remain at Mecca until we make arrangements for Mr. Caine."

"I can take her down tomorrow—"

"Not you. Someone else. You'll be busy. With our friend here."

Morgan straightened up. He was conducting a board meeting and he knew how to do it. His hard eyes were fixed on me.

"Here is what we're going to do," he said.

He was only halfway through explaining what we were going to do when Helmut Nasenklammer interrupted him.

"It's impossible, sir. Grasshopper Glacier is eight hundred miles from here. We'll be putting down for fuel every two hours—"

"Nothing is impossible."

Nasenklammer wasn't buying it. "It'll be dark by the time we get there," he protested. "I'll have to land on ice or rock. Has it snowed up there? Snow would be worse. There are no skids on that chopper. The wind's terrible—"

"You're an accomplished pilot, are you not?"

"Yes, sir. Of course. But let me take care of him myself. I won't need any lead pipe. I'll dump him. I can take him out with Bidet in the morning."

Morgan's eyes were on the ceiling. He was ignoring Helmut Nasenklammer, not an easy thing to do unless you're really the Boss and Helmut Nasenklammer knows it.

"Are you done?" Morgan's eyes said.

Nasenklammer shrugged.

"I've given it a great deal of thought, Helmut. My mind is made up. There's no need to try and change it. Bidet will be found in the spring, or perhaps next summer, the victim of an unfortunate accident. It will not do for Mr. Caine to be found. Not in the spring, not in the summer. Not in the fall or winter. Never. A man without a past is a very dangerous thing. We cannot trust him, not even when he is very dead. Perhaps he has a guardian angel. We cannot take a chance. Do you understand, Helmut?"

"Yes, sir."

"Do you understand, Rashad?"

Maybe he did, maybe he didn't. Rashad didn't say.

"I will be occupied in the morning," Morgan continued. "We're finally acquiring Corvex Steel. I must meet with the lawyers. But Rashad and I will be free to leave here by two o'clock. You will have left before that, Helmut. Can you find Bosack?"

"Bosack?"

"Your hearing is excellent. Your manners I merely tolerate. Sometimes you forget who is in charge here—"

Morgan's smile was cruel.

"Find Bosack," he said sharply. "Find him tonight. We have the jet. Hunker can drive Rashad and myself down to the airport after lunch tomorrow. Leave the details to Mr. Bosack. He's familiar with the area. He took me up to the Spider, and he provided a very useful shuttle service for Miss Carpenter. We'll want to be there by midnight, and we'll want you there, Helmut. With Caine. Are you attending to this? Near the glacier there is a small shack. Used for equipment, I believe. It's set back off from the trail, but not so far that it can't be easily seen. I noticed it when I was there to supervise Allison Carpenter—"

Morgan suddenly turned to me.

"Another very modern woman, Caine. But one without the courage of her convictions. No doubt you're familiar with her. You seem to be familiar with all of Mr. Rashad's little peccadilloes."

I glanced over at Muhammad Rashad. His eyelids were pressed down smoothly over his eyes.

"My schedule is very tight," Morgan said. "My time is not my own. And Mr. Rashad needs to get back to his work in the laboratory. We have had enough diversions. We have rescued him from his folly, so that he can make important contributions to our enterprise—"

"I can't do it."

"Pardon me?" Morgan snapped.

Rashad's pale hands fluttered helplessly over his lap. "I—I can't do it," he said meekly. "I can't go back to that glacier."

The blood rose in Morgan's face. "You're a fool!" he sneered.

He turned toward Nasenklammer: "Remember this, Helmut! The fool has resisted me every step of the way. He thought that keeping his eye on the Fraser girl would solve his problems. And worming his way into Miss Carpenter's affections! A fool! He opposed my participation in this company. He resisted my plan to frighten Miss Fraser away. He couldn't see the beauty of going along with Margot Fraser's own plan and adding a few touches of our own. You're a coward, Rashad. The Fraser girl had more courage in her little finger—"

Morgan didn't try to hide his contempt. Rashad did. It was only a family quarrel but I was glad I wasn't part of the family.

Morgan finally got himself under control. He turned in his chair so that he faced me.

"It's time that Mr. Rashad recognized his precarious circumstances in life and acknowledged his benefactors," he smiled. "I believe I could settle things myself, Caine. But it's better that we involve Mr. Rashad. Perhaps in the future he will be less likely to resist the reality of his situation."

He slapped both of his palms down on the desk.

Rashad shuddered.

"That leaves the Fraser girl," Morgan said. "Mr. Rashad's great fear was that she would recall him. From an earlier life." He smiled to himself again. "She hasn't yet, but perhaps she will. Her memory may be as good as mine. But where is she? Helmut did the best he could. He led us to Caine—"

"Thanks for the flowers," I said.

Morgan was still smiling.

"Bidet did his usual job," he went on. "I should have removed him long ago. He was a coward. I'm sure Mr. Caine has more courage. Perhaps you can enlighten us—"

"Sure," I said. "Glad to help. I can give you his number."

"Whose number is that, Caine?"

"The man she's with."

"Yes?"

"Dr. Lew Diamond. Chief of detectives. Or homicide, I forget which."

It wasn't a veil of irritation that crossed Morgan's face this time. It was a shroud.

"You have your instructions," he said tartly to Helmut Nasenklammer. "Find Bosack. You will have Caine up at Grasshopper Glacier by tomorrow evening."

He waved his hand in front of his face as though he was bothered by a fly. The meeting was adjourned.

I spent the night in a small anteroom next to Morgan's spacious office. Not that I'd recommend it. They had me strapped tightly down on a hospital cart and pushed off into a corner. They didn't leave any room for error. Nasenklammer must have been a Boy Scout.

I knew it was morning when I heard the thundering noise of the helicopter lifting off the mountaintop. The same rifle-shot chops of noise filled the little room a half-hour later, when the helicopter returned. Goodbye, Martin Bidet.

I twisted my head back to look out a small window. The view wasn't worth it. Nothing but sky, scrubbed clean by the wind.

Nothing but silence.

The anteroom door opened softly a few minutes later. I knew I was going to have company sooner or later. But I never figured on Muhammad Rashad.

His head swung carelessly from side to side as he walked past me to stand at the window. He didn't even look at me. His eyelids were twitching. He couldn't help it.

I didn't have much time, but I made the most of it.

"He's squeezing you dry," I said quickly. "It doesn't take a genius to figure it out. He must have known you from Chicago, either you or Douglas Fraser. He kept it quiet all this time just like you did. For different reasons. When he tried to take over and you put up a fight, he had a little talk with Benny Rader. Then he came aboard, the silent partner. Only he's not a partner. He's the Boss. Where does that leave you? Nowhere. No way out. And for a guy who's got more brains than Douglas Fraser ever dreamed of. All these years it's been a masquerade, Benny. Now it's a nightmare. He's walking all over you just like Fraser did. It would be easy for him to take care of you just like he took care of Allison Carpenter or Flossie Cappelman or Maureen Fraser. A bullet in the head would do it. Why doesn't he? He needs your brains. Electronics, that's the future. Without you he's just another guy selling mops to the hospitals. And what do you get out of it? That's a good question."

I twisted my head to see whether he was listening. All I could see was his back.

"I had a gun when I came in here," I added. "Before you found the proper angle and hit me over the head. With a pipe. Exemplary. It's called a Special—a Margolin Special—and it sure works sweet. Even though it hasn't turned up. What the hell. I don't know where it is. Maybe you do? I could use it."

Muhammad Rashad didn't say anything.

He stood silently at the window, looking out over Mecca and the mountains and the high sky beyond. His little hands were clasped tightly behind his back.

His fingers were turning white.

31

I was right about Mecca. It was only the tip of an iceberg. Helmut Nasenklammer ran me downstairs on the hospital cart. He never heard of kid gloves. He unbuckled the straps on the cart, propped me up against the wall, and tied my hands and feet. Then he put his shoulder into my stomach. I knew how Dr. Lew Diamond felt.

The chopper was just what you might expect, an Aerospatiale AS-350 equipped with a mini-FLIR system for night vision, a real fancy number. It was sitting on an elevator pad in the basement.

Nasenklammer put me in back like he meant business. There was nothing fancy about it.

I don't think I broke anything important when I landed on the floor behind the aft seats, next to a large wooden box filled with safety flares. If I had broken anything, I wouldn't have been able to tell anyone about it. Not with the way he had that dirty blue rag tied across my mouth and drawn securely behind my head.

The best I could do was gargle.

Helmut Nasenklammer was talking to himself. None of it was very nice.

I gargled.

I wanted to ask him where he picked up that Southern accent. It didn't go with his name, Noseplug.

He wasn't in the mood.

The elevator took us for a ride, helicopter included. The steel cover on the surface rumbled open to let us through and we got a taste of the afternoon. If it weren't for the company it would have been a nice day.

Nasenklammer kicked the chopper off the pad and we swung out into the bright cold sky. The nose dipped. Mecca swam into view below us. It swam right out again, as Helmut got used to the wind, but not before I caught a glimpse of all those pyramids and angles, the house that blood built, and two workers in cream-colored overalls standing next to the heliport and looking up at us, shading their eyes with their hands, and the wide parking lot running straight to the edges of the mountaintop and scraped clean and deserted except for three cars, two of them very long Cadillacs and the other one a beat-up Chevy of undetermined age, which didn't look like it belonged. Actually, I had a fairly long glimpse.

The chopper rattled and groaned against the empty sky.

Noseplug didn't go with the wind, he went against it, or in at an angle. He had his hands full and he had big hands. I worked my way into a corner against the bulkhead. All I could see was the sky. It gave me plenty of time to think.

What I thought about was the Grasshopper, high and cold in the night mountains to the north. Solid with its secrets of ambition and death. I thought about a girl with gold-flecked eyes and a crooked smile, locked away in a glass cage with no way out. And a dark-eyed girl who was free to go but had no place left to run. I thought about Muhammad Rashad, and those tiny brown eyes, and the ancient knives that sharpened themselves and came to life behind the twitching lids when he came into the little anteroom next to Morgan's office one more time and slipped the Margolin Special into my holster and walked out without saying a word. It was a fool's game and he was playing me for a fool. I didn't buy it.

I thought about Herbert Lehmann Morgan, a movie star if there ever was one, whose pleasant smile hid a cruel hook of deceit and careless dying.

I thought about a thug named Noseplug, all muscle and bone, who was fighting his own instincts. His own instincts were to settle things the easy way, smash out the windows, a bullet in the side of the head, a swan dive from the open door of an Aerospatiale AS-350 deep in the mountains.

No wonder he was talking to himself.

He was still fighting the wind after a couple of hours but he stopped ignoring me. He twisted around in his seat and noticed me sitting up in the corner of the cabin. When his big paw forced its way back between the seats it was wrapped around a very large handgun.

"Not here," I said. It sounded like I was gargling. I went flat on the floor and lay still.

Nasenklammer brought her down for a drink. He stood at the door while they filled her up, just to make sure no one peeked in. No one did. Then he got back in his seat, looked at the maps a while, and scratched his head, and we lifted off again.

The light started going out after our third stop.

Darkness came on fast, and when darkness came he activated the floodlight that was mounted under the belly of the chopper, near-infrared, and he slipped the night-vision goggles over his eyes. Morgan was right. Noseplug was an accomplished pilot. Exemplary, you might say.

But the goggles did nothing special for his looks.

It was hours later when I felt the chopper hovering in the night sky and then slowly descend. I would have checked my watch, except it was on my wrist. My wrist was still tied behind my back.

The wind was trying to rock us to sleep, but it wasn't a lullaby.

The wheels touched gently against the hard ground. The rotors fought back, and then we sank deep on the shocks. When he turned the chopper off, the silence of Grasshopper Glacier rushed down to meet us. The silence and the wind.

Noseplug scrambled back into the cabin. He had a hunting knife in his hand and he used it. First on the rope around my ankles, then next to my jaw.

I tried working my jaw. It worked before my feet did.

I said, "You're pretty good, Noseplug. Where'd you get that Southern accent?"

"Huntsville," he said without thinking.

He went out the door first. He had a little leather kit in his hand and the gun jammed into his belt and he waited for me. He had to wait a while, but I finally got the toes working, and then the ankles.

I slid out after him.

The moon was out, the moon and the wind. Noseplug poked me in the back and we started down the trail in the faint light.

Morgan must have drawn a good map, because we had no trouble finding the small line shack just off the trail. Nasenklammer opened his leather kit, extracted a hammer and a chisel, and went to work on the padlock.

"Government property," I said.

"Don't move."

"What the hell time is it?"

"Don't bother me."

"I think it might be my birthday."

He grunted. I turned my head to look at the face of Grasshopper Glacier, high and cold in the wan light. A few wisps of dry snow blew down from upstairs. You could still see the chunks of ice where the boys had dug out Douglas Fraser with their buzz saws a week or so earlier.

Ice worms.

I shuddered.

I turned around again when I heard the latch pop off the door and noticed that part of the door had come with it. Helmut Nasenklammer wasn't very fussy.

Two was more than company, it was a crowd. His flashlight looked things over inside. He spotted a kerosene lantern on a wooden shelf in the back and fired it up.

"Pick a corner," he said. "Away from the door."

I did.

He picked one, too, and went to his haunches. The gun was still sticking out of his pants. He looked like a guy who spent a lot of time on his haunches.

He groped around his feet without looking and found his leather bag. He fumbled with it a moment, took out a small walkie-talkie, turned it on, and set it gingerly on the shelf above my head.

It made beautiful static.

"You look like a smart guy, Noseplug. Except for your face."

"You're not so pretty yourself," he said softly. "And not so smart."

He shifted a little on his haunches and got himself comfortable.

"You're a good pilot, though. Can you tell time?"

He looked at his watch.

"Forget it," he said.

"Maybe they're not coming."

"Shut up."

We listened to the static and the wind. I didn't like the sound of either. But it's all we had. Helmut Nasenklammer couldn't carry on a civilized conversation.

Another hour passed before we heard a distant, sing-song voice trying to fight its way clear through the static. It rose and fell:

"Nosey . . . Nosey . . . Nosey . . . Nosey . . ."

It brought Noseplug to his feet. He glared at the radio.

"Nosey. . . . This is Bosack. . . . Do you read me, sweetheart? . . . Nosey . . . Nosey . . . Nosey . . . Nosey. Make a funny grunting noise if you read me, sweetheart . . . Nosey . . . Nosey . . . Nosey . . ."

Nosey grabbed the radio from the shelf and squeezed it in his fist. He made a grunting noise but it wasn't funny.

When Bosack answered, he sounded even farther away.

"On their way up, sweetheart . . . forty minutes ago . . . so they ought to be . . . tough old birds . . . unless a bear got them. . . . Nosey . . . Nosey . . . Nosey. . . . Do you read me, sweetheart? . . . They walkie, I talkie . . . tough old birds . . . bring them down, Nosey . . . let them walk . . . plenty of room . . . plenty of light down here, sweetheart . . . moon's out . . . Nosey . . . Nosey . . ."

Nasenklammer used his thumb on the radio. Then he used his fist. He didn't like the way Bosack referred to him. "Noseplug" he could tolerate, but "Nosey" offended his sensibilities. He dropped what was left of the radio on the dirt floor of the shack.

"They're coming," he said to himself.

He returned to his haunches.

He was still sitting on his haunches when the door suddenly flew open and slammed shut behind him. Just the wind. But it scared the hell out of him. He'd had a long night. The gun jumped from his belt to his hand and stayed there.

When the door opened the second time, it didn't slam shut. The doorway was filled by Herbert Lehmann Morgan.

His cheeks were rosy. The hood on his Eddie Bauer down jacket was flipped back from his neck. His eyes were bright with reflections from the kerosene lamp.

He looked from Nasenklammer to me and back to Nasenklammer, who suddenly got off his haunches.

"Exemplary! Splendid! You did it! One week off, Helmut. With pay. We'll send you to Tortola!"

Morgan followed his smile into the little shack. That made it more than company and more than a crowd. But it gave Muhammad Rashad a crack at the doorway.

It framed him like a portrait.

Behind the ruff of his hood his face was stiff and dark. His skin was leathery. His eyes were shrunk to tiny, lifeless points. They met mine for an instant, then shifted to my chest and drifted away. A fool's game.

I heard the wind crying, somewhere far away.

"None the worse for wear," Morgan was saying. He had bent over, and his face was next to mine. The smile was gone. He nodded toward the door and I took his advice.

Outside, Morgan's eyes took in the face of the Grasshopper and the moonlit helicopter parked at a slight angle on the ground beneath it. He grimaced and turned to Rashad.

"Does it seem the same?"

"Cut his wrists," Rashad said quietly.

"What?"

"The rope around his wrists," Rashad explained. "Cut them free."

"Wait a minute," Nasenklammer protested. His lips twisted back and he shot a glance at Morgan.

"I am not a coward," Rashad said firmly.

Whatever Noseplug saw in Morgan's face, I didn't. But it told him what to do. He grabbed me roughly by the shoulder and turned me around. In a moment my hands were free. I rubbed my wrists and then let my hands drop to my sides, useless.

Rashad's lips had split apart. I suppose it was a smile.

"Yes," Morgan said. "Exemplary. We have to climb that? Very well. Go down to the helicopter, Noseplug. We won't be a minute."

Nasenklammer looked at me, his eyes narrowed, and he turned quickly and walked down the trail toward the chopper.

Morgan had already started the other way, along the rough trail of boulders and scree that led upward along the side of the Grasshopper. I followed, looking up to see the moon sailing high above the ice.

"I'll lead," Morgan called back over his shoulder.

He meant it.

I could hear Rashad behind me, breathing heavily as he scrambled over the rocks. The wind ripped his breath away, I lost the sound for a moment, and then it returned. I wondered what was in his head, behind that shrunken face and those polished little mahogany eyes.

He'd been there before, up to the top of Grasshopper Glacier with Douglas Fraser. He'd started his own little bloodbath up there in the crying wind—a desperate gamble for power and all the things he didn't have. Now he was helpless, beaten at his own game, broken by a man with a lantern jaw and calm eyes and a quick smile that wished death on everyone who stood in his way—Herbert Lehmann Morgan. A man who could have put Rashad himself on ice a thousand times but didn't, and wouldn't, because Rashad in the laboratory was money in the bank.

Because Rashad was beaten. Because Rashad was harmless. That's the way Rashad wanted it to look.

A fool's game.

I reached my hand inside my jacket and touched the grip of the Margolin Special. It was ice cold. Nice of Rashad to provide it.

It was also empty. And I knew it. It had to be. There was no way Muhammad Rashad was going to hand me back a loaded gun—not if I was going to be a pawn in his last masquerade.

The trail narrowed. The pale ice shouldered in on us from the left and forced us up against a dark rock wall. I heard the wind scraping the sky overhead. From out on the glacier came the distant sound of melt-water trickling over the lip of a moulin. Soon it would freeze over. The wind would stop. Soon it would be silent forever.

Which is worse? A man who kills, or a man who cheats someone else into killing for him?

I looked back at Rashad. His hands were empty. His face was a dark mask. Morgan was far ahead of us, waiting. He had his own dreams—dreams of power and influence and death.

We reached him and looked out upon the surface of Grasshopper Glacier. The moon sailed above it, a silent unseeing eye of ice in the black sky. Wisps of snow drifted in the back-eddies of the wind, curling upward like pale ghosts.

Rashad's breath came in short gasps. He looked at Morgan.

They didn't speak.

Morgan sucked in air and put his chin to his chest. Then he headed out upon the glacier. Carefully. I knew what he was looking for. A shadow that would mark a crevasse, the hump of a serac on the icy surface, the soft white burial mound of snow that would hide a descent to death.

I followed behind him, letting the distance between us slowly grow. I had only one chance, and Morgan was going to give it to me.

He stopped, a silhouette against the snow, and turned to face us.

"Rashad!" he called. His voice boomed across the glacier and came back to him: ". . . ashad! . . . ashad! . . . ashad!"

The wind tore his words apart.

"Found it. . . . ound it. . . . ound it. . . ."

Behind him I could see the sharp thin shadow of the crevasse, the far edge raised a little higher than the one at his feet.

I sensed Rashad moving away from me. Then I saw him out of the corner of my eye, circling around to the right. He was moving toward Morgan, one hand in his parka pocket.

"Morgan!" I shouted.

The word rang out like a shot.

I was in a low crouch, feet spread, arms straight out in front of me. The Margolin Special was pointed at his head. He leaned forward, squinted, and saw the gun.

He spun toward Rashad.

"You fool!"

His hand made a futile gesture toward his coat and then fluttered helplessly in the air. He was too late. Rashad's bullet caught him clean between the eyes. His head snapped to one side and he fell limply back into the darkness.

Rashad's head turned.

His gun—gleaming in the moonlight—swung toward me. Just the way he planned it. But it was too late for Muhammad Rashad. Even empty, the Margolin Special is a nice number. Especially if you can throw it.

A faint smile was beginning to curl up from his lips as the butt end of the Special caught him on the bridge of the nose.

I heard the crack of bones breaking.

Rashad coughed.

He staggered backward. His hands were splayed outward, grabbing wildly at the empty air. And then he too disappeared into darkness.

His screams followed him down.

The wind cried, like another weeping woman.

32

Two weeks later, at two o'clock in the morning, you could forget almost all of it. Or try to.

There are arguments the whole way as to which is tougher, up or down, at Grasshopper Glacier. I still vote for down. A lot of people go up. Not everyone comes down.

Forget about Noseplug. I heard him overhead on my way down, but he didn't file a flight plan. Maybe Tortola. Maybe for more than a week.

Forget about what happened to Bosack, sitting down there all alone in the dark campground where everything started, playing with his radio. He let me call him sweetheart. He never knew what hit him.

Forget about the two Indians who picked me up outside of Hungry Horse when Bosack's rented car ran out of gas, Harlan and Roy, and how they figured me for a cop when they saw the Margolin Special sticking out of the shoulder holster, and how scared they got. A good trick, because they were both drunk. I asked to drive and they let me. But forget about that.

Margot Fraser? She's hard to forget about. She couldn't go home. There was no home to go to. Lew Diamond took care of her. He talked to me, and he got bits and pieces, and he took the rest on faith. I think she's in Berkeley, a face in the crowd. It goes to show, a cop is man's best friend.

Forget about Cynthia Farmer. How she got down from the mountain is simple, and I wish I had thought of it. It would have saved me a lot of trouble. Col. Hunker didn't drive Morgan and Rashad to the airport after all; the lovely receptionist did—the one with the starched white dress and the thick black shoes. Before they left they turned Cynthia over to Hunker. She suggested a bottle of Mogen David. He agreed. After the fourth glass she hit him over the head with the bottle, went outside, got in a beat-up Chevy of undetermined age, and drove herself on down. But forget about her.

Two o'clock in the morning, and the last of them finally decided to leave—Dr. Lew Diamond, Tracy the Blonde, and Michael Moro. Tracy was on the steps, Moro was on the sidewalk next to Delgany Street lighting up one of his New Jersey stogies, and Dr. Lew Diamond turned to me and said:

"The whistling fisherman."

I bit.

"The whistling fisherman?"

"You've got it, Nick. Damnedest case I've ever had. Can't sleep, can't think about anything else. Why would a fisherman whistle?"

I stopped him right there.

"Don't tell me. Not interested. I lead a nice quiet life—"

He didn't hear me.

"I thought tonight might get my mind off it. The lamb *shashlik* was pretty good, by the way. I never had that before. Tasted like chicken. But it didn't."

"No?"

"It didn't get my mind off it. The guy's head was mashed in with something. You tell me what. And why the hell was he whistling? Christ! I forgot my bag!"

"Stars are out," Moro said. He looked at the blonde.

She had one hand on her hip, one foot on one step, the other foot on another step. Short skirt.

"Dr. Lew forgot his purse," I announced to the crowd. "You can be on your way. Thanks for coming."

"He queer or something?" Tracy said. "A cop with a purse?"

"Stars are out," Moro said quietly.

When Dr. Lew Diamond came back out on the porch, he left the front door open. But he had his bag over his shoulder and one of my books under his arm.

"Don't work up a sweat on the way home," I said.

"Christ! I have to meet a guy at three o'clock this morning. What time is it? Did we finish the vodka? Says he knows something about J. Thomas Dalton."

"Thanks for coming by, Lew."

"Real name's Junior Thomas. Dalton is his wife's maiden name. Miss Texas, down there where they raise grapefruit. He's the fisherman. Worth about ten million. Why the hell was he whistling?"

"I don't want to know. There must be an answer for everything. Will you get home all right?"

"Sure," he sighed. "Why not? Why go home?"

He nodded his head in the direction of the front door, which was open, as stated, and the woman who looked so good there with her shoes kicked off and her legs tucked comfortably beneath her on the sofa in the drawing room, all of which we could see. The light hit her face just right, showing off that faint, crooked smile and those gold-flecked eyes. Even the aureole of honey.

"She stays, Lew. Never says goodbye."

He sighed again.

"Almost never," I added.

He tottered down the steps, whistling.